WHAT READERS LOVE ABOUT *THE HUNTER SERIES*

"Don't miss this SF series! It is no mean feat to create a riveting science fiction plot that explores philosophical themes without being heavy-handed. But this trilogy does it! I was engaged from the get-go and it just kept getting better. The writing is superb—I highly recommend this series."

"What a ride! The first book would rank well among I. Asimov's works, the second had me hoping that Hunter would have a career at least as long as Holmes did, but the third is a class of its own."

"Highly recommended! I only found this author a few months ago and have since read and enjoyed all his fiction. With interesting conflicts, great writing and fascinating science fiction plots I look forward to his future fiction!"

I0593314

TITLES BY ROBIN CRAIG

The Hunter Series
Frankensteel
The Geneh War
Time Enough for Killing
Leonardo's Child

Time Travel and Alternative History
The Time Surgeons
Hannibal's Witch
The Passion of Judas

Short Stories
Past, Present Future

Non-Fiction Philosophy
Dialogue on the Two Chief World Systems
Good Without God
Cloning Around: The Ethics of Human Cloning and Stem Cell
Research

For the latest news visit robin-craig.com or follow on
fb.me/authorcraig

Leonardo's Child

Book IV of *The Hunter Series*

ROBIN CRAIG

Published by ThoughtWare Books.
Printed by Amazon.
Available from Amazon.com and other retail outlets.
Available on Kindle and other devices.

Chapter titles from Nietzsche's *Thus Spake Zarathustra* (T. Common translation)

Cover art by Kira Craig using images from Pixabay with fonts from 1001 Fonts.

Author's website: robin-craig.com

ISBN 978-0-6484972-8-8

Once you have tasted flight, you will forever walk the earth with your eyes turned skyward, for there you have been, and there you will always long to return. — Leonardo da Vinci

CONTENTS

ACKNOWLEDGMENTS

My thanks to my wife Sonja for reading and enjoying the drafts of this novel and for encouraging me to complete it, and to my daughter Kira for developing the artwork.

Chapter titles are from Nietzsche's *Thus Spake Zarathustra*, as translated by T. Common (source: https://en.wikisource.org/wiki/Index:Thus_Spake_Zarathustra_-_Thomas_Common_-_1917.djvu)

Chapter 1: The Song of Melancholy

On his eighth birthday, Albert received a gift from his father.

He did not know about the gift. Not in the moment when he opened his eyes on that morning to the soft yellow light of a warming dawn. The light was real, but the dawn was imagined, for his window opened on a scene as unreal as it was beautiful. It had been a long time since any window of his had literally opened at all, let alone onto the real world. Technically one could argue it did show the real world, but it was a world far away, and as inaccessible to Albert as friendship and love. But the psychologists had decreed that the sight of a natural garden and sunshine was good for a growing boy, so that is what the window showed.

His keepers wanted Albert to be well adjusted and happy, as long as the mechanisms did not interfere with more important goals.

Albert hated his father. Or thought he hated his father. Perhaps the hate was merely the frustrated face of his love for a father he had once adored with the single-minded devotion only a child is capable of. But whether he hated his father or loved him, it was his birthday. He had a tradition, if tradition was the right word for what he had done on his seventh birthday and on that day decided he would do every one thereafter. He thought about his life and the parents who had betrayed him.

He believed that if he did this he would never forget. But whether he wished to remember out of love or out of hate, for happiness or from regret, he could not say. He just felt in some inchoate part of his being that he must never forget.

~~~

Albert had not been fully cooperative in his birth. Perhaps it had been the first signal of a future of intransigent independence, or perhaps it had been mere restlessness. Whatever the cause, he had refused to settle into the desired head-down position and spent the last few weeks of his fetal life in frustrating—to the adults if not himself—indecision on whether his head or tail should be the part presented to the world on his arrival. Even in this day a breech birth was to be discouraged, so when the doctor had again caught him head down, he picked this date eight years before as the day to induce the fetus to become a child, hoping he would stay in position for the few days required by the intersection of scheduling and predictive guesswork.

As it turned out, between the doctor's decision and the appointed birth day Albert had again turned away from his exit to the outside world. Fortunately, he changed his mind again, and on the last night had conveniently decided to investigate the lower portion of his mother's womb for the umpteenth time. Yet even so the birth did not go smoothly. That may not have been his fault, for while his mother was young, fit and limber she was not entirely standard in either internal or external construction. Whatever the reason, the birth was difficult, and his mother needed some post-birth care and attention.

Thus had his father found himself sitting alone in a room, a fragile bundle nestled on his lap. His father was an intelligent man, but he felt somewhat lost. This was not the first baby he had held, but it was the first that shared half his genes. He looked into the future encapsulated in the bundle with both apprehension and excitement.

The small punched-in face did not look especially pleased to be out of the comfort of his former home, but one eye was open and gazing out at his new one, nonetheless. The other eye was partly glued shut, but a regular flicker showed that it too was struggling to pry open its eyelid to look at this strange new world of light and color from a slightly different angle. The eyes were the deep blue of the newborn but had a strange tinge to them, as if the blue had inherited some of the green of the sea surrounding their home. What went into those eyes was discernable to his father, but what the brain behind them made of it was not. He expected it was the same as any newborn, a wash of color and movement with interest but no meaning, but something in the deep wells of his baby's eyes made him wonder.

Then Albert's mother finally came into the room and lifted him to her, and whatever he made of the world was lost in the comfort of her warmth, the familiar if softened beat of her heart, and the pleasure of his first taste of milk. Having nutrients supplied passively might have been convenient, but there were surprising pleasures in working for it even when it was on tap. He sucked with gusto.

Albert remembered none of this, but his father had told him the story and he remembered it. He treasured it, for it told him that whatever had changed in the years since, his parents had loved him then. Though they could withdraw their love, they could not erase it from having existed.

When he was two, Albert was happy. Children accept the world as it comes. They must, for there is too much unknown to question reality as anything more or less than what is. He regarded his father's lively dark eyes and unruly dark hair as simple facts unworthy of special notice, as did any child. And if he noticed that no other woman had eyes the golden yellow of his mother's, or that her catlike tail was not shared by the mothers of his friends, then he made no comment. It was what his mother was, and all he cared about was that, when he gazed into those yellow eyes, they shone with the reflection of the love he felt for her; and that when she stroked him with her tail it was a delight, not only for its ticklish softness but for the motive that impelled it, the emotion it embodied.

But when he was four, Albert looked at his mother's yellow eyes and realized they were not the same as other people's. He looked at her tail and wondered even more. Then he walked to the bathroom and stared into the mirror at his own emerald eyes, thinking of all the other eyes he had seen. While eyes varied in color, none were like his mother's, and though he had seen other greenish eyes, none were the precise shade of his own. Yet feeling his own tail bone, it was as truncated as any other of his species.

Albert went to his net access point. He read some articles on child development and genetics. When he did not understand, he investigated further. There were many paths to follow through the tree of human knowledge, so this took him some time. Then he went to see his father.

His father was a busy man, but he often worked from home, and he greeted Albert with a ready smile when he came into his office. He always had time for Albert, except when immersed in the most difficult of problems or the direst of emergencies.

"Daddy?" ventured Albert.

"Yes, Albert? What's the matter? You look… strange."

Albert said nothing, merely came up to his father and climbed onto his lap. His father held him gently and lightly kissed his hair. He could tell something was troubling his son but said nothing. If Albert needed advice, he would ask in his own time. If all he needed was the wordless comfort of being enveloped on his father's lap, Daniel would give it. Albert could never be the entire world of a man like Daniel, but in moments like this, he was world enough.

Finally, Albert sighed and looked up at his father with his intense emerald eyes.

"Mummy is a geneh," he announced softly.

His father started as much at the announcement as at the irrevocable certainty with which it had been made. He stared at Albert with sudden intensity, but lightened it with that smile adults use when a child uses a grownup word they might have heard but not truly understood. "Do you know what a geneh is?"

"A genetically engineered human. Mummy is one. Her first name is Katlyn. She is *the* Katlyn, isn't she? The one the government tried to kill before you came here. You are a famous genetic engineer. Dr Daniel Tagarin," he pronounced slowly and precisely, as if stepping on unfamiliar ground. "You made her."

"Does that worry you, Albert?"

Albert thought about it. "No. But…"

His father waited, but Albert remained silent, reluctant to open the next door; feeling without knowing why that when he opened it, he must go through, and in going through would change his world forever. Wondering in his child's way whether knowledge was worth the price; but also wondering in his own way whether that ever could be a question.

"But?"

"I am a geneh too," he finally replied with the same quiet certainty.

Daniel had known this day would come, but not that it would come so soon. Other parents might wonder when their children would finally see that the Santa Claus or Tooth Fairy they had been told was real was not. Daniel and Katlyn had wondered when their child would finally see that the never mentioned was real. It was not that they were ashamed or wanted to hide the knowledge; they simply thought the knowledge might be too much for a child to understand, or if he did, to bear. They had hoped that the knowledge and the strength would arrive together.

"Yes," said Daniel, the simplicity of the reply underscoring the certainty of the revelation.

Albert put his head to Daniel's chest and cried silently. He did not know why he cried. His father simply stroked his hair gently, waiting for it to pass, knowing that more must follow.

"Why?"

Daniel did not hedge by asking what he meant; he knew it. "Your mummy and I wanted our own child, like most couples do. But since she is a geneh, it would be too dangerous: our genes too mismatched. So, after you were conceived, I repaired the incompatibilities. But we knew how to do more than that: things to make you better. We talked about it, your mother and I. It wasn't an easy decision. But for the same reasons your mother exists, I had to give you the best I could. You were already a geneh: you had to be to live at all. So, I made you better. We believe we did the right thing."

Albert thought about this. "Was that fair? To me? Am I just an experiment to you?"

Albert was looking at him solemnly, but Daniel could not help smiling at being in the position of arguing the ethics of genetic engineering with a four-year-old. The smile turned tender. "Albert, you are far more to us than an experiment. As I said, we wanted a child, someone part of both of us. When you are hungry, we feed you; when you are sick, we take you to a doctor. This is no different. It was within my power to make you better than you could have been just from our genes. So, I did it. Not as an experiment, but for you. Because even though you did not yet exist, we loved you."

"How could you love me, before I was?"

"We loved the idea of you. And we knew that when you were born, we would love the reality."

Albert silently hugged his father, but he was not finished. After another minute he added, "But genehs are still illegal. They still want to kill mummy. They still want to kill me. You love me. But the whole world hates me."

"Son, to live at all you had to be a geneh. And your mummy didn't decide lightly: she herself grew up under that sentence of death, but she never regretted living to do so. Those laws are stupid, and stupid laws can't last forever. And you are safe here in Capital, a country that loves the individual more than anything: just as your mummy is safe. Don't worry. You are the future of the human race: one day, and I don't think it will be too long in coming, the human race will realize it. You will have a good life. A wonderful life."

Albert had another question, but something stopped him from asking it. Perhaps it was fear of the answer. But that night as his mother sat on the side of his bed singing a soft song of trees, birds and freedom, he convulsively grabbed her hand.

"What is it, Albert?" she asked, surprised at his intensity.

"Do you love me, Mummy?"

Her golden eyes looked deeply into his. "Always and forever, Albert," she had replied tenderly. "Always and forever."

But his mother had lied.

When Albert was six, he had been exploring the margins of Capital. The wild areas that would become the floating foundations of the next wave of settlement of the city on the sea were still growing, home to all manner of fascinating ecosystems and the creatures that comprised them. His parents worried when he did this. Albert knew they disapproved; so, he sneaked out. His parents knew it but thought this small degree of rebellion and freedom was worth the risk. They knew a line had to be drawn somewhere, a line all parents drew between the risks of independence and the apparently safer but perhaps more dangerous ones of cosseting their children in a suffocating safety.

Perhaps they were wrong in where they drew the line. But they thought they were safe. Nobody knew his true nature, or so they thought. The rumor that genehs could not breed with normal people was widely believed and encouraged by his parents. It was, after all, true—almost. They also encouraged the misapprehension that Albert was the son of one of their loyal bodyguards, not their own; Katlyn a doting aunt, as happened so often with women who would have liked a child but could not have one of their own: not a mother.

In addition, Capital's reputation abroad as a freewheeling anarchy was belied by the physical safety of its inhabitants, for if Capital detested laws to control its citizens' lives, it also abhorred attempts to curtail their life, liberty and pursuit of happiness. For much the same reasons.

It should have been enough.

But one minute Albert was trying to catch a particularly interesting crab, which was trying with equal persistence to remain uncaught, and the next a black-clad figure arose from the sea and the crab had a reprieve.

"Who are you?" cried Albert, surprised but not at all afraid of this apparition.

"Are you Albert?" the figure asked.

Albert nodded dumbly, and that was the last thing he remembered.

He opened his eyes to a concerned face peering into his, a long narrow room behind the face, and a faint noise which he later learned was the sound of a jet slipping through the sky at supersonic speed.

The nurse smiled at his open eyes and said, "Welcome back, young man. I was getting a bit worried. But it's OK now, you're safe."

Albert jerked his head around. "Where am I? Where's my mummy and daddy? Who are you?"

She patted him gently on his arm. "There, there. It's OK. Your mummy and daddy are fine, it's just that they thought you were safer with us. Now rest, little one."

"No! I want my mummy and daddy!" he wailed. He wondered at the curiously intense look of sympathy from the nurse, but his eyes felt very heavy, and he slept.

When he woke again, he still felt disconnected as he allowed himself to be led out of the jet and into the maw of a great building that opened from the enclosed hangar.

He wondered what this place was, but decided to just observe and learn. A few people asked him questions, but he just stared blankly as if unable to comprehend. He could not interpret the strange looks that passed between them. But his composure broke as he was led along a corridor, and he saw, through the door of an open office, the back of a familiar body and wild head of hair.

"DADDY!" he yelled.

The man spun around, but instead of happy recognition there was only a look of faint irritation on his face, as if an annoying insect had insinuated its presence where it wasn't wanted. "Daddy!" Albert cried again, but when he tried to run to him his escort gently held him by the arms and said, "No, lad. You can't."

Then his father simply stared at him for a few more moments before turning back to the man in the office and gesturing abruptly. The latter shot a look of poisonous reprimand at Albert's escort, as if to say *Why the hell did you bring the kid through here?* —before getting up and shutting the door. His father never looked back again. He did not have to. Albert had already seen the look in his eyes. It was worse than a look of hatred, worse than a look of repudiation. It was a look of such indifference that it said more than *I have no son*; it said *I never had a son; I do not know you.*

"Daddy!" Albert cried again, softly this time, as if to a memory rather than a man. His escort turned him around and crouched down to his level. "I'm sorry, Albert. You weren't supposed to see that. But…" he looked around, as if to check he wasn't being overheard. "Look, I'm not supposed to tell you this, but… Well, the reason you're here is your parents don't think they can look after you anymore. I know it's hard for you to hear, but they're scared of you. They don't want you anymore. But don't be too hard on them: they've made sure you'll be looked after. They've given you to us to look after. They know we can do a good job."

"No! Let me go! Let me see him! Or my mummy!"

The man just looked at him with sickening pity. "I'm sorry Albert, I can't. He doesn't want to see you. He's just here to validate the formalities. Your mother isn't even here. She didn't want to come."

The words dripped like an acid counterpoint to the memory of his father's eyes, and for a moment the man was worried by the blank look on Albert's face, as if there was no longer a person left within. But then Albert shook himself slightly and nodded his head, in understanding if not acceptance. The man led him unresisting to a room, pointed out the amenities and left, softly locking the door behind him. Albert fell onto the bed and cried as he had never cried before. It was such an immense betrayal that he could neither believe it nor bear it; but the betrayal had been there in his father's eyes, a betrayal so deep not even guilt or regret remained. If he could have, he would have damned the supernal perceptiveness of his own eyes, eyes that would not let him forget what they had seen.

Albert knew about lies. His parents had never lied to him, but they had taught him about lying. He knew lies were dangerous because any lie was a contradiction to the reality that stood serenely beyond men's ability to fake it, as untouched by their wishes as a mountain. Yet he knew that people lie, that sometimes you had to lie when dealing with an enemy, and how best to lie if you had to without suffering the revenge of a violated reality. But for all that he was a very unusual child, still he was just a child. The depths of deception that adults were capable of were outside his experience and understanding, and the evidence of his own eyes too devastating to refute.

~~~

In the twenty months since that day, Albert had matured. His escort on that day had tried to be like a father to him. He had done so surreptitiously, as if that duty was beyond the level of care and concern that his superiors wanted or would have approved. But he had talked to Albert when he didn't have to, comforted him more than he was required to, even sneaked in the occasional gift or treat. Albert in his turn had taken him into his confidence. But there was always a distance that the man could not reach across.

Albert had been betrayed, and he never needed to learn the same lesson twice. He knew he would never trust another adult again.

His new home had taken on the task of his development with a zeal that exceeded his parents'. Without saying it, but indirectly by expressions and overheard comments, they had made it clear to Albert that his parents' laxness was inexcusable and an early indicator of their true feelings for him. It had not been to let him find his own way in his own manner, but from a desire they would not admit even to themselves: to hold him back from his true potential, which they were responsible for yet feared with the atavistic fear of the unknown.

There were lessons. There were tests. His teachers expressed their disappointment openly if he did less well than they hoped; his surrogate father accepted such results, but Albert could tell he was disappointed too, like he was disappointed that Albert would never fully accept him as a father figure.

Though Albert despised his parents, he still knew when to take their advice, especially in the area in which he had discovered they were experts: deception through omission rather than commission. He knew that his new home expected great results from him. But he also knew that he should keep his true abilities hidden; that this would give him an edge in any future conflict between their interests and his. There was no reason to expect such a conflict would arise: but he had never expected his parents' betrayal either. So, hide he would. Yet he felt, without quite knowing why, but with a grim certainty, that to disappoint them too much was dangerous; that they wanted something from him and if he failed to provide it, they would discard him as his parents had, only more permanently. Hence, he excelled, bearing their disapproval that he excelled less than they had hoped.

~~~

All these things he thought on the morning of his eighth birthday, until his reminiscences were interrupted by a knock on his door. The knock was unnecessary, as Albert well knew. But it was one of the polite touches his mentor, Mr Ward, had come to use routinely.

"Come in!" he called.

Mr Ward entered, presenting Albert with a small cake. "Happy Birthday, Albert!" he said brightly. "And I have another surprise for you. I've persuaded management that since it's your birthday you should have the day off. You can do anything you like!"

Albert gestured toward his window. "Can I go outside?"

A small frown flowed across Ward's face and vanished. "Sorry, Albert, you know I can't do that. We're just not allowed. You know how special you are: it is just too risky to let you outside."

Albert pouted like a frustrated child. Not too much, just enough to convey part genuine disappointment and part playing a game: as if to say, *I'm sad but I don't take it too seriously*. "That's OK, Mr Ward. You know what I never get?"

"What's that, Albert? You know we try to give you everything you need."

"I never get to be alone. So that's what I want today. I just want to go to the playground and do whatever I want. Some climbing, some swimming, some reading. Just me. On my own."

Mr Ward smiled. "I'm sure I can arrange that! Just leave it with me, and someone will come and get you soon." It wasn't as if he wouldn't be watched every second anyway.

"Thanks, Mr Ward," said Albert happily, sitting up to eat his cake.

~~~

So that was how Albert spent his eighth birthday, until in the middle of the afternoon he was lying on a float in the pool, eyes closed, equations mating in his head to produce mainly sterile offspring, as he trailed one arm through the cool water.

His father—his true father, not the substitute Mr Ward—was in no way superstitious, but he appreciated the meaning and power of symbols.

Albert had been born at 3:20 PM.

And at 3:20 PM, Albert felt a strange tingling, as if the arm trailing through the water was an antenna collecting vibrations and channeling them into his body. His father's birthday present had arrived.

Chapter 2: The Vision and the Enigma

Albert held his breath at the strange feelings coursing through him but gave no other external sign. This was part of his inner discipline. He had learned that knowledge was power, and he never shared it without good reason. Especially with those who appeared to love him, for love was the greatest trap of them all.

If he had felt in danger he would have cried out. But the feelings were strange rather than unpleasant, lambent with power rather than febrile with disease. He stretched his arms, as if simply stretching, to feel the fire in his nerves. Then he began to see images in his closed eyes, as if a symphony that had been gathering itself for years was finally beginning to play its first slow movement, and he watched in silent fascination.

His father had given him this gift years before. He had not done it with this circumstance in mind but with any number of circumstances like it. He had not expected it would be needed and, if it were, much later than at this tender age. But he was a cautious man, never playing one strategy at a time: never limiting himself to one plan, but always having a backup, and a backup for the backup. That is what had brought him, beyond all odds, to create Albert's mother, save her, bring her to Capital, and thus in time create Albert himself.

And whatever his son thought of him now, Daniel had loved him and implanted a gift for him that might be used in two years or fifty, perhaps never. But would be there for him in his time of need.

His father was not only wealthy but an eminent scientist with many contacts. He had access to many advanced technologies, and this was one of them. As originally implanted, it was as good as undetectable: mere microscopic organic fibers spread throughout parts of his body. But the fibers were complex micromachines, the skeleton of self-assembling devices, using the energy of his own body for their power and molecular memory for their instructions. Over the years, their complexity had grown, incorporated into bone and muscle but not yet integrated into a whole: still undetectable, except by direct search or exceptional diagnostic luck.

Albert's nervous system had been studied when he was young, and the relevant pathways mapped and understood. Now one of the machines nestled in his optic nerves played those nerves like a conductor leading an orchestra, and what he had become was played into Albert's amazed sight.

He did not know why his father had given him this gift and then abandoned him. He did not know why his father had not told his replacement family about it. Perhaps he had, thought Albert; perhaps this was another test, and hidden watchers were even now smiling at his childish attempts at deception. He dived into the water, to hide an expression that was both a snarl of challenge and a smile of grim determination. *Let them.* It changed nothing. He would assume they did not know and do what he had to do. Not trying would be worse than failing, for at least trying had some chance of success.

His father had hoped he would be there when this long-planned present arrived. He had hoped to share in his son's surprise, answer the eager rush of questions he expected. But he was not here. Yet as the lesson came to an end, Albert emerged from the water to rest his arms on the side of the pool; and as the display in his eyes closed, a voice spoke into his ear: *Happy Birthday, Albert, my beloved son.*

It was his father's voice. Albert knew this meant nothing; knew this gift had been implanted years in the past, long before his loss of love and betrayal. He thought he did not care, that his father's long dead words meant nothing to him. Still, he was glad of the water running from his hair down his face, so that nobody could see his tears.

CHAPTER 3: THE STILLEST HOUR

Albert knew he was now in danger, if he had ever been truly safe. Now that it was complete, his new equipment, while not detectable externally, could be found more readily. A medical problem or some decision to scan him for routine purposes might well reveal his father's gift, and then it might become a curse.

If knowledge was power, knowledge in other hands was danger. He owed his new family nothing. *No, not my family: my captors.* His parents had given him to them, but there was no right in that, therefore these people had no more right to hold him than if they had caught him in a net. If they were truly his family, they would let him go outside, not keep him here for his 'protection'. Even his parents had let him wander. And if he was to do this, he must not think of them as a family who cared for him. So, captors they were, who only cared for him in order to achieve their own hidden purposes. Even Mr Ward. If his own parents could betray him, he would trust nobody. He was on his own, as he always had been. The only difference was he now knew it.

He wondered if he was watched. He thought he must be; he supposed he would find out soon enough in any case. He rang for dinner; he still did not want any company and he knew Mr Ward would indulge him for the rest of the day. He ate, barely tasting the food and barely remembering it afterwards, so lost were such secondary stimuli in the buzz of plans in his brain.

He thought for a long time. Finally, he sighed, curled up and went to sleep. Tomorrow he would see what his new toys could do. *The game is afoot,* he thought, his ever-active mind simultaneously pleased at this homage to his favorite detective, a man who out-saw and out-thought his fellows, and excited at the possibilities of the game itself.

~~~

A little after two in the morning, his remote watcher was startled to see Albert's limbs begin a wild thrashing, his eyes open and staring, before he fell out of bed to the floor, mouth foaming. Then the wild thrashing ended, replaced by a shivering quiver.

"Hell!" the watcher cursed, hitting the alarm.

A bleary-eyed doctor dashed into Albert's room, accompanied by some security guards, and quickly ran some diagnostics over Albert's unconscious body. He looked up with an expression of alarm just as the night supervisor rushed in to join them.

"Sir, we're going to have to take him to a hospital! His heart is racing but his blood pressure is way down; pupils dilated and unresponsive. I don't know what the problem is, and we have no way to properly diagnose or treat something like this here. Christ!"

"Can he be faking it?" the handler asked.

"Nobody can fake something like this! These are all autonomic functions, nothing a person can control!"

"A normal person..."

The doctor shrugged. "He's never shown any ability to control his autonomic functions before. I suppose anything's possible—but I doubt it. As you say, he's not a normal person. But isn't that part of why he's here? Who knows what can go wrong when you tinker with a human body? It looks like he's suffering some kind of organic breakdown, maybe some congenital defect. The only other thing I can think of is poison, but who could poison him here? It's your call... but if you don't take him to hospital, and this continues, he'll probably be dead by morning."

The doctor then fixed him with a dead stare. "I formally recommend hospital. You can over-rule me. But then it's your responsibility if he dies."

"Dammit! You sure you can't treat him here? We've got our own clinic, for Chrissakes!"

The doctor shook his head. "If he'd broken a leg, sure. But not for something like this. If we knew what it was... probably. But we need a hospital. We need high tech diagnostics and treatment, the kind of things only a proper facility has."

The handler chewed his lip. "Watch those damned eyes of his," he instructed the doctor quietly. He walked over and slapped Albert hard on the cheek; there was no response, other than Albert's head just lolling away and spittle escaping his lips.

"No conscious reaction," advised the doctor.

The handler made a decision and brought his wrist to his mouth. "Get us an ambulance. Now!"

They rushed Albert to the public entrance of the facility, the doctor doing his best to stabilize him. Within minutes of their arrival, an ambulance wailed up to meet them, Albert was hustled inside, and it sped off.

No sooner had it hit the road than Albert began shaking violently, eyes flickering, but he subsided within seconds. The doctor had just lifted his eyelid when Albert cried out; his hand shot to the doctor's face; then Albert's flailing arms struck him on the nose and he fell back against the side of the ambulance before falling to the floor, stunned.

"Christ Almighty!" swore the guard as he rushed over to try to stop Albert from harming himself, as he bucked violently on the bed. He grabbed Albert's arms, but one slipped from his grasp and seized the man's neck. Then the man gurgled and fell to the floor.

Albert sat up shakily and looked around.

~~~

In the hours before sleep, Albert had thought about possible courses of action. He had thought about his fears: *a medical problem could lead to discovery*. He had rolled over in his bed to hide his smile in the pillow. *Sometimes a problem defines its solution*.

His plan was bold. That meant it was also risky. He knew he could be caught; and that would give his owners knowledge they should not have. He thought about the carefully crafted picture of himself he had cultivated during his captivity—*how easily the word comes now*—and fretted. Then he relaxed. His plan was not too far beyond the abilities they would expect; a little, but people often reached more deeply into the well of their powers when motivated enough by fear or rage or love. If he failed, he would not defend or explain, yet he would be able to persuade, nonetheless. He smiled again. He considered his plan to be intelligent and bold. It didn't take much change in perspective to make it look stupid and foolhardy, the reaction of inexperienced youth whose bravado and arrogance exceeded its ability. Perhaps it would downgrade rather than upgrade his captors' opinion of him.

If he failed, his father's strange gift would no doubt be taken from him. But if he did not use it now, it would soon be discovered and taken anyway. His possible futures all converged on the fate unleashed by the decision he made now.

There were many unknowns. He didn't even know for sure that he was monitored. But in a world of incomplete information, he could only use the information, clues and guesses he had. *Assume as little as possible, but don't let doubt paralyze you: assume what you must then act.*

Night was always better for dark plots. There were fewer people, and the few who were awake were more likely to be tired. Whatever adaptations they had made to living at night, the legacy of hundreds of millennia of evolution as day-loving hominids had left its indelible mark. Better, there would be fewer people around everywhere else as well.

And so, in the early morning hours he woke up, gave an attention-grabbing act, and then his new internal chemical plant released a poison into his bloodstream. It was not undetectable, but he was counting on his captors having no means of detecting it in the short time available. In any case the doctor had been right: he was not faking anything by then. He was barely conscious, his body fighting for his life, when the doctor had rushed into his room.

But the initial examination over, his real symptoms eased enough for him to act. When the ambulance was underway, he staged a fit to let his flickering eyes take in the scene. One doctor hovering protectively over him; one burly guard to keep him company. No paramedic: presumably they thought the doctor was enough and extraneous people too great a security risk. Fortunately, fitting more guards in would have been difficult; and how many burly armed men do you need to guard one boy? Even a boy like him was no match for one guard, given the imbalance in bone and muscle. Or so they would assume.

Albert had a few plans. If he had to, he would wait to get to the hospital and try to escape from there. But with just two men present it was better to act now. His flailing arms briefly grabbed the doctor's face and a tube flicked out from under his fingernail to inject a powerful soporific; then he knocked the man violently on the head to hide his collapse. The guard received similar treatment. By now the last of the poison in his own body had been almost neutralized, and Albert sat up, alert and ready for action.

He smiled. An ambulance had all kinds of useful supplies. He quickly scanned those supplies, selecting painkillers, scalpels, scissors and the other things he needed.

He looked sadly at his pajamas. He had chosen them because the shirt could pass as outdoor wear, though the trousers wouldn't do at all; but he could hardly have gone to bed in outdoors gear. He studied the two unconscious men. Working as fast as he could, he pulled the jeans off the guard and cut the legs to fit: the raggedy look had never gone completely out of style among the young, and never would. He debated about shoes but decided bare feet would look less out of place, especially with his ragged jeans, than oversized shoes that made him look and walk like a duck. One of them had a cap which fit well enough and would help hide his hair and face from view.

Albert briefly scanned the unconscious men again and chose the guard as the most suitable candidate. Working quickly, he injected local anesthetic into the guard's arm and then his own. He had known for many months that there was a tracker under the skin there; he hoped it was the only one. He quickly made an incision in the guard's arm, sliced the tracker out of his own and inserted it into the guard's in one smooth movement. He did not know if that would work, but the most likely thing was it would transmit an alarm if it cooled down or otherwise failed to detect an environment of living flesh. So, he gave it a new host, hoping that was enough and would help buy him more time. If its brief transit time itself caused an alarm, nobody should be surprised given his apparent medical emergency.

He bandaged both wounds, grabbed some painkillers for later, then banged on the panel between him and the driver's cabin.

A woman's voice issued from a grille, "What's the banging back there?"

"Stop the ambulance! We have a problem here, something's come loose. We need you in here," Albert replied in a passable imitation of the doctor's voice.

The ambulance slid to a halt. When the driver flung open the back doors, Albert dispatched her in the same way as he'd done the others. He dragged her inside, shut one of the doors and peered out the other. They were in a residential part of town next to a well-wooded park: perhaps already near the hospital.

He turned back inside to look down at his erstwhile captors, now lying helpless at his feet, plotting his next moves.

~~~

Liliana jogged through the night. She couldn't sleep and hoped that the combination of exercise and cool air through her hair and lungs would drive the insomnia away. This was a safe neighborhood, so she was unconcerned by the hour, but the can of mace in her pocket gave her extra comfort.

As she emerged from a path through the trees, she was surprised to see an ambulance, lights flashing, stopped by the roadside with its back door hanging open.

She stepped cautiously towards the door. "Hello? Hello? Is anything the matter?"

A boy crawled to the opening, head down, blood on his hands and arm. "Help me," he coughed pathetically. "Are you all right, kid?" she asked in alarm, stepping forward.

Then like some giant trapdoor spider he lunged out, grabbed her by the neck, dragged her bodily inside and slammed the door.

~~~

Albert looked at his growing collection of captives, wondering if he should leave a clearer message for anyone tempted to track him. He smiled coldly, then did what he had to do with calm precision. When he was done, he examined his work with satisfaction. *It would be rude to leave without a farewell letter to my masters.*

He peered carefully outside again but nobody else was in sight, so he hopped out, slammed the door and went around to the front. As he had expected, the ambulance was still ready to go. He sat in the passenger side, set the auto navigation to follow a winding route passing within a block of the hospital before continuing to the coast, then turned the flashing lights off and sent it on its way. After it had passed the hospital and was meandering through another large, leafy residential park, he briefly slowed the vehicle, stepped onto the outside, slammed the door, then jumped.

The ambulance rapidly accelerated and sped off. Albert did not look back as he bounded away into the cover of trees and darkness.

CHAPTER 4: THE GREETING

The Department of Human Genetic Integrity, or GenInt as it was more commonly known, was not as powerful as it had once been. It had been given enormous powers at its founding, at the height of public fear of genetic engineering of humans. Powers that had eroded only slightly over the years, an erosion slowed by periodic news releases carefully cultivated to keep the fear at least simmering.

But the years had passed and then an operation had gone terribly wrong. Somehow a geneh had not only been born but grown to adulthood, despite the power GenInt had been granted and the numerous controls they had put in place. In GenInt's view the police had bungled the case appallingly; their own role in the debacle was minimized in their internal reports. In any case the geneh and her maker had escaped.

Worse, the two had escaped to Capital, the only country depraved enough to give them sanctuary. To itself and its supporters, Capital was a free country, the freest on Earth. But GenInt knew it for what it really was: an anarchy and a danger to right rule and good order. The people, GenInt's hierarchy knew, needed to be led. Left to their own devices they were like a rudderless ship, or worse, a ship with a hundred rudders and a hundred captains, destined for the sharp rocks all around. The escaped geneh was a case in point. A few videos of the happy-looking creature playing with children, and suddenly too much of the world loved her and thought genehs weren't so bad after all. *Idiots.* The people were happy for GenInt to do whatever it took to protect them from their fears but were extremely unhappy to be shown any unpleasant consequences. They were like birds raising a cuckoo. They thought it was cute and wanted to care for it and tend to it, stupidly unaware that it had killed their own babies, and when grown would do the same to their children's babies.

But GenInt's powers had come from the people, and a telling blow had been landed against it by this one woman and her seeming normalcy of spirit in her abnormal yet harmless body. The active opposition was bad enough. Worse was how much of their remaining support was now infected by suspicion and mistrust. So GenInt had learned caution.

For all the good it did them today.

~~~

Isabel had been leaning back in her chair, savoring the scent of her midafternoon cup of Earl Grey tea and daydreaming about her boyfriend, when a ping alerted her to an incoming message deemed important. *Important my foot*, she thought, having accumulated years of experience in the department and the mysterious evaluations of its message-filtering AIs. So, she kept her tea at the ready in one hand while she opened the document with the other.

She sat up straight at the name of the sender. *What the hell?*

Isabel read the document, first with puzzlement then with growing alarm. Her tea sat cooling on the desk, lonely, fragrant and forgotten.

The document had no title except for the large letters *DRAFT*. Isabel sat in her chair, tapping her desk in a faint drumbeat as she thought about what it said and why its author had sent it. There was no note, no explanation, just the sender's identity and the text of a speech. The speech revealed more than anyone should have known about the recent escape debacle; and far more than GenInt would have wanted revealed, which was nothing. The attendant denunciation of GenInt was enough to make Isabel literally blush. But *DRAFT*. That implied it could be changed, but was it an olive branch or a threat? The speech had a time and date already fixed. *Tomorrow night*. It was only afternoon now, but if the speech was going to be altered there wasn't much time. Its author clearly knew that bureaucratic wheels moved slowly, but he had allowed no more than the minimum time for them to roll in the right direction, defined as the one which would permit desirable changes on its journey from *DRAFT* to *FINAL*.

Isabel thought some more. The message had come through the Anonymizer, the service GenInt and other government departments used to allow untraceable reports. Yet the sender had not only identified himself but validated his identity. The two facts together implied that he wanted them to know that the message was serious, but he did not need a reply. So why did he send it? Why not just dump them in it when he gave his speech?

Fortunately, one consequence of her years in the department was that Isabel had risen to a position of some seniority. In fact, the number of people higher than her could be measured in the tens, not the hundreds. Thus, she was privy to things that most were unaware of. She knew that was why she had been chosen as the recipient—the damnable man knew all kinds of unlikely facts and wanted a target who knew he knew. She knew what the speech was about. She knew why it was labeled *DRAFT*. She knew what the sender wanted.

The conclusions were inescapable. He was not happy and had made the consequences of his unhappiness clear. He expected action that would change his opinion, he expected it fast, and there would be no negotiations and no excuses.

She felt sick.

She composed a summary of the document with her evaluation and recommendations, attached the document itself so the recipients could make their own judgments, and hovered her finger over *Send*. She hesitated. She had risen high in the department, but if she stuffed this one up, she might find herself in Alaska. She shrugged and sent it, adding her own much shorter mental summary of her more formal written one.

We're screwed.

CHAPTER 5: WAR AND WARRIORS

Miriam Hunter lay in bed, her mind for once ensconced in the warm pleasure of relaxation. She had lived through many things in her life, and often enough they reached their dead fingers into her dreams to revive the fear, the fire, or the blood of their time. The arms that held her tonight were usually unaware of the rampages of her internal demons; only becoming aware if the bonds preventing imagination from becoming action loosened enough for her to jerk or moan in her sleep. Those arms and the pleasure of their embrace were part of why the monsters of the past did not stalk her mind tonight.

Tonight, she simply flew free, soaring through a sky of clouds and sun, looking down on a world as full of promise as it was remote. She moved her arm, and arrowed down through canyons of white, her wrist trembling as it trailed through the tendrils of mist. She wondered how something so insubstantial as cloud could cause such a strange sensation and frowned, feeling there was something important about it. As if even here the world was calling to her.

She awoke, prizing one eye open to peer at the phone silently but insistently vibrating on her wrist. Part of her mind wanted to just float back into the clouds, but she knew it must be important. *It damn well better be.* She prized her other eye open. The blinds were closed but she could tell by the quality of the light that it was still pre-dawn. *And damn it, it must be.* Her eyes focused on the time, and she saw it was only a little after four.

She gently levered her companion's arm from her and slipped out of bed. She was naked, but the room was warm and the carpet soft.

She could tell by the rhythm of his breathing that he was in a deep sleep, and she knew he wouldn't wake; he had been known to sleep through earthquakes. Nevertheless, she moved quietly with a smooth grace, grabbing what she needed without turning on any lights; finally stealing from the room like a cat on a secret mission.

She set her car on auto and tried to find out more about the emergency, but there was nothing. She frowned at the terse command to get herself in to see her chief as soon as humanly possible if not sooner. *What the hell?* She took control of the car and sped up. *Your wish is my command, Master.*

But when she arrived and took the elevator up to her floor, she was surprised. With the urgency of the message, she had expected to encounter a crowd of tense cops crackling with coffee and nerves, but the building held no more people than usual at this hour. The absence of a crowd was matched by the absence of tension.

At least when she walked into the Chief's office he was there too, along with a single man as nondescript as he was nonuniformed. She looked carefully from one to the other searching for clues, but while they returned her gaze, neither of them looked interested in giving her any. She frowned, kicked the door shut and sat down. She crossed her legs, allowed her eyes to pass over the stranger, looked at the Chief and simply asked, "Well?"

The stranger allowed himself a slight smile, as if acknowledging her composure. The Chief looked at him expectantly, but the smile neither moved nor showed any signs of allowing his mouth to open to speak. Finally, the Chief gave up and sighed.

"OK, Hunter. No doubt, despite your surprising lack of curiosity, somewhere in there you are dying to find out what's going on, and it looks like I've been elected to tell you. This gentleman"—the slight inflection in his voice ensured the word was well bracketed with ironic quotation marks— "is one of our colleagues from GenInt."

Miriam's eyes widened and darted to the man's, but his only response was a slight widening of his smile. Her relationship with GenInt, formally the UN Department of Human Genetic Integrity, had not been smooth. They had never forgiven her for her part in the Katlyn fiasco, when both the catlike geneh and her creator had escaped after being on the verge of capture. From her side, she had never forgiven them for the laws that had made the whole episode necessary; nor for how their agent had insinuated himself into her affections and her bed in order to spy on her investigations. In a more recent case, looking into the fate of mysteriously vanished drifters, Miriam had lost her limbs and almost her mind as well, when that mind had been suppressed so her brain could be used to control a deadly war robot who came to call herself Kali. Then, to the world's surprise, the geneh master had offered to restore her mangled body via his advanced cell therapies and proceeded to do so. The public relations boost he earned via her participation did not mend any fences in her relationship with GenInt. Miriam did not care; she saw nothing but positives in the entire transaction. Including any embarrassment suffered by GenInt.

As the man made no comment and thus chose to remain outside the conversation, she felt free to speak of him in the third person. "So, does our colleague have a name? Or is he just a flunky with a stick?"

"You can call me Adams," he finally replied in a gravelly voice. "There is no need for hostility. We're all on the same side, are we not?"

She inspected him coolly. "I don't know. Are we? If you would be so kind as to tell me why you dragged me out of bed at this time of night, maybe I could decide."

Adams steepled his fingers. "This is a matter of great delicacy. No doubt you are wondering why, if this is an emergency so important to interrupt your sleep, you and Chief Pike are the only police here."

He paused for comment, but she remained watching in silence. "Detective, I understand why the police in general are suspicious of us, and you in particular. No doubt you wonder why, in that case, we especially want you on the case. The thing is, in some sense it is because of you that we are in this predicament. I don't mean in any blameworthy sense. Quite the reverse. As you know, that whole Katlyn affair was very bad publicity for us. It emboldened certain factions within GenInt, factions you might approve of, or at least disapprove of less than others. It led to a softer approach. Not that we in any way compromise on our core principles, mind you. But you could say we became more interested in study and understanding than in immediate and strict enforcement."

"So, what's blown up in your faces this time?"

Adams grimaced. "So you don't jump to understandable but wrong conclusions when you hear some of the surprising details, first I should show you the damage."

He summoned some images into the air. Miriam had seen many things over her career, but even she paled. They were bodies, two men and two women, lying on the floor of an ambulance. They were arranged as if sleeping yet were covered in blood, and the spray on the walls was mute testimony to the violence of their end. Morgue close-ups of three of them showed they had almost been torn apart. Something about them gave the impression that the tearing had been intended to keep them alive and suffering as long as possible; that when death had finally come, they had welcomed it.

She looked at Adams, her earlier bantering hostility forgotten in the commonality of two human beings facing such ruthless barbarity.

"The men were ours, a doctor and a guard, escorting the killer to hospital. The women were not part of GenInt, just an innocent ambulance driver doing her job, and some unfortunate passerby."

Miriam didn't ask for details, she just stared. She knew what the involvement of GenInt implied and she knew the details would not be long in coming.

"Yes, you understand. The killer was a geneh. He pretended to be dying—quite convincingly, according to witnesses at the facility he escaped from—then, by means we aren't completely sure of, he knocked his two escorts out with some kind of drug. But that wasn't enough for him, as you can see. Not content with escape, he did that to them."

She mutely examined the images. "I see four bodies in the ambulance but only three close-ups. What happened to the fourth?"

"He is the guard and is still alive. The killer transferred an embedded tracker into him, and we assume that is why he left him alive. If the tracker doesn't feel a pulse, it sends an alarm."

"Terrific. Any other physical evidence?"

He handed her a piece of paper in a protective sleeve. "It appears he wanted to leave us a written message as well," he explained. Written in what looked like blood were the words 'Don't come looking for me.'

"This is a victim's blood?"

"Yes, the one still alive, ironically enough."

"Do you know why he targeted the second woman?"

"We don't know how she became involved. I suppose genehs could well have a grudge against GenInt, but that doesn't account for what he did to her. Obviously, he had to leave the ambulance at some point, so perhaps she was just in the wrong place at the wrong time. An inconvenient witness, eliminated not only without qualm but with unnecessary cruelty. Underlining the lesson and warning, perhaps."

"Maybe that was his first mistake. Do you know where she was last seen?"

"Approximately. However, it doesn't help, other than marking the earliest location on the ambulance route he might have run from. We expect that he kidnapped her, killed her while still travelling, then escaped somewhere else."

A terrible thought intruded into her mind, but she suppressed it. *Don't jump at shadows, find out the facts first.* "So, who is this geneh? Where did he come from? I haven't even heard of any investigations lately."

"Yes, well, I did mention our change of emphasis. A year and a half ago in Asia, our operatives discovered an illegal operation. Not a one-man show like your man Tagarin, but a small government extra-legal initiative. It is best if I do not reveal the government but suffice it to say it is one of the less reputable ones. As you know, GenInt has a lot of reach even in places like that, and in this case someone informed. We like to believe it was an honest citizen doing his duty, but frankly it was more likely the result of an internal power struggle, or plain revenge over some personal quarrel. Be that as it may, we found out about it and raided the facility. The scientist in charge blew up the lab. We presume he was trying to destroy the evidence, but his creation must have been alerted by all the noise and had hidden. He might also have been aware of the explosives, for he was protected enough to survive."

He looked into Miriam's eyes. "In a past age, I imagine our agents would have killed him on the spot. But in this age, they did not. They took him under our protection. We brought him here, where he was to be looked after, raised as normally as possible, and studied."

"How old is he?"

"We aren't entirely sure. You know from your own experience that their rate of development can be altered. Unfortunately, the scientist did succeed in destroying all the records of what they were trying to do, and everyone involved is either unknown or dead. But he now looks eight years old, so we estimate he is somewhere between six and ten in actual years."

"You've had him for over a year. What are his modifications?"

"Unlike your old nemesis Katlyn, he has no obvious external signs. But he is exceptionally fast, strong and quick-witted. Unfortunately, also more ruthless than we ever imagined, as if he has no conception of morality at all, or if he does, believes he is beyond it. So ruthless that we now wonder whether the destruction of his lab and records, rather than being the work of his creators, was engineered by himself."

Suspicion again prickled Miriam's scalp. "May I see some images of this child?"

Adams complied without hesitation and Miriam studied the images. "Caucasian? Why a white child in Asia?"

"We believe, given his enhancements in a body that would pass as normal, that what they were after was some kind of super-spy. We suspect the target was the USA or perhaps some other Western country. Even in our day of worldwide travel and ethnic mixing, the camouflage of the majority can help."

"These images… they vary a lot. Were they taken over a long period of time?"

"No. They are all recent. He has a very… mobile face. It lets him change his appearance. Not infinitely of course, but significantly, as you can see. Which also fits the spy theory."

"He seems to have a different eye color in some of these too?"

Adams smiled grimly. "At least that part isn't a natural ability. He is quite partial to color-changing contact lenses, and we have indulged him. We think it may partly be admiration for, or perhaps solidarity with, Katlyn, with her startling yellow eyes. His favorite color is a bright green, though that doesn't seem to have been captured in these. Maybe that's because his natural color is blue."

"You've had him eighteen months, you said? Exactly?"

"Closer to seventeen. Why?"

"I was wondering whether it had made any difference. How was his relationship with you while you had him? Friendly? Hostile? Do you think he came to think of you as his family? Why do you think he turned into… whatever he became, to do this?"

Adams spread his hands. "He showed no signs of psychopathy if that's what you mean. Not a normal boy, of course, and rather suspicious and reserved. But friendly in an aloof way if that makes any sense."

"What's his name?"

"He calls himself Chao. I'm told that in Chinese it means 'surpassing'."

Miriam studied Adams, wondering about his story. But there wasn't much on the side of her suspicions, just the coincidence in age, the white skin, and the intermittently green eyes. But none of those were exact matches and against it were all the details of the story and, while the face could match amidst all that variability, it nowhere did exactly. She felt relieved at that conclusion, provisional as it was, for otherwise the extra tragedy of the child's manifest evil would be even harder to bear.

"When did all this happen? His escape, I mean."

"A week ago."

"So why are you coming to me now? When the trail is cold? Why come to us at all now? What do you think I can do that you can't do yourself?"

"Obviously we had hoped to catch him quickly without causing either a panic or, frankly, our own embarrassment." He produced a frank, embarrassed smile as evidence. "However, as you point out, the trail is now cold, and the hunt has reached a stage where your expertise is greater than ours. And of course, besides your well-deserved reputation at catching criminals, you are one of the few people with actual experience in hunting a geneh on the loose. True, this one is quite different. But nobody has any better experience. Also…"

"Yes?"

"I know your history with him is rocky. But the esteemed Dr Tagarin appears to have forgiven you, and his treatment of you brought him a lot of good press. As the world's foremost expert in the subject of genehs, he is a resource without price. We had hoped that while he would see us in hell before he would help us, you might be able to talk to him when nobody else could."

She stared at him. "Are you serious?! There's not a chance! If you have any hope that he might one day be useful to you for something else, don't even think about it: if I tried what you're asking he'd probably never speak to me again."

She gave him a penetrating look. "I know you have suspicions about me: it is in your nature to be suspicious. But do not imagine that Tagarin and I are friends, and I can leverage that friendship into him helping me, let alone you. He saw an opportunity to use me, in a way I could hardly refuse, and he used me to his benefit. If there is a bond between us, it is the bond between enemies who respect each other enough to be civil as long as neither crosses the other. But to help me help you? He'd see me dead first."

"Even with something as… barbaric as these murders? I know Dr Tagarin and GenInt are enemies, but to give him credit he has always acted ethically according to his lights, and he has always avoided bloodshed. I imagine he would be as horrified by this as we are."

Horrified? Oh yes, especially if… but no. It can't be. Deal with the horrors you know, not the ones you imagine. "No doubt. But as you say, I know him. Even if he believed your story, he would blame you, not Chao. He would say you made him what he was."

"And," she added after a pause, giving him a steely look, "Far be it from me to tell him he's wrong."

They must really want me, she thought, when his only reaction to this provocation was an apologetic shrug and the comment, "Well, I had to ask. We would like your help, with or without Tagarin. And I do not need to point out that you are an officer of the law, and GenInt is still part of that law. I will admit that your notoriety gives you a measure of freedom in your dealings with us, but there are limits you would do well to not overstep."

"You come here to ask my help by threatening me?"

He shrugged. "You have a well-deserved reputation for putting both logic and law above your personal feelings. I do not mean to threaten you, merely remind you of some facts, which are facts whatever either of us feel about them."

"There is one fact you are avoiding mentioning."

"Yes?"

She waved the message written in blood at him. "It looks like anyone who goes looking for him is likely to end up horribly dead."

"Be assured that we are not trying to get rid of you, if that's what you're suggesting. You are highly able, and I am sure you can look after yourself."

She stared at him, stared at the message, stared at her boss.

"So, if I agree to this, where do we go from here?"

"If we thought we could tell you that, I wouldn't be here. Just do what you do. Find him. Stop him before anyone else is hurt."

"Parameters? Is it secret or can I talk to whomever I need to? Dead, alive, or you don't care? What help will you give me?"

"We would like to keep it confidential, but not at the expense of failing to catch him. So, we would appreciate as much discretion as you can reasonably maintain. We will give you access to all the information we have that is relevant—any information obtained *will* be classified, however—and your department may bill us for all reasonable expenses. As for dead or alive—I think that if we told you to bring him in dead, you would be unlikely to obey. So, we give you no instructions: if you find you need to kill him, do so; if you find you *want* to kill him, you may do that too; or you may bring him in alive. It is entirely up to you. *But bring him in.*"

"I'd like access to the bodies and any other physical evidence."

"You can inspect things like the ambulance and locations. The bodies, I'm afraid, have been cremated already. We do not think that will inconvenience you. All physical evidence had already been collected, of course, and you are welcome to it."

She gave him a look that left him in no doubt what she thought of that.

"I suppose it will have to do. I assume you have this boy's genome sequence; can I have that?"

He looked uncomfortable. "I am afraid that would be against GenInt's strict rules. We exist to protect the world from genehs, not reveal how they were constructed, not even to other government agencies. I do not think that will inconvenience you either. Any samples or DNA sequences you think are relevant, you can simply send to us for analysis and comparison. That might even be faster than using your own overworked resources."

"For someone asking for help, you are not being all that helpful, burning evidence and withholding relevant information."

"I believe I made it clear that we don't think any of that will inconvenience you. The cremations, well, we did not intend involving the police, and we had already collected all the data. The genome, as I have explained, is accessible to you in the only way you really need."

She looked at him for a while, slowly drumming her fingers on the desk. "Well, can I at least interview the surviving guard? Today?"

"Of course."

After the previous, she hadn't thought it would be 'of course' at all. "And whomever in GenInt knew the boy best?"

"Of course. That will be Mr Ward."

She stared at him a while longer.

"All right, Mr Adams. I'll help you. Not for GenInt, and not for your pogrom against genehs in general. But for the sake of his victims and their families."

Adams nodded and attempted a friendly smile. "That, Detective Hunter, is all I ask."

Privately, she doubted that was all they *would* ask, but she would cross that chasm when she reached it or, more likely, it opened under her feet.

~~~

After Adams had gone, Miriam sat back in her chair, eyes closed, considering all he had said and shown her. She knew he had been honest about wanting her help, yet felt sure there was more to it: that they would have preferred not to involve her at all.

She studied the images of Chao. *More than one of him, and there'd be Chaos*, she thought with grim amusement. *And are there more than one of him?* She did not trust coincidences, even somewhat loose ones, but this time, looking at the carnage Chao had left behind, she hoped that was all it was.

Now that she was alone with her own thoughts, she allowed her earlier fears back into her mind, and thought back to the call she had taken nearly two years ago, wondering.

~~~

Miriam had been at home. Not at Beldan's home but in her own apartment high above the city. They had not married. Not because they did not love one another with a passion that ran deeper than infatuation or lust, and not because either feared commitment, but simply because they were both so committed to their jobs that too much of their lives was forced to be separate. Sometimes she thought that they might get married and have children, but no urgent need forced the issue. When they were in the same city they lived together and they shared their lives, their minds, their hearts and their bodies. For now, that was enough. Perhaps it always would be.

Her apartment had always been an extravagance for someone on a police salary, even someone as senior as her. But she had not paid for it, except by the character that had earned her uncle's love and respect enough to bequeath it to her. Now even as Beldan's wife she would keep it. It was hers and held many memories that deserved to be kept alive.

Sometimes she and Beldan would come here, if it was convenient or they felt like a change. Sometimes she liked to come here when Beldan was away, for the solitude and to live in her own space. Today she was alone.

It was late afternoon when an encrypted call pinged insistently on her private line. The AI in her phone might be relatively simple, but it was assuring her this was a call she would want to take, so she accepted.

The man who appeared looked out at her with his usual intensity, except now it was distorted by a terrible urgency. She began to smile in greeting, but he cut her off with no greeting of his own.

"Miriam! Sorry to call you like this. But something has happened. Something terrible."

"What... what is it?"

"I must apologize that we never told you what I'm about to. It is something we thought better to remain unknown, not that it did us any good, as it turns out. Katlyn desperately wanted to tell you, but we agreed it was too dangerous. But you see... we have a son."

"A son!"

He nodded, his haunted look the opposite of the joy such announcements usually entailed. Her own heart sank at the implication. "I... I see. Please go on."

"It is safe here, and you can't keep a child locked up. He was out wandering this afternoon. He's gone."

She sat up straight, automatically locking her own feelings away so they would not distract her. "You must have reported this to your local police. What's the status?"

"No clues. He had a tracker: we might let him out, but there are some routine precautions one must take. That's how we knew he had gone: he seemed to be staying in the one spot, but he would not answer any calls. When we went there, we found his tracker inside a physiological simulator, so it would give no medical alarm. The police couldn't find a trace of him. Someone has taken him."

"Where had he been?"

"Playing on the outer reefs."

"The presence of the simulator proves he didn't just accidentally fall into the water, or into a crevice, obviously. Any clues from the tracker?"

"The detailed transmission log from the tracker showed a brief loss of signal, then its resumption. So, we assume someone used a signal blocker then covered things up before that became suspicious itself. There is only one reason for that: someone took him, someone who put in a lot of planning and resources."

"Why?"

He looked at her, agony on his face. "Because he is my son. *Our* son." She knew what that emphasis meant; she knew why they had not revealed the boy's parentage. The son of the geneh Katlyn would be a symbol and an affront to half the world.

"So, no clues at all?"

He shook his head. "Whoever did this was professional and at a high level. We guess they came out of the sea and left the same way. Probably an airplane-borne stealth submersible. Either that or…"

Or he's already dead, Miriam completed in her mind.

"What can I do to help?"

He shook his head again. "I don't know. But I just wanted you to know. So that you knew… and if you hear anything, you'll know what it might mean. We don't know who took him, or why, or what they did to him or want to do with him. Or even if… even if he's still alive. So just… keep your ears and eyes open, I suppose."

"I will."

She looked at him and allowed the door in her mind to open a crack. "Oh Daniel! I'm so sorry!"

She turned her attention to Katlyn, who had been sitting on the arm of his chair, silent and staring into the distance with an empty expression, as if part of her soul had vanished with her son. "Katlyn! I don't know what I can do—but whatever it is, I'll do it."

For long seconds she was afraid that Katlyn would not reply. Then she turned her eyes to Miriam's and bared her teeth in a feral snarl, which brought back memories of what she had been when she had first caught Miriam and nearly killed her, the first fatal casualty of her lone war against the world. "If you find who did this and Albert is dead, kill them. Promise you'll do that. Promise me." Her voice was as implacable as Death himself.

"It won't come to that," she answered in a whisper. "He's not dead. If they wanted to do that, they'd want to make a statement. Show off what they did. You must believe that."

But Katlyn didn't answer, merely turned her eyes back to the distance. Miriam realized that their new sheen was tears she would not yet cry.

She turned back to Tagarin. "Daniel, is there any reason he would have been taken, I mean besides just being the son of a couple as famous as you and Katlyn?"

He looked into her eyes and the agony in his own was worse. "He is a geneh, not just the son of a geneh, but one in his own right."

Her eyes widened again. "Oh my God, Daniel. What kind? What

did you do to him?"

"Nothing external; there's nothing to set him apart from anyone else except his emerald-green eyes. Unlike Katlyn, I wasn't trying to make a point, just a son. A human son, with all that means."

He paused and she waited, wondering what more was to come.

"He has some less visible improvements. He is strong and fast, like his mother. But his main enhancement is that he also may be the most intelligent human who ever lived."

"What?! You can do that?"

"We don't know everything about the genetic basis of human intelligence or how far we can take it. Even with unplanned natural variability we've had the rare blessings of a Leonardo da Vinci, an Isaac Newton, an Einstein or an Aristotle. Based on what we do know, I tried to do better even than them, and I believe I succeeded. Of course, he has not yet reached his full potential, but even now his talents are remarkable.

"Imagine if Leonardo had a child. Not a child of recombination and dilution, as is normal, but one where his genius was purified and refined, all dross burned away, and its essence amplified by all the power of science. He is that child.

"I suspect from your face that you do not fully approve. I understand, few do. But appreciate that improving the human race is my passion, and, like all parents, I wanted the best for my son.

"I just hope that I have not destroyed him instead."

~~~

The boy's age was rubbery but within the right range. His appearance wasn't right but was close. His origin was different but could be a lie.

But why would GenInt lie about it? Did they want the boy found, or not? GenInt knew about her history with the Tagarins, though she hoped not all of it. As far as the world knew, Katlyn was still her enemy and, while Daniel had saved her, his announced reason was civic duty and altruism, and his unstated but obvious motive the spectacular public relations victory it gave his cause. Few knew he had also done it out of friendship, and none of those were likely to rat her out to GenInt. Still, he had done it, and GenInt might suspect her loyalty or efficiency might be reduced if she knew she was hunting their son. Or perhaps they really had hoped for Tagarin's help and knew they would never get it if he knew they had taken his own child.

She decided there was no benefit in telling Daniel and Katlyn about this development. Any hope they gained from his being alive would be crushed into pain by what he had become, and any hope still remaining after that might end up cruelly dashed if it were not him after all.

For in any case, she did not know it was him. She evaluated the alternatives dispassionately. GenInt might be lying, and there was no Chao, only Albert. If GenInt were telling the truth, things got complex. Chao and Albert could be different, in which case Albert's fate remained unknown: he could be dead or a prisoner elsewhere or even within GenInt. But the alleged timing allowed the possibility that the Asian group had kidnapped Albert, who had then *become* Chao. Miriam felt the last was perhaps the greatest tragedy: a lone child, abducted by one group only to be snatched by another, and somewhere along that journey being twisted from an innocent child playing at the seaside into a vicious killer.

That thought led her mind back to the victims, and the tragedy of lives cut short and the grief which that caused their loved ones, and in the glare of that calamity it did not occur to her to wonder what other things GenInt might be lying about.

Chapter 6: The Convalescent

The man who was ushered into an interview room later that morning was solidly built, with a wide head fastened to a thick neck; he had short, curly light brown hair and imperturbable grey eyes. He wore a short-sleeved shirt from which muscular arms emerged; a tattooed serpent wound around the left one. When he sat down, his eyes lazily scanned the room while his strong hands rested calmly on the table, moving only to scratch at a dressing on his arm.

As Miriam walked in and sat down in front of him, she saw his eyes flicker briefly over her body, but she had the impression it was habitual threat assessment, not something prompted by more common and less savory motives.

"Hello, Mr Gagliardi," she said. "You know why you are here. Can you tell me what happened?"

"Not much to say, ma'am. There was me and the doc in the ambulance when the boy had a fit. The doc tried to help but the kid was flailing all over the place and knocked him down. When I went to help, he stabbed me in the neck and that's the last I remember."

"What did he stab you with? Did you see a syringe or anything? Where did he get it from?"

"I didn't see nothing in his hands, though he was so damn fast it's possible. But it felt like he stabbed me with his own fingernails, like he had poison claws or something."

"Did you see what he did to the others, or know why he killed that passerby?"

"Sorry ma'am. I knew nothing until I woke up in hospital. But there's one thing I do know, ma'am. Things like him shouldn't be running around. Folks shouldn't make 'em, and other folks shouldn't keep 'em. Know what I mean?"

"Have you shared that opinion with your employer?"

"I'm just a guard, ma'am."

"You are also the only one he left alive. Do you know why?"

He rubbed his dressing. "He had some tracker he stuck in my arm. I guess he just left me alive to fool it."

"Did you know the boy at all?"

"Not really. Saw him around sometimes. Never spoke to him. I did bring some food to him and Mr Ward once, but all he did was look through me with those damn green eyes of his."

"Green?" she pounced. "I thought his eyes were blue?"

Gagliardi shrugged, looked uncomfortable. "I hear he can change 'em. Only saying what I saw, ma'am. I'm just a guard."

~~~

Mr Ward came in later and presented quite a different image. He was of medium height and build, compensating for his average physique by being nattily dressed and sporting carefully groomed shoulder-length brown hair and a narrow, precise mustache. Bright brown eyes regarded the world and all its works with amused benevolence.

When Miriam entered the room, his eyes remained properly fixed on her face, and their mode switched to friendly, open and sincere. She decided she liked the guard more.

"Good morning, Mr Ward," she began. "I understand you were closest to the boy, Chao? What is your position in GenInt and your relationship with him?"

"Good morning, Detective," he replied. "I am a psychologist. I am, or tried to be, a mentor and father figure to the boy. I thought I had succeeded at least to some extent, but it appears not so well."

"Why did you keep him? I thought GenInt were opposed to the existence of genehs?"

"GenInt is not as ruthless as it once was, and more tolerant elements held sway in this case. I admit I am one of them. It was thought that tracking his development would give valuable data on what happens to a modified human being growing up, especially regarding possible negative side-effects including mental, physical or developmental instabilities. Sadly, we might be seeing the effect of such instabilities here."

"How would you describe his physical state?"

"He was unusually strong and fast, with excellent balance and dexterity. Seemed healthy. Unlike your Katlyn, there was nothing exotic about his appearance. From the outside he looked much like any other boy, though of course with the uncertainty in his age one can't make precise comparisons."

"She is not 'my Katlyn'," she replied curtly. "But that aside, how would you describe him mentally?"

"Very clever. The higher the intelligence the harder it is to measure. Fewer points of comparison, you see. But I would say he was one in a million. Arithmetically there must be thousands of comparable brains among the world's billions, but it's still exceptional. He displayed both rapid thinking and the ability to solve complex problems. However, he wasn't consistent. It was as if he was a high-performance engine that had cracks in its construction. He was brilliant, but had odd failures and weaknesses, yet never consistent ones."

"Emotionally?"

"He was not happy, but nor was he depressed. He fluctuated much like a normal person, though sadder than average. But no indications of buried rage, delusions or psychopathy. I was surprised that he wanted so badly to escape, let alone what he did upon doing so."

"You are surprised he wanted to escape? Surely you would have expected it, given he was a captive?"

"I did say, 'so badly'. He appears to have somehow poisoned himself to get out, then went on to exact a terrible vengeance on everyone within reach. That goes beyond a generic wish to be free. Perhaps there was some trigger we did not observe. Perhaps the monster was always there, lurking. Perhaps both."

"You mentioned poison, and of course he knocked out his guards. Mr Gagliardi told me he had poison claws. What do you think happened?"

"Surely if he had something as melodramatic as venomous claws, we would have noticed before this. No, I think Mr Gagliardi has too much imagination. The boy must have found something to use. Or maybe," he added uneasily, "he had inside help."

"Is that likely?"

"No, but nor was his escape, so it must be considered. Be assured we will tell you if we discover anything like that."

"Thank you. Please transmit any other information about the boy that you think could help, especially if it gives any clues about where he might go or what he might do. For now, I have only one further question. You said that his intelligence was one in a million, but that it was inconsistent. Perhaps that was part of the instabilities you mentioned. Or could he have been fooling you?"

"You mean, was he even more intelligent, so much so that he could plan and execute a pretense that he was less intelligent, if one in a million can be called that? That would imply..." His stopped and his eyes gained a touch of alarm. "I certainly hope not!"

"So do I," murmured Miriam. "So do I..."

CHAPTER 7: THE SHADOW

The news report was prominent, but not too prominent.

It declared that a dangerous geneh had escaped from a GenInt holding and research facility. It urged the public to be alert but not alarmed and that the geneh, being still a mere boy and a fugitive, was unlikely to hurt anyone unless cornered. Photos were shown with the admonition to report but not approach.

GenInt took full responsibility for the incident, and internal investigations were proceeding. GenInt reaffirmed its dedication to protecting the public and rooting out dangerous genetic engineering wherever it may occur.

Celebrated detective Miriam Hunter had been appointed to the case and was already on the trail, so the public could be assured that all that could be done was being done, and a swift resolution was hoped for. A brief resume of her stellar career was included to support these assertions, wherein the embarrassing escape of Katlyn was reimagined as 'driven from the country'.

There was no mention of the carnage of the geneh boy's escape, that being considered by the authorities to be too alarming.

In their homes, bars and offices, people saw this and shivered, frowned, cursed, or reacted in any of the other ways people react according to their predilections. In one office, a man read it and smiled; his smile held victory, with a dash of cynical contempt. *Speech version two then,* he thought with satisfaction but not surprise.

CHAPTER 8: JOYS AND PASSIONS

"A story is told in the Word of God. It is the story of Babel and the great Tower men built there. The lesson of the story is not that men should not build. No, my brothers. The lesson is that men should not imagine that their puny efforts can equal the glory of God; the lesson is that men should not try to exceed the works of their own Creator. For when men tried, he cast down their tower and confused their tongues, creating all the languages of the world."

The preacher paused, raking the audience with his gaze. "Some believe this story is literally true. Some of the enemies of God say it is but a myth from the dawn of mankind, a tale of folly born of ignorance. And I?"

He paused, eyes gently stroking the audience for long seconds, an audience who jumped as one when he thundered, "Do you think the Word of God is hostage to the science of man? Do you think that if a man finds a shard of pottery in the ground and says, 'This contradicts *Genesis*', that we should put away our Book and worship at the Shrine of Science? No!"

Then he continued in a softer voice. "But do not think that we can read the literal history of the world in God's message. Do you know how big the history of the world is? Do you think God cares to tell us the details, as if we were children around the campfire? No. No, my children. God tells us the stories he wants us to hear, not as a schoolmaster wishing us to memorize who did what to whom when, but as our Father who wishes us to understand Him, and how we may find Him.

"So no, I do not insist the Bible is true in the sense of opening a book of dry history. I merely insist that its message is true."

He stood still, as if communing with God himself. The audience waited, the only sound a susurration of breathing that swelled and fell like the waves.

"The Word of God is as true now as it was then. Tonight, I will tell you another story. You have heard me speak before of the demon Katlyn." The susurration drew its collective breath as a hologram appeared. It was the first image ever taken of the geneh as she leapt across the rooftops in a city years ago. It had been enhanced, less for clarity than to subtly alter her expression, sharpening her face and yellow eyes. If demons existed, it was not hard to imagine that she was one of them.

"Once there was a great genetic engineer. I will not speak his name, for you know it. Many of you will wonder why I call such a man great."

He looked tenderly at them, like a shepherd at his flock. "My children, do not be deceived. There was greatness even in bright Lucifer, the most gifted of angels, deceived by his own brilliance into renouncing the light. If only this man had learned that lesson. Perhaps then he would have known not to repeat the Devil's mistake, but to resist it."

He sighed. "Like Lucifer he was a brilliant light in the firmament. Like Lucifer, he was seduced by his power—a power given by God—into thinking he could exceed God.

"Some say we, we of the Church of His Image, are anti-science. That is a lie. We approve of science, because it is how men learn of the glory of the Lord's creation and gain dominion over it. And do not mistake me. This man was great. He could have brought great healing to God's servants, achieved mighty works in His name."

He removed his glasses, wiping them as if to clear a mist, and the bright lights reflected off what looked like tears. "But instead!" he thundered, "Instead he wished to better God! He created life in his own image! For no reason except he wanted to and craved to flaunt his own glory! Flaunt it in the face of God himself!"

His voice dropped to a whisper. "And so, the Lord humbled him. His works were scattered, and his demonic creation died in the inferno, as it must. Do not damn those who had to destroy his demon child. Damn only the man who made it necessary, the man who made a thing that could not be allowed to live.

"But instead of being humbled, instead of accepting God's discipline and returning to the service of humanity: what did this man do?"

He glared at the audience. "He withdrew his gifts from the world. In bitterness, he retired to his fortress. No, not in humble repentance. Not in contemplation of his sin and how he might repay his debt to man and God. But to plot revenge, revenge against those who had done their holy duty! And to achieve his revenge, he doubled down on his sin! He created the fiend Katlyn as his personal scourge to bring his enemies down!"

His voice again dropped to a whisper. "Bright Lucifer fell, but for him falling was not enough. Having started his fall, he would not stop until his darkness was complete: until he ruled over Hell itself. As did this man. I grieve for his soul, my brothers. Look into your own souls and learn. There is no giving a fraction of your soul to evil. You cannot be good for six days and think you can escape the evil you commit on the seventh. Once you open a chink in the armor of light, the evil will enter and grow until it devours your soul.

"So, this man did not only create another child to his design, a child even more twisted than his first! No, my friends. He took this female child as his lover, calling her his wife! To the sin of pride, he added the sins of lust and incest! Once upon a time, men feared the succubus, the female demon who would sneak into a man's bed in the darkness of night to seduce his body and devour his soul. What level of depravity must a man descend to, to create his own?"

The audience growled. If that man had been present, they might have torn him apart. The preacher waited until the growl faded to a sigh.

"But this is old history, and some if you might wonder why I retell it now. A cautionary tale? Yes. A lesson in how the oldest words of the Bible still have intimate meaning today? Surely."

He stopped, looking sadly around the hall, his gaze stopping on one, then another, then another. Then he sighed and continued. "If only that were all."

The audience was silent.

"I do not know if this man was responsible for what has happened. Oh, he is, whether it was done by his hand or inspired by his example!"

Again, he raked the audience with his gaze, daring them to draw the conclusion.

"For as many of you will now know, there is a new demon let loose amongst us," he continued in a whisper. "Another geneh has invaded the world of men."

He waited for the roar of dismay to fade. "I wish I had happier news for you, my brothers and sisters. You know I have criticized GenInt in the past, for their errors of judgment and fading of their zeal. Perhaps I could criticize them now. But I shall not, for now is the time we need them.

"GenInt gained knowledge of a geneh child, a mere boy. Why he was coming here, perhaps we will never know. They laid a trap and caught him. We have little knowledge of his abilities. All we know is that, though less than ten years of age, he somehow escaped. And what you will not know, but I know, is that he mercilessly killed a number of GenInt agents in the process!"

He shook his head sadly. "Too many people, perhaps even some of you, dear listeners, have been seduced by the blandishments of Satan, that Master of Lies. You may have seen recordings of this Katlyn, may have wavered in your resolve upon seeing what looks like an innocent and friendly young woman. You forget that Satan dressed up his temptation of Eve in fine words and juicy fruit. He is the master of cloaking evil in pretty raiment.

"Katlyn was a thief who tortured the brave policewoman sent to find her. She was fast and powerful. But look at what this boy has done. Whatever he is, we can know this. He is both more capable than Katlyn and more evil.

"So, I have one message for you. One message for the brave men and women of GenInt."

He gazed somberly at his audience and at the world beyond.

"This abomination must die."

~~~

Charles Denner had been an unusual boy. He was not especially strong, not especially athletic, and not especially interested in anything physical. But he had been intense.

A boy like him could expect to be bullied. He was, once. The tough boys had gathered around him behind a building at school and begun laughing at him and shoving him; they had pushed him to the ground, hoping to provoke a fight. They were bad, rough boys who had not yet taken the jump into a deeper evil. In their ethos it was unmanly to beat up on someone without cause, though they had no compunctions about provoking the cause.

But Charles had said nothing, merely picked himself up off the ground and looked at them with his mad intensity. His manner said he was hurt but did not care. His gaze held neither anger nor hate nor fear, just a look that implied his tormentors didn't even exist in his reality. The bullies did what they did in order to declare their existence to a universe that, left to its own devices, would ignore them; but their sense of existence was too fragile a construct to survive the dismissive depths of Charles' eyes.

The leader of the bullies had looked away, uneasy without knowing why. He turned back, looking Charles up and down contemptuously while carefully avoiding his eyes. "Ah *merde*," he'd drawled, demonstrating his command of the French language to his gang. "This dickless dope ain't worth it. Let's go." The others were happy enough to titter at his wit and even happier to obey his suggestion.

Charles was left alone after that.

He had many interests but no passions except religion. His parents were believers, but not fervent. They looked at their son with alternating pride and alarm, wondering if he would grow up to be a saint or a madman.

Once, Charles read a story about St Thomas Aquinas. Thomas also had been an unusual boy, intense and religious. Charles wondered if he would be like him. He did not think he could ever equal an achievement like the *Summa Theologica,* for he doubted he had the wisdom, and sometimes he wondered what calling God might have in store for him instead.

Puberty was not especially kind to Charles. He did not like desires he could not control nor passions he did not understand or seek. He found himself in the odd position of not being especially interested in girls as a topic of thought but finding his eyes and other parts of his body unaccountably drawn to them on the most unsuitable of occasions. He did not like to sin, but to his chagrin, he found the sin of lust occasionally inescapable. He wondered why God would torment him so, but believed with the intensity he reserved for his beliefs that it would all make sense in the end. He remembered the story of Job and took comfort in the hope that if God or Satan found him worth testing, then they must see in him a worthiness equal to the trial.

Charles may have underestimated his intelligence for, while he was not very popular, others often sought his advice when they did not understand a lesson or some homework. But he was surprised when one of the girls in his class, Rachel, asked him to tutor her on religion, a topic about which he would not have thought she cared.

The school was not allowed to teach any particular religion as the One Truth, but they did have a course on comparative religion that managed to put Christianity in the best possible light. In their view there was nothing wrong with this: it was impossible to do otherwise when their religion was in fact the right one. Most of the students were blissfully bored with the topic, but young Charles loved it. He loved the very idea of religion, whatever the specific beliefs. He was surprised when the girl asked him to help her, for she had never shown much interest in the classes, and it was a course that few could actually fail unless they really tried. Its true purpose, after all, was not the grade points but the health of their souls. But even Charles had some need for the approval of his peers, and increasingly the female ones, so he happily agreed.

When he knocked on the girl's door and she answered it, she had changed out of her school uniform into a softer outfit that hugged her young body in ways that Charles would have found delightful if his mind wasn't already engaged in thoughts of God. Her parents, she explained with slightly pink cheeks, were still at work, so the two of them had a couple of hours of privacy at their disposal. He nodded absently, not caring either way; he couldn't see how her parents' presence could interfere with their studies. She sat at her desk and sat him next to her, then in the opposite of the usual way these things progress, bumped her chair next to his and sat with her thigh pressing lightly against his.

Charles barely noticed, continuing to explain some abstruse point in the text that the girl cared as much for as Charles apparently cared for her thigh. She sighed inwardly. She had done this for a lark, and she was in equal parts amused at what his indifference said about him and annoyed at what it might say about her.

The course of history can turn on the smallest of decisions. If Rachel had made a different choice, who could have told how Charles' life would have turned out? Perhaps the diverging lines of choice would have rapidly converged back, and history would have been none the wiser for the detour. Or perhaps he would have become a better or a worse man.

None of these thoughts were in Rachel's head as she debated whether to let things follow their natural course, disturbingly in this case to nowhere, or hit Charles over the head. In the end, freed by the indecisiveness of her brain, her own hormones grabbed their chance and made the decision. She was amused by Charles, and not at all revolted by him as some girls professed to be, considering his oddness to be intriguing rather than repellant. The thought that in mere minutes she could be having sex with a boy, instead of learning about the depravity of the Phoenicians, sent exactly the same shiver up her middle as she had hoped would afflict Charles from the touch of her leg. The thought was rapidly followed by the resolve to make it so. *Screw you, Charles,* she thought, grinning at her own double entendre. *Let's see if you can ignore this.*

"Charles?" she asked sweetly.

He looked at her, puzzled at the interruption in the middle of a sentence where no question made sense—if one assumed the listener was in fact listening.

"Yes, Rachel?"

"Is it true that the Bible says God made men and women to be together?"

"Well… yes. But that's got nothing to do with this passage," he replied, his puzzlement increasing.

She managed to sigh and smile at the same time. "Charles. I think you're smarter than you pretend."

"Uh… what do you mean?" he asked, his confusion real but his reddening cheeks indicating that some level of him was starting to get the hint.

"I mean this," she breathed, lifting his hand and placing it on her breast. "And this," she added, leaning over to plant a long slow kiss on his lips.

When she finally let him speak, both his confusion and his redness were complete. "What… what?" he managed to get out.

"Charles, you putz. It was very sweet of you to teach me this stuff. I'm grateful. Really. So let me teach you something *you* need to know."

Even if Charles had been in a mind to resist, resistance was useless. She led him to her bed and showed him exactly what she meant.

Afterwards, he lay on his back next to her, body buzzing with pleasure. But his lust sated, guilt rushed in to fill its place. He loathed himself. He knew what this rite was, that it was meant for marriage, the sacred institution set down by God himself. He knew what sin he had committed and that his previous sins were nothing in comparison: for surely the greatness of the sin was measured by the magnitude of the pleasure it had given him. He was afraid to open his eyes. He did not know what he feared more: the sight of triumph in the eyes of a temptress, who had lured him into sin through his own kindness and love of religion; or a look of guilt to match his own, the look to prove his own depravity in damning both of them by his weakness.

But he would not hide. Some would have called him a fanatic, others a lunatic, but he knew his soul depended on never turning his face away from the truth as he saw it. If he was damned, he was damned by his own actions, and he would face his damnation as a man.

But when he opened his eyes to look at her, her own eyes were still closed. And the expression on her face was neither smirking triumph nor crushing guilt, but a simple look of happiness. As if the pleasure that had filled them in the last frenzied moments of their lovemaking had not fled in the face of guilt, but rather guilt could gain no foothold in its precious afterglow.

He did not understand.

He knew this girl. There was nothing exceptional about her. But where some of the kids he knew were cruel, or mean, or liars, he had never seen that in her. He realized that was part of why he had so readily agreed to this tryst, not knowing it was a tryst. She was just a friendly, uncomplicated girl, and if he had seen her cry in sadness and shout in anger, he had never seen her deliberately hurt anyone.

The word that came to his mind thinking about her as a person and the expression on her face now was *innocence*. But they had both just shared in a great sin that was the diametric opposite of innocence. It made no sense.

If things made no sense, he knew, it was because you were making a mistake. But what mistake was he making? His train of thought was derailed when she opened her eyes and smiled. "Ah… Charles. That was better than books, wasn't it?"

He could not help but smile in return. His guilt was temporarily powerless in the face of the simple innocence of her eyes. "I… but… I…"

She put her finger on his lips and laughed. "Don't worry Charles, we're not going to hell. Do you really think God would make us this way then condemn us for it?"

He shook his head dumbly. She was so simple: the issues were far more complex than that. But the pleasure had not fully left his body, and it was linked to hers, and through that to her innocence and uncomplicated joy. He could neither forgive himself nor condemn her.

"Oh, Rachel. If I were God, I wouldn't send you to hell. I'm not so sure about me though."

She laughed delightedly, then sat up, covering her breasts with the sheet. Apparently, what she was happy for him to see and touch in the throes of passion was still subject to shyness afterwards. "I think we'd better get dressed. Unless you want another lesson?"

She laughed again at the redness that rushed to his face, but it was a laugh of amusement not cruelty. He turned away and got up, not hiding his nakedness; he could not hide now. They both dressed silently. Then she reached out her hand to his.

"Thank you, Charlie."

Nobody ever called him Charlie. In the face of his intensity, it seemed an impertinence. But from her lips it gave him a strange pleasure.

Two totally different narratives played in their heads as he walked home.

~~~

Rachel watched Charles go with the echo of a smile on her face, then lay back down on her bed, hands behind her head, just enjoying the remnant sensations of the afternoon. She reminisced how it had come to this. She had been sitting having lunch with friends one day when Charles walked towards them. Jason, who was popular with the girls and casually contemptuous of people unlike himself, had hooked his thumb in Charles' direction and slyly commented, "Watch out, girls." The girls had tittered obediently, and Julie had leant back against a tree and called out in her best throaty voice, "Hi, Charles!"

Charles had looked at them with his fathomless eyes. He did not ignore them or spurn them, just said "Hi" with a faint smile and walked on. Julie pouted and Jason laughed. "Losing your touch, Julie? Don't worry; nobody has a chance with him. He has no dick."

Rachel didn't know why she'd felt she had to come to his defense. "And how would you know, Jason? Been checking *up* on the competition, have you?"

Jason smirked. "What's this? Does our Rachel have a thing for Charles?"

"No, I just think you're being unfair. He's OK, just a bit odd."

Jason's smile broadened. "Well, if you like him so much, prove me wrong. See if those cute tits of yours are enough to make him discover he's a man."

"Screw you, Jason."

"At least you *can* screw me."

She glared at him. "All right, you're on. Maybe he's better at it than you are!"

~~~

Charles had walked home deep in thought, his body alternating between the glow of forbidden knowledge and the flame of guilt. He found no answer that day or in the days that followed.

Outwardly, he was the same intense but quiet boy as always, but inside his mind remained a battleground between temptation and shame. When three weeks later he had been wandering aimlessly after school, thinking he was thinking about a point of theology, he looked up and found, first to his surprise and then to his horror, that his feet had taken him to Rachel's house. He wanted to run but could not. He could not tear his eyes from her door.

Then he bared his teeth at himself. He would face his fears and his temptations. God would not allow him to be tempted beyond his ability to resist: that he knew from his Bible. He had fallen before, but he had been taken by surprise. He would prove his strength! He would beard Lucifer in his den and emerge victorious! Then, perhaps, his sin would be redeemed.

So, he walked to her door resolutely, but by the time he knocked, he discovered he was half hoping that she wouldn't be there and half hoping that one of her parents would answer the door. Then Rachel herself stood there, looking at him with faint surprise; when she smiled, Charles realized his mistake.

"What are you doing here?"

"I... I was just wandering around, found myself in your street. I thought I'd say hi."

She looked him up and down and his belly did somersaults, knowing what her eyes were remembering. "Um. Hi, Charlie."

She waited, but he just stood there, unable to speak as his face filled the silence with its redness.

She sighed. "Look, Charlie, I'll let you in on a secret. If you want me, you just have to ask." She held up a finger as if in stern warning.

"I don't mean that's how it is between a boy and a girl. Other girls, well that's between you and them. But we've already broken the ice, if you know what I mean. And I like you, Charlie. I like even more what we did the other day. So, if you ask, I'm not going to bite you. I might say no. But more probably I'll say yes."

Charles looked at her with something like agony in his eyes, trying without much success to keep those eyes pointed at her face where they belonged. "I... I mean... I... um..."

She sighed again. "You're much more articulate in class. I suppose I can help you out this once. She pushed her body gently against his, entwined her fingers in his and said huskily into his ear, "Do. You. Want. Me?"

He opened his mouth, but his tongue was unable to respond. But a different appendage had already given its answer and she giggled and dragged him inside.

After that his battle continued. On one front it was manifested by his determination to fight it, the slow erosion of that determination by the sight of her at school, and his final capitulation to the idea that if he could only get his burning lust out of his system, it would at last let him be. Lust proved remarkably resistant to that theory.

She never said no. She was not in love with Charles, and she had other boys, but she found him intriguing. Also, she found that his palpable reluctance and her power to overcome it added to her own pleasure; unlike other boys, who brought a less challenging fun. And if Charles had thoughts of saving her soul from Satan, perhaps she had thoughts of saving his from God, or at least from his twisted version of God. She had meant what she had said that first time. She did not know if there was a God or, if there was, what He was like; but she could not believe any God would give his creatures the need and capacity for such joy then punish them for indulging in it.

Perhaps history would have turned out differently if on that first day Rachel had shrugged, laughed inwardly at Charles' stupidity, and borne an afternoon of boredom instead of passion. Perhaps then Charles would have continued on his way, ever an intense young man but one whose passions would never ignite to change the world.

Or perhaps history would have turned out differently if either of them had been less than they were. Though most could not see it, Charles had a big heart, but even so there was no room in it for the love of a mere mortal woman, so given was he to his God. Rachel was not the prettiest or brightest girl in the school. But she was long limbed and soft bodied, and she had opened the door to an appalling glory. He adored her, feared her and hated her. But he could not do the one thing that would have freed him, which was to despise her. If Rachel had displayed anything other than her simple happy innocence, had given even a hint of reveling in his fall, he could have blamed her, despised her and forgotten her. But he could not: he could only blame himself, despise himself and never forget his failure.

Under the circumstances, Charles would have laughed bitterly if anyone had called him pure. But if he had been less pure in his devotion to his beliefs, he would have done what most people did and compartmentalized his life; perhaps officially planting his flag in the camp of God or of the world, but largely treading a middle path that avoided the highs and lows of both. He might have accepted his sin.

But Charles was pure. And the only way he knew how to cope with his falls into depravity was to equalize things by a counterbalancing increase in the passion of his devotion to God. He had always been serious about religion and had chosen a Church that encouraged such earnestness. It exhorted its flock to share and, if they felt the gift in them, to preach. Charles had preached before in the youth group with some success. But now he found new depths to his soul and passion. Now he came on fire. The previous moderately gifted speaker became a firebrand whose words struck the congregation on the face and lifted them to glory. They forgot the boy in the sight of the birth of an Angel.

Charles reveled in his new power. But then he would seek out Rachel on the playground and look at her shyly, and she would smile and nod. Or he would walk her home from school and into her home and into her bed. And the guilt would always come, but instead of overwhelming him it would purify his passion like gold in a furnace and drive him to even greater heights.

Unbelievers shook their heads at yet another huckster preacher. But among believers, his fame and with it his power grew. He started his own study group, which grew into his own organization. He spoke of many things. If he spoke of the depravity of man, it was because he knew his own depravity. If he spoke of the glory of God, it was because he knew that glory too.

At first, he preached about many topics. But this was an age of technology that was expanding in all directions, beyond the dreams of the last generation let alone the last century. Some saw it as the birth pangs of a new age; others feared it heralded the end of humanity in a blaze of uncontrolled power. When he heard some speak of the coming 'technological singularity' as salvation, Charles saw in it a different kind of singularity, a black hole that might swallow all the world, the death of all Light.

One night, Charles watched a report on the advances in genetic engineering, enthralled and appalled. Had his passion been science, it might have inspired a career in the laboratory. Instead, it inspired his calling in the Church.

The theme that now kept recurring in his sermons like a growing drumbeat was that Man was made in God's image, and while that was his glory it must also be his humility. Man should not seek to better the image he had been made in. Man should not seek to make his own creations to rival that image. Man was not worthy of such heights. And so, the Church of His Image was born.

Charles still knew the thrilling, thralling sin of lust but, with Rachel now removed far from his life, for a while his native shyness with women saved him from sin in the actual flesh. But as his fame grew, he discovered what he should always have known: that others shared his lusts. There were women in his congregation whose flesh was consumed by the power of his speeches as much as their spirits were; who sought him out for private discussions; who raised him up to Heaven only to cast him down to Hell.

After these sessions, Charles felt the same crushing guilt he had with Rachel. But he bore the weight of that guilt himself. The women sometimes felt the same shame and guilt he did; sometimes the pride of achieving union with a man, or perhaps the idea of a man, they admired. In either case Charles forgave their weakness, for how could he condemn those who shared his own? He told them it was man's nature to sin, that he regretted his own part in that sin, that God would forgive if they repented and sought His forgiveness. Often they would pray together, to seek it; inevitably, on occasion this led to repetition rather than absolution.

In years to come a journalist would ferret out some of these women and throw his deeds in his face. But Charles would simply smile sadly and note that if man was able to resist sin by his own power, God would not need to save him; that he knew and accepted his sinfulness; that, like Job, Charles had been tested and through the tests been purified and humbled: until God saw his humility, reached down and lifted him out of his sin.

He would then look at the journalist and add, "I speak for God. I did not choose this: God chose me. He chose a weak vessel to show his own power. He chose a sinner to show his mercy. The worst sin of our age is the sin of hubris, of pride. All you have said is true and I have no right to pride. Perhaps that is why God chose me."

Charles had been known to destroy journalists who went after him. Whether this one had done it out of courage or folly did not matter. Charles left him alone, for he had only spoken the truth.

It was said that St Thomas Aquinas resisted the temptation of lust and as reward God gave him the gift of perfect chastity. Charles Denner failed to resist temptation but received a better gift: God gave him a wife.

Juliana Rodriguez was religious in an outwardly unassuming but inwardly passionate way. When she first saw Charles Denner preach, she saw not a man but a vessel of God. She knew she had to be with this man, but she never suspected it would be so intimately. She was talented in IT systems and could have made a good living in the secular world, but she chose to give her gifts to the Church of His Image in return for material wages the secular world would have scoffed at, but spiritual rewards that world could neither see nor understand.

She was little like Rachel except in the shape and sparkle of her eyes, but such shape and sparkle were what Denner had seen so many times in that first passion he'd had besides religion. He was drawn to her, but where Rachel's innocent sexuality had caused the collapse of his resistance, Juliana's innocent purity made her untouchable. When he left her, he wanted her; but in her presence he knew it was impossible.

Yet he was drawn to her presence and her eyes. When he looked closer, he saw in those eyes, not what he had seen in Rachel's, but a devotion to the Spirit of God: and from it to the spirit of the man He spoke through. He did not know why one day he proposed to her. He did not know why she looked at him for long moments then accepted.

Juliana would have done anything he asked. If he had asked her to sleep with him, she would have done it; if he had then asked her to leave, she would have done that too. It was not that she loved him, though in her way she did. Like Charles, there was little room in her soul for mortal love. But her love of him was just a lesser face of her love for God. When he asked her to marry him it was like a door opening on an unexpected world. She could no more refuse to go through that door than she could refuse to breathe.

Her desires were at a more refined level than Charles'. Where his passion burned, hers smoldered; where his rhetoric soared, her advice was calm; where his lusts had once borne him into sin and shame, she had been a virgin: yet she happily let him have her as often as he wished.

If his passion for God left little room for lesser passions, so it left little room for happiness. But for the first time in his life, he was as happy as he had the capacity to be.

~~~

The boy who had known Rachel and the young man who had married Juliana were now years in the past, and the leader they had become looked out at the crowd. He knew the warm bodies present in the flesh were a tiny fraction of the audience who watched, to whom his words and expressions were borne swift as light by human technology. But he also knew that a crowd had a life of its own; that the passions of its individual members fed on each other to bring into being something much greater; that it formed a nucleus that spread that passion around the world.

He could have sat in his office and given the same speech and reached the same number of eyes and ears. But it would not have reached the same number of hearts.

His message to GenInt had had its effect. Left to their own devices, they would not have admitted the existence of the escaped geneh. He did not know the whole story, but he knew enough: that wherever the geneh had come from, they had taken it, but instead of sending it back to Hell, they had kept it for their own purposes. That could not be permitted. He had been prepared to publicly name their crime. They had neatly avoided his threat by admitting to part of the truth and appointing Miriam Hunter as lead investigator.

He had had his run-ins with that Detective himself, and he had to admit a grudging respect, not only for her ability but for her integrity, at least according to her own lights. He knew there was a school of belief which imagined that God would take such things into account, and while the sweet rewards of Heaven were closed to her, perhaps her fate would be less appalling than the full fires of Hell. He admired her enough to confess his own weakness: a wish that it was true. But his God was as uncompromising as his faith and, no doubt, her unbelief, pride and fleshly immoralities would doom her soul. *Still, who can tell God what he can do?* He wondered whether that thought came from humility before God or weakness in his own resolve.

In any case, GenInt's response was enough: it was more important for this thing to be caught and killed than for GenInt to be punished. He smiled grimly. He would keep his eye on them. Their punishment might come later.

Now he sat alone, pondering the death sentence he had pronounced. He himself had found his last words hard to write and harder to say. The crowd had responded with a roar, but it had an undertone of uneasiness. Yet the words had to be said.

He knew he could have argued more. After all, the Lord himself had said 'you shall not suffer a witch to live', and the creature now at large was far worse than a witch. But he needed to shock people, not dilute his words with justifications. The pendulum had swung too far: there was too much sympathy for Katlyn and the cause of geneh rights. Denner had always faced the truth and he knew that too many other people did not; and more, that if people did not want to face the truth, he would have to face it for them. He knew his words would have their effect; he knew a storm was coming. Then would be the time for arguments, debate and nuance.

He sighed. People could be their own worst enemies. The people had approved the Geneh Laws. In the hidden corners of their souls, they must have known that those laws might be used to kill children and probably had been. But they did not like their faces rubbed in the implications of their own decisions. They wanted more than to be kept safe and protected: they wanted to be kept safe from the knowledge of how they were kept safe.

But there was a cost, even for him. Perhaps it sprang from the same well as his weakness in desiring divine mercy for Miriam Hunter. He had a vision of this boy, running from the world, hidden in the dark places. Evil he might be, but the evil had not been of his choice. He set his mouth in a grim line. If there was a cost, he would bear it. But he knew he would go to his wife tonight. He needed to lose himself in her arms and forget for a moment all thoughts of sin and duty and price.

CHAPTER 9: THE PALE CRIMINAL

Robot cleaners had come a long way since their evolutionary ancestors, the small disks that had scurried around carpets and usually avoided falling down the stairs.

That and innumerable other advances in scientific and technological fields, from automation to materials science, had changed society enormously and in manifold directions. Those many directions were pushed and pulled by as many motives, but the types of motives were limited. People wanted to eat, sleep, love and make love; they wanted warmth and comfort balanced by excitement and thrills; governments wanted control and monitoring, while citizens wanted freedom and anonymity, though more for themselves and less for those they disliked.

Thus it was that as governments' ability to spy on their citizens grew, the citizens' opportunities for escaping it also grew. Governments duly complained that they needed greater powers and limitations on those opportunities, lest criminals thrive. The citizens duly complained that the innocent should not suffer just because the government couldn't do its job properly without the weapons of tyranny. The innocent were, of course, themselves; any peccadilloes they might indulge in were needed and no worse than anybody else's, including those in power; and thus were properly beneath the attention of the leviathan State.

This tension played itself out differently across the globe. In Capital, the government was locked in its room and only allowed out to defend the people's individual rights to be left alone, especially by the government. In darker countries, the citizens were metaphorically locked in their apartments and only allowed out to do what they were told. The United States stood somewhere between these two worlds. If its Founding Fathers woke up today, they would start another revolution; yet the one they *had* started had left a deep vein of freedom in their country. While the balance had tilted one way or another over the years, sufficient people guarded their liberties strenuously enough that the government was far from all-powerful. If the cracks this left in society helped criminals follow their dark paths, they helped far more innocent people just live their lives unmolested by busybodies who confused a desire to rule with the qualifications to do so.

These thoughts went through the mind of one such seeker of freedom as he watched a robot cleaner dart adroitly around his apartment before vanishing through a hole in the wall. His path to this apartment had been equally tortuous but far swifter.

One of the more successful attempts to evade government meddling was encrypted digital currency, of many varieties but collectively called cryptocoin. Albert had no phone, his captors regarding that as unwise. But part of his birthday present had been $250,000 of cryptocoin spread across three identities, each as anonymous and secure as cryptocoin itself. Supposedly even the lost father who had given them to him could not track them. Albert wondered if that was true; he wondered if it was not just another part of a choreographed game he was playing for the pleasure of hidden watchers. *Screw it,* he thought; then said it out loud, darkly delighted at his power to speak the forbidden curses of adults. He could only do what he could do.

He could access his accounts over the net, but only if he had a secure connection. Hence, his first need was a phone; but he could not go to a shop and buy one, and to buy one online required being online. Thus, his first task was to find a way to bootstrap his way to independence.

In the ambulance he had looked longingly at the phones around his victims' wrists. But he had known he had no time to use them in the ambulance, and if he removed them their anti-theft features would probably give him away. In any case he'd almost certainly be locked out of them.

These thoughts had gone through his head as he dashed into the park after his rolling jump from the ambulance. In the absence of good information about where he was and what might be there, the possible ramifications were too numerous even for his intellect. He knew that the one thing more dangerous than lacking a backup plan was to have no plan at all. *But sometimes, you just have to take your chance and run with it.*

So, he literally ran. He was no superman, but his enhanced body was fast and had good endurance; he raced through the night, scanning for any opportunity to seize.

He saw a lightening in the sky to the north, and its faint flickering indicated it was probably a shopping area. It would not be well populated this time of night, but with automation reducing the costs of operating to little above the costs of just sitting there idle, most places stayed open all the time. These days most cities never slept, even while most of their denizens did. He changed direction instantly, heading towards the beckoning lights.

When he left the park he slowed his run to a confident jog, hoping it would broadcast hurried purpose rather than harried flight. People would wonder what a child was doing unattended at this time of night; he hoped to give them neither the chance to ask nor sufficient cause to report the sight.

Then he saw what he had hoped to find: a public library. These were both more common and smaller than in ages past, excepting those still clinging like limpets to their heritage of physical books and videos. Most were glorified net access providers; most didn't have staff, especially at night, relying on security AIs to keep any villains at bay. All the automated ones were free for basic services, though some charged for special services. Depending on local political sensibilities, this was achieved through government programs or by private individuals and foundations who understood the value of wide dissemination of accurate knowledge. Libraries provided better, deeper and faster access, with more sophisticated fact-checking AIs, than was available for free elsewhere.

Albert slowed to a walk and the door whispered open at his approach. As he strolled inside, its lone occupant looked up from a station. She looked slightly surprised to see him, but showed an admirable lack of curiosity when she bent her head back to do and mind her own business.

He slipped into a comfortable seat in front of a net access point, turned off its AI, tunneled through an anonymizer service and did some quick searches. He ordered clothes and shoes in his size, special contact lenses and, most importantly, an expensive phone with top security features. He had chosen his suppliers carefully: another result of advancing technology was providers who would deliver anywhere, anytime, for a fee. It was a fee he was happy to pay.

Delivery would take fifteen minutes. He fretted about spending too long in any one location, but decided on prudence, deleting all his history from the browser then doing more searches and deletions to help confuse any trail that might remain.

He was just about to leave when a voice spoke behind him. "Kid, what are you doing here this time of night? Where are your parents?"

Apparently, the woman was less admirably incurious than she'd seemed.

He turned slowly and looked down his nose at her through narrowed eyes. He roughened and deepened his voice and drawled, "I sure do appreciate your concern, ma'am. But I'm what prejudiced people like you used to call a 'midget', though we prefer 'little people'. Look it up. I'm eighteen years old. So, bugger off!"

She jerked her head back, surprised and somewhat affronted by his rudeness but even more mortified by her own lapse. This man certainly looked like a boy, but... "Er, sorry mister," she stammered, red-faced. "Good night then."

No doubt a medical expert in growth disorders would have seen right through his transparent lie. Fortunately, as Albert had hoped, whatever suspicions she had were less than her reluctance to commit another social faux pas.

He graced her with a forgiving smile, rose, tipped his finger to his forehead in farewell and left. He had considered using a rather different configuration of his finger but decided he was better served making her feel better than encouraging anger. Both brought less risk than more vigorous solutions.

Then he made his way to the alley he had specified and waited for the delivery drones to arrive, breathing out in relief when first one then the others hovered, verified his assumed identity, gave birth to their burdens then hummed back into the sky. He ran to where he couldn't be seen, quickly dressed then activated the phone in full security mode.

But he had been seen in the library. The woman may well have noticed the green of his eyes, narrowed or not. His work might then be tracked. Staying on the move, he ordered another phone through yet another anonymizer portal and in ten minutes had it on his wrist.

He erased the original and later would leave it in plain view. Between tracking his movements, identifying where he had been, obtaining warrants then actually finding the data, his enemies could not find it for several hours at worst, more likely days. If his erstwhile family did go to that effort, some unsuspecting soul would discover they had not been quite as lucky as they'd thought in finding it, not that it would cost them more than some inconvenience.

He repeated that exercise several times over the next few days, the fates of his phones ranging from fire to water. He swapped among hotels with fully automated services. These were also common: cheap housing for the poor and relatively dispossessed, or those who wanted to hide. Finally, feeling safe enough at last, he booked a room in a similar but better hotel using a different identity. In the early morning hours when nobody else was around, he let himself into this longer-term shelter.

He allowed himself to sleep for many hours.

Then he went to work.

CHAPTER 10: ON PASSING-BY

'OMG. So embarrassed! Thought I was helping, but all I did was insult someone differently abled! Note to self: not everyone is tall!'

Miriam rubbed her eyes wearily. *So, this is what it has come to.*

She still occasionally cursed the week's delay in the hunt for Chao. *I must think of him as Chao, not Albert. I must hope the distinction is real.* Every day made the trail go colder.

She had had to make assumptions. She had to think of him as a child, a brilliant child but a child nonetheless; lost and alone in a strange city; neither a superman nor a master criminal with an organization behind him. Then she had a chance to catch him. If her assumptions were wrong, she had lost him already.

She worked out the probabilities of where he had started; the reasonable distances and directions he might have taken from there; what he had to do to hide and survive, the two necessities imposed on him before he could thrive, and by thriving, vanish. She had sent out questions and feelers for any clues there might be within the geographical and time limits: thefts, disappearances, even crimes of violence. The criteria were vague. Many witnesses had come forward, many clues were received, and none of them led anywhere. She was reduced to casting a wider and wider net for subtler and subtler indicators.

Somehow, one of her AIs had decided that the combination of 'differently abled' with 'tall' indicated 'short', and 'short' might indicate a child; somehow, the person who posted that note in her social feed was either poor at privacy settings or imagined the whole world was interested in her social gaffes; somehow, in the complex and tortuous filtering of a sea of raw clues too vast for human comprehension down to a list small enough to be useful, this particular hint had survived.

Shows the quality of all the other clues, she thought grimly.

She read the message again. The date was the same night as the boy's disappearance, in a place close enough to the ambulance's route. Miriam sighed, muttering to herself, "What are the odds?"

"The probability of relevance to the current search is approximately 2.31%, taking into account…"

"I wasn't talking to you!"

The computer fell silent in a way that almost seemed offended.

~~~

"So, Ms Flanigan, isn't it? Tell me as much as you can remember."

Miriam had managed to track the woman down and arranged to meet her at the library where the embarrassing incident had occurred.

"Well, he was sitting at that terminal over there, doing whatever he was doing. I thought he looked like a lost kid, maybe running away from some bad situation. I thought I should help. All I did was put my foot in my mouth. He was quite rude to me about it."

At least you weren't found disemboweled on the floor with that foot jammed into your mouth. "Do you really think he was a grown man, not a boy?"

The woman thought. "Well… I don't know. Not a 'grown man' in the mature sense, just eighteen he said, so still a youth really. He did look more like a boy, but he had some cap on his head and was usually looking away too, kind of shifty now I think about it, so I didn't get a great look. Maybe it was just his size that made me think he was a boy. He did sound more like a man. But I really couldn't say for sure."

"Did you happen to notice his eyes?"

"Well, as I said, he didn't look at me except when I spoke to him, and then he was squinting at me, offended-like. But they did look kind of funny, like they were some bright shade of green."

Miriam got no more useful information out of her and called in the techs.

~~~

"Hi, Miriam," said the image when she accepted the call.

"Hi, Jett. Did you extract any clues for me?"

"No, nothing."

"Well, you're useful! Thanks for calling! So why are you smiling?"

"Sometimes nothing means something. And I mean *nothing*: the search history of the computer was wiped. It had some records after the night in question, but nothing before that. Really wiped, like whoever did it knew what he was doing and wanted to be sure nobody would know what he'd been looking for."

"But you, of course, self-described genius as you are, have somehow managed to restore the missing data?"

"Sorry."

Miriam sighed. *I'm doing a lot of sighing lately.* "That's OK. We do what we can."

His image vanished, and Miriam pondered the news. *So let us assume our midget was indeed our boy. He was after something and did not want us to know what. He is alone with few resources, or he wouldn't risk using a public library. He might have been searching for an address, someone or something that could help him. But who would he know in a strange country?*

She gasped as one possibility struck her. *I might be opening a wound best left untouched, but I have to do it. They're probably expecting this anyway. They'll have heard about this now and wondered.*

So, she put through a call to Daniel Tagarin. With GenInt being involved, she would be surprised if such calls weren't being monitored, and she hoped he would realize the same. If GenInt were telling the truth, they may well not know that Tagarin had a son or that he was missing, and it would be best if they remained in ignorance.

"Detective Hunter! Consorting with the enemy?"

"Hello, Dr Tagarin. I know this is presumptuous, but would you answer a few questions?"

"I will at least listen to them," he replied abruptly, as if feeling she was pushing the boundaries and should know why.

"Thank you. I expect you have heard of the recent escape of a violent geneh here?"

His eyelids flickered, but he simply answered, "I have."

"You are famous in this field. Have you, by any chance, heard anything from or about this person, or any other young geneh, recently?"

"No, Detective, I have not. Can you tell me anything about him?"

"Only what GenInt told me, which is that he was made in some Asian lab, so they do not suspect you were involved."

"Don't they? I suppose I can take some comfort from that," he replied softly.

"Yes. I thank you for your consideration," she replied formally; her expression and tone of voice spoke of the unstated. "Sorry to have disturbed you."

"Goodbye, Detective."

So not that. If Chao is Albert, surely he would have contacted his father by now; surely his first goal would be to return to Capital. So where are you, Albert? Are you still out there somewhere, imprisoned and alone? Or are you dead? Or is madness your fate, at the hands of men or genes, and the lost boy that was Albert has become the psychopath Chao? I suppose it makes no difference. I must find Chao. And perhaps in doing that, I shall find Albert.

She thought some more. *If he wasn't looking for a person, what then, and why hide it? I doubt he was ordering pizza and didn't want us to know he likes it with pineapple. But he needs resources. Things to help him. Perhaps he went shopping.*

She began to construct new search parameters. She knew it was a long shot, supposition upon supposition. *But I can guess that whatever he wanted, he ordered it then and wanted it soon, so we have narrow windows in both time and space. If I am chasing a mirage, it is the only mirage in town.*

Such a search would not be easy. Courtesy of GenInt's pull, she had a warrant that could open most doors. But that only helped if she found the right door. Large, reputable stores would be the easiest, with good databases and a polite, nervous compliance when faced with the demands of the law; but for that very reason, he may well have avoided those. In this era, it was easy to set up a small online dropship store in your bedroom with drone delivery direct from a warehouse service to the customer, that might or might not respond to demands of 'who did you sell what to when?' Technology gave many options for commerce with possibly vague compliance with the terabytes of legal regulations they were nominally subject to. In the abstract, Miriam approved of that opportunity for freedom. In her present capacity of searching for a mouse scurrying within the vast walls of chaotic commerce, she was less pleased.

She realized one flaw in her plan was that he couldn't buy anything without money, or at least credit. And where would he get either? She set a similar search in progress for thefts, starting from a few days before his escape until his night in the library.

CHAPTER 11: SCHOLARS

Albert had a lot to think about. First there were questions of survival and liberty; perhaps, he thought grimly, now that he had cast his dice, those were now the same. At a fundamental level, maybe they always were. His surrogate family would not be happy with him, and he had long suspected his position with them was perilous. He supposed it had now tipped from the perilous into the fatal.

Thus, he had taken steps to make himself safe for a while. Jumping from phone to phone and place to place should be enough: each step of his way had been theoretically secure, and though nothing was impossible, his multiplication of the improbabilities told him he was more likely to die by a freak meteorite falling on his head than being traced to his current location.

Yet immediate safety wasn't enough. Like a drowning man finding an air pocket, it was necessary but only the first, perilous step. To survive long term, let alone achieve anything beyond hiding, he would need substantial funds. He remembered a quote from an old movie: that to turn a dollar into ten dollars was a miracle, but to turn one million into ten million was inevitable.

His father had not given him that much funding. In this matter, if not in others, Albert held the man blameless. He knew the accounts were intended as emergency funds for use by an adult with many other resources, not for the circumstance in which he had thrust himself. Still, he regretted it. The amount would have meant little to his father; he wondered if his father even remembered it now. He shrugged. Until you were able to stack the deck, you had to play with the cards you were dealt with, and he would have to work with it.

But how? He considered crime, but the thought made him uneasy. He felt crimes had been committed against himself, did not like it, and wondered whether that was just the standard 'every boy for himself' or perhaps shrouded a deeper principle. He was not convinced there was any morality, that the concept was anything more than yet another means for the powerful to control the weak. That was one of the issues he would have to unravel, but he had more pressing things to solve first. In any case, he was in enough trouble already with the law. Having expended so much effort to erase his trail, it would be foolish to trigger any fresh alarms now. Especially when he thought that successful crime, defined by lots of money, would be much easier if he already had much greater wealth to invest in it.

No, he should stick within the law for now if he could. So how?

He could hardly go out and get a job. He could get a remote job, but that would just be a salary: it would no more be the ticket to riches than it was for any other mere employee. He knew his desire for rapid wealth was hardly unique to him; he knew that get rich quick schemes followed that desire like unfaithful hounds; but he knew the people who got rich out of them were invariably their promoters.

He shrugged again. *When you don't know something, find out.* How to make money had not been of interest to him before, and nor was it something he could have done before his escape without raising all kinds of red flags. He began his search.

~~~

Interesting. Way back at the turn of the millennium, a prize fund had been established to award a cool million dollars for solutions to interesting mathematical problems that had long eluded proof. Most remained unsolved, and the prize was now five times higher. *If there is anything I can do that other people find impossible, this must be high on the list.* He looked over the problems, read about the issues, and thought. Was it worth the attempt? He was not a mathematician, though he had certainly learned a lot about the subject over the years. He smiled. Even if he could not do it, it would be an interesting puzzle; little enough recreation was available to him, and this was better than most. He looked over the problems again. *That's the one: the P versus NP problem.*

'P vs NP' had been a thorn in the side of mathematicians for a long time, not that people didn't think they knew the answer, but that nobody could prove it. Some problems in mathematics could be *solved* quickly, others could not, while others were such that any proposed solution could be *verified* quickly. The question was whether all in the second class were also in the first: that is, does quick verification imply a fast solution? The question quickened his own pulse, for it had critical implications if true.

Modern encryption relied on certain calculations being easy to do but hard to reverse. While faster computers made cracking easier, they also allowed tougher codes, so the code makers had remained well ahead of the code crackers. That was vital, now that encryption of data was so important in so many parts of life, not only financial but in business and people's personal lives.

The shortcut of quantum computing to crack such problems via massive parallel calculations remained a dream. A useful quantum computer had to have very many entangled quantum states, by one way of looking at it. But the reality under that was it involved a quantum wave of staggering complexity. The very nature of the quantum realm, which enabled such things as 'tunneling' of 'particles' via their extended wave definitions, meant that the more complex a quantum device, the less likely it was to retain sufficient integrity to be useful. The more complex it was, the less its peaks could rise above its valleys, and the more vulnerable they were to being drowned by the fluctuating quantum realm they stood in.

So, quantum encryption remained a tool for the wealthy or for special applications, and most encryption still relied on the P vs NP conjecture being false: on the two not being equal, so a cipher was easy to decode when you already knew the key but impossible to crack if you didn't. His excitement mounted at the further idea that practical applications would rapidly follow, which made the value of the prize pale in comparison to the potential of using it. Especially if the possessor of the secret was an outlaw already.

His excitement was tempered by the fact that he found himself agreeing with the majority view that they were not equal. If that was so, the potential reward was the prize money only. He smiled at the thought. *It took me five seconds to get greedy! I think I could live with five million dollars. A good start, anyway.*

The majority, he knew, were often wrong. He thought about the issue, about why he instinctively thought they were right in this case, and frowned. *It is only mathematics: my hesitation stems from reality. What is the relationship between the two? Is there one?*

He sat still for a few minutes, rolling the issue around in his mind. Of course, there is a relationship: that is why the question of P vs NP has any significance; it is why mathematical science works. *But why do I feel it cannot be so?* Then the answer came to him. *Because it looks suspiciously like getting something for nothing.*

He knew that in the real world you could never get something for nothing. To live, you had to do what your life required. To do something, you had to spend effort, energy and time. To solve a problem, you had to engage your brain on it. If P=NP, too many things that were hard became easy and for no particular reason. It was like getting a free ride on the universe: and the universe always demanded payment.

He drummed his fingers on his leg. *Fine, but how do I prove it?* And for all that his intuition looked true, intuitions are often wrong.

It wasn't even obvious where to start. He already knew that mathematical proofs were often found in the most unexpected places. Formulations that on the surface appeared to be about quite different things could share deep commonalities, and lob in a proof from left field. So, what fields could be relevant? He had looked askance at the mathematics of infinity: not the concept per se, but the notion that it could have a physical reality: that infinities could be extended in any meaningful sense beyond that simple symbol that just meant *indefinite: stay away, for you can't get here anyway.* And infinity had the same kind of anything-goes problem: once you allowed infinity, anything could be made to seem possible.

So perhaps the most fruitful line of enquiry lay in its opposite, in finite mathematics? His pulse quickened again, as he caught the scent. He was not yet on the path to a proof, but he could smell where it might start. He would learn about finite mathematics; he would investigate related fields, anything that hovered around the margins of *you can't get something for nothing.* Perhaps in that tangled world he would find his answer. The history of mathematical proofs was littered with failure and with unsatisfying successes: not an elegant proof, but a nightmare computer-generated 'proof' no human being could actually understand. He wondered if he could do better.

He smiled at the irony that the problem might simply be easy to believe but too hard to prove.

CHAPTER 12: THE FLIES IN THE MARKET-PLACE

Miriam felt like a cat chasing the world's fastest mouse, and worse, a chameleon mouse who could blend into its background.

Her feelers had discovered that a phone had been delivered near the library where the boy had last been seen. The financial side yielded no clues: payment had been from a cryptocoin account now deleted. But that, plus delivery to an alley in the middle of the night, so close in time and space to her suspect, was surely not only the next link in the chain but further evidence of nefarious intent. The thought that she was truly on the trail of Chao awoke in her the old thrill of the chase, whatever her misgivings about the case itself.

The thrill dimmed when she considered that she had little information on the phone, no idea of how long he had kept it, when and how many times he had used it, or, therefore, from where. If the trail of the ambulance had given her a map of overlapping circles in time and space; if the incident in the library had managed a rather tighter map of circles; then now the possibilities might be too many to calculate or contemplate.

Still, it might be a thin, worn thread but it was the only thread she had. This time she was lucky, or her target had made a mistake. It was an expensive phone rather than a cheap burner, and one of its location security features was not disabled. This led her AI hounds, in sifting data and correlating times and locations, to zero in on one particular device. After that, it was only a matter of waiting until a firm location popped up. Unfortunately, the team of over-armed police who burst into the apartment ended up as disappointed as its occupant was surprised.

Miriam looked sourly at the gangly youth in the interrogation room as he sat slouched in the chair, legs stretched out and with a surly look on his face. His only similarity to the case was that he was a boy of eighteen, as the person in the library had claimed. But he was of normal height.

"So, Mr Henderson. Where did you get this phone?" she asked, waving the device at him.

"I done nothing wrong! I found it! I didn't steal it! And since when do you cops have time to go chasing after a phone? Don't you have any crimes to solve in this city? And who's going to repair my door?"

"A good citizen would have handed it in, thinking someone had mislaid it, or perhaps been robbed. Then nobody would be breaking down the good citizen's door."

"Yeah, right. I done nothing wrong."

"So you said. Now this is important. Where, when and how did you acquire this phone?"

"Why should I tell you? What's in it for me? I hate cops. What are you gonna do? Arrest me for finding a phone? That'd be a lark. I'd get one day's probation or something."

Miriam sighed. "Look, Mr... Henderson. I'm not actually after you. I just need to know about the phone. As for what's in it for you, besides being a good citizen helping the police, if you don't help me then I can make a good case for accessory to murder."

"Murder?!" His bluster vanished, and suddenly he looked more like an 18-year-old boy and less like an embittered street thug. "I know nothing about no murders, lady!"

"So, tell me about the phone instead."

He scratched his head. "Well, it was a while ago now. I just found it on top of a bin in some alley. Slick phone, looked nice, worked fine. No identification on it at all! I would surely have handed it in if it had," he said, projecting sincerity. "But as it was... finders keepers, eh? Rule of the street, lady."

"Can you tell me exactly where and when, or as best you can remember? Then we can let you go."

"Well, it is a bit vague. I might have been a bit high at the time, know what I mean, lady?" This time he projected a man-of-the-world air.

She sighed. "Just do the best you can."

He proceeded to do so, suddenly feeling more helpful. The location was more precise than the time, and the result was a broad set of possibilities during which its previous owner could have travelled far and wide. When she looked at the resulting map of probabilities, she groaned. She set the AIs searching for further leads but with little hope of more success.

Her attempts at finding a money trail were even worse. It was like looking at the waves on the surface of the sea and trying to work out which were caused by an individual shark's path. Surely the shark left waves and ripples, but so did too many other things, most of them not sharks at all. Combining the two searches in the hope of reinforcement achieved nothing that survived investigation.

Even the AI told her she might as well give up. Miriam was not used to giving up. But as the days went by, she knew that unless Chao did something exceptional, she would never find him. *He could be anywhere, doing anything. I can almost hope that he really is a psychopath who enjoys killing, just to give me a body. But how many serial killers have gone for years without being known or caught, in a world of so many often-anonymous people? And how many have been as intelligent as he is? If only I had some idea of what he wanted, maybe I could predict something. But what if all he wants to do now is hide? And if that is all he wants, why should I try to find him? Let him live his life, if he can. Except… except for the victims he already killed. They deserve justice. But how can I give it to them? Perhaps the only justice anyone can hope for in this case is to let sleeping dogs lie.*

She composed her report to her superiors. The many pages of theories, data, actions, results, deductions, speculations and recommendations amounted to nothing. She sat looking at her conclusions, spent, empty of ideas, empty of motivation. Her face was expressionless; she felt unable to muster enough emotion even for a frown. From somewhere in her mind floated the ancient words of Martin Luther: *Here I stand; I can do no other.*

CHAPTER 13: THE SOOTHSAYER

Gregory finished his analysis and sat comfortably back in his chair. As befitted both his position and opinion of himself, he had a corner office with not one but two windows at right angles to each other, commanding a spectacular view over the city. *And at this time of the afternoon, the light is just right, the way it makes the stone glow and the glass sparkle,* he thought poetically. He wondered if he should go home early. He had the prerogative. After all, he worked enough overtime that a bit of undertime was acceptable.

Oh well, first better check there's nothing so urgent it can't wait.

His eyebrows rose a fraction at the appointment that had insinuated itself into his calendar. He knew about this agent. Once he had been one of the golden boys, but an operation he was running had, on the verge of triumph, crashed into a disaster whose repercussions were still felt. Not really his fault, but it had to be someone's fault, and he'd had the fatal flaw of proximity. Professionally, Gregory recognized the necessity. Personally, he reckoned it had been a waste. After all, the guy was good enough and smart enough to have the leverage to not get sacked. But they had taken their pound of flesh more subtly and by degrees.

So, he was surprised to see his name on the appointment. *Not only smart, but enough balls to come to someone at my level.* He smiled. This could be interesting. He pressed the button to admit the supplicant.

Gregory supposed the man was going to beg for something and was quite prepared to send him packing, balls or no. If he wanted to use a stick, what leverage he had was surely getting old and weak; if he wanted to use a carrot, what talents he had must have atrophied from misuse by now.

"Good afternoon, sit down."

"I want in."

"In what?"

"You know."

"I suppose I do, since you came to me. But you're just a mid-level agent with, shall we say, an unfortunate reputation. I don't think I could justify putting you on. Especially when you have gone over so many heads to talk to me."

"My reputation is why you want me."

"Really?"

"Really. Part of my reputation is that I know certain things that should not be said. Obviously, as a loyal agent, I would never reveal them. But I mention them for background."

With that, he showed Gregory a list.

"Interesting speculations, but not relevant to this case or why you should be on it."

"More than speculations, I can assure you. I have always been very meticulous about having proof for my assertions. That is also part of my reputation."

"You realize that if this is a serious negotiation, there will be repercussions. Adjustments. Ironclad guarantees. Your currency will have been spent, as it were. Vague threats—if I may be so blunt as to call them threats, I am sure this is just a friendly discussion—held over our heads might have been tolerated in the past for mutual ceasefires, but not for something as hot as this. If you leave things alone, you can look forward to a comfortable, pleasant career, though not a shining one. Why risk it all on a single throw of the dice? Are you sure you want it that much?"

"I do."

"Why?"

"Because in a real sense it might finish what I started years ago: redeem the so-called mistakes that made my career less than the stellar one I had hoped for. You will recall that for all my 'failure', were it not for unanticipated protections I would have succeeded in killing my target. And that target is an example of why I am uniquely qualified. I have more, and intimate, knowledge of the players in this case than anyone else."

"The relevance of that knowledge is uncertain."

The man gave Gregory a narrow-eyed look that chilled him: it said that the knowledge was relevant, and they both knew it.

"Maybe, but can you risk that? There is more to this case than dry evidence. The people and their relationships may prove critical, especially at the crucial point. You need me."

"Hmm."

"And Gregory," he added with a tone of sincerity, "this is not just for my career, not just the usual jockeying for personal advancement. I want to do something that matters. Really matters. This is my chance, and I deserve it."

Gregory sat regarding him for a long minute.

"All right, let us say I agree. What are you proposing to do?"

CHAPTER 14: THE SECOND DANCE SONG

Miriam had had a long week. After she had submitted her report on Chao, she kept on working on the case, wondering why nobody had come back to her with either acceptance, pleas or condemnation. Perhaps they too had no ideas and were content to let her run, like some engine that would keep going until they turned her off and might as well be left alone.

Now as she entered the lobby of her apartment building, she knew she was tired. It was not the tiredness of mere fatigue, but that of wondering if further motion was worth the effort. She had loved her career. There were times when she had danced close to a line perhaps only she could see, the border between the law and her own sense of right and justice; times she had crossed it. If the world had known all she had done during those dances, she may well have fallen from grace long before today. But this didn't even have the virtue of such drama or the joyous fear of taking a stand. In the vacuum of leads she'd had time to brood about the larger issues. She thought she was doing the right thing, chasing Chao. She thought she was doing the wrong thing, if she was chasing Albert. She thought none of it made any difference, since she couldn't find him, whomever 'him' was.

But the worst of it was she wasn't sure she cared any more. She had fought her battles and made her compromises believing that her job served justice. Now she wondered if it served anything other than the ambitions of men who saw others as stepping-stones to their own advancement. Whether they defined their advancement by the simple venality of their growing paycheck, their rule over others, or the imposition of their crazy religious beliefs, made no difference to her.

And I don't even know why I suddenly feel this way. I don't know whether I am serving justice or its opposite, but I've been there before. I feel I've given up, in a sense, but that's because there is nothing I can do. Maybe I'm just tired, and it will be better in the morning. God, I need to sleep.

She threw her bag onto a chair then stopped in shock. A man was sitting on her lounge chair, the slanting brim of a hat hiding his features. Not hidden was the gun he held in his hand. It was not quite pointed at her, yet was held in such a way as to make it obvious it could be pointed and fired in an instant. Something familiar about the line of his jaw pulled at her memory but would not be caught, like the nibble of a fish at a bait it refused to commit to.

"Who are you and what the hell are you doing in my apartment?" she growled.

The face smiled and recognition clawed its way to the surface of her mind, receiving its final shove into awareness when a familiar voice drawled, "Direct as always, I see," as he lifted his face to the light.

"Amaro! My God! Would you like to put that gun away?"

He smiled crookedly but made no move to holster it. "Ah, yes, sorry about that. But I know your reflexes. I didn't want you shooting me the second you saw a handsome stranger in your room."

"I don't see it moving."

"I'm not convinced you won't shoot me anyway, now that you know who I am."

She chuckled. "Once I might have, you lying, heartbreaking bastard." Then she sat down opposite him. "But I got over it—as you said I would. So, what are you here for? Did GenInt not like the message I sent? Have you come here to twist my arm—or to shoot me?"

Amaro sighed and holstered his gun, and she realized what had seemed off about his manner. When she had known him, at the start of her career, he had been funny, dazzling, self-confident. Now he had aged, as if he had become tired in the same way she was feeling tonight. As if the wind had left his sails and worse, as if his sails no longer cared to catch the wind.

"What's wrong, Amaro?"

"Perhaps I am tired."

She sighed and granted him a crooked smile. "Is this how we end our careers then, Amaro? Together again, but two tired old campaigners giving up the fight? We both started out so full of fire. What happened to us?"

"Pah! Look at you! You have done well—as I knew you would. And as far as I can tell from your career, what I see is still the young idealist you always were. Frankly, I didn't think that would last, didn't think it could last. But here you are, still fighting for truth, justice and what passes for the American way."

"And what about you, Amaro? Your career is less public than mine. I am afraid I quite lost track of you." The old pain poked its head up just long enough to add its steely addendum, "Though frankly, I did not care to find out."

"Others losing track of me is part of my job, even when the trackers aren't as glad to see the back of me as you were. You know that GenInt would gladly have had both our scalps after that Katlyn fiasco. It is fortunate we live in a world where displeasing our superiors merely leads to a reduction in career prospects rather than height. In a former age, at best I would have ended my days digging ore in the bottom of some cold mineshaft. I can't complain. I extorted a good deal out of my employers. But I paid a price. Sure, I had interesting work and was paid well enough to eat good food, drink fine wine and bed pretty girls. But I always felt I was sidelined, never seeing the best cases or being privy to the highest councils."

"So, what are you saying? You led a life of comfortable boredom? As tragedies go, I've heard worse."

"Oh yes, I have had a pleasant enough life. But if you haven't changed—well, perhaps I have. I know you find it hard to believe, but I was a young idealist too, even if my ideals weren't yours. I believed in GenInt, believed in what we were doing."

"You speak in the past tense."

"Ever the detective, my dear. But I will tell you the truth. I told myself I still believed. I accepted my superiors' caution concerning me, telling myself they were unable to fully trust me. But I believed they believed too. Do you know why I am here? No, of course not, though I am sure you suspect several possibilities. I have heard rumors, you see, rumors about things GenInt, or perhaps factions within it, have been up to. My career bored me. So, when I thought about the issues and your involvement, I gambled on a hunch and went to see the highest level I had access too. I feared what they might do to you. Especially knowing your penchant for putting ideals above prudence when dealing with such people."

She gave him a cynical smile. "Do you expect me to believe you care? Come on, Amaro, what's your game?"

He returned a smile as sad as hers was cynical. "Oh, I do care, for reasons I will tell you in due course. I feared what they had done and would do, and I was bored with my work, so I bet on my suspicions and growing disillusionment. I reminded them of my expertise in the matter of genehs and, frankly, you; and that while our failure was an embarrassment to them, we came damn near to success. Hell, I actually shot the bitch."

"If you are trying to weasel your way back into something like my affections with your charming frankness, don't call her that."

"Just testing, my dear. Like old times, eh?" He smiled at her charmingly and she glared back dourly.

"Speaking of Katlyn," he continued seriously, "before I go on there is one debt I must repay, not that I can. I said I was an idealist, and I was. I believed. But what we did, what they did, what happened after—and what GenInt has become—has made me wonder whether I was on the right side."

She just looked at him silently, wondering where his lies were leading this time. He sighed. "That was a brilliant masterstroke by our old sparring partner Tagarin, by the way. Repairing your horribly abused body after that nastiness in South America—a public relations tour de force. So noble when you were literally his sworn enemy; such a moral giant, to put aside personal animosity in honor of your honor! A man so great he would put aside his feelings for an enemy who almost brought him down, in tribute to her virtue and nobility!"

He gave her a penetrating glance, and for the first time she saw the old Amaro, not in his incarnation as Lover but his true one as Spy. "Of course, I didn't believe a word of it. I know which side of the fence you fell that night."

"I don't know what you're talking about. You know what happened to me."

"You always were a lousy liar. But I take my hat off"—she was amused to see that he literally did— "to the adroitness of your performance back then. Bravo!"

"Believe what you want to. It makes no difference to me. Or to anyone."

"Oh, but that's where you're wrong!" he replied earnestly. "It matters a great deal! You see, you don't have to admit anything. But I know there is some affection between you and Katlyn; I believe you will be seeing her again. When you do, I would like you to do something for me."

"Why, and why do you think I would?"

"It isn't much. But if you would tell her that I was wrong. Just tell her I am sorry I shot her. You were right. She did not deserve it."

For long seconds Miriam stared at him wide-eyed, struck by such a surprising statement. "You're kidding, right? What's your game?" A thought occurred to her on exactly what his game might be, so she added, "And are you crazy? Obviously, she deserved it! They were both criminals!"

He laughed. "Oh, I'm not fishing for a confession or recording anything to entrap you. For once in my life, I'm being honest. I don't ask or expect her to forgive me. But I just think it would—balance the ledger somewhat, perhaps—if she knows that, in this little way, she won her little geneh war."

She stared at him a while longer before replying. "Sure, Amaro, whatever you say. I'll tell her—if I ever see her again. But why do you think I will? What do you think we are, tennis buddies? And speaking of buddies, I can't imagine this is the story you told your GenInt bosses."

He laughed but did not reply.

"Enough, Amaro. Why are you really here?"

"You know GenInt's interest in the matter of Chao. You can guess they are disappointed in your progress. You will not be surprised that they have some suspicion that your dedication is less than they'd like, though they are unable to poke holes in your report, fortunately for you. Officially, I am here to help you. Unofficially, I am to keep an eye on you. To spy on you. GenInt have two hopes. Ideally, you will do your job in your usual exceptional manner: for them. Or you will do the same except that you will betray them: but then I will be watching, ready to betray you in turn."

"Just like old times, eh?" she replied softly.

"So that's why you laughed!" she added, more sharply. "You *did* tell them that story! That you'd spin some yarn like that to make me trust you! As if! Surely, they aren't so stupid as to believe I would?!"

He shrugged. "It doesn't really matter, does it? It doesn't change what any of us will do, whether I am telling you the truth, or told them the truth, or you believe me, or they believe me, or nobody believes anybody! In any case, I'm with you, and will be spying on you, and they believe it improves their chances of the result they want."

"However," he added grimly, "perhaps they will be disappointed."

Miriam stared at him, trying to sift truth from lies. "What if I decide the easiest way to get rid of you is to report this conversation to GenInt?"

He spread his arms and shrugged. "Then my plans will probably fail on all levels, assuming they believe you. But I do not believe you want my plans to fail, as I think you can see that our interests align. If I am telling the truth, then I'm on your side. If I'm not, what is that old phrase...? Keep your friends close, and your enemies closer?

"Anyway, I shall tell you the full truth, whether you accept it or not. I did not tell them such details as you accuse me of. If you think about it, you will know that it is not in my nature to reveal all my cards. I merely said that because of our history, you would trust me enough to work with me, and I could counteract any distrust because I won't trust you either."

He put out his hand to her, but she ignored it.

"The last time I touched your skin with mine, it was to slap you in the face," she said, "and I prefer to leave it that way. But yes, Amaro, for now let us pretend we are allies."

Chapter 15: The Famous Wise Ones

A lbert spent weeks with his mind inhabiting the realms of higher mathematics, while his body remained safely ensconced in his lair, acquiring food and the other necessities of life by means calculated to leave no trail visible amongst the activities of his neighbors.

His initial interest in finite sets and finite mathematics in general soon expanded to include complexity theory and related fields. A particularly significant set of algorithms he found was in a paper by one Samantha Allende on the maximum amount of information that can be extracted from noisy sources. Her name rang a vague bell, and when he discovered that she had been involved in the hunt for his own mother in her time, he laughed. *So, we meet again, old family friend! You helped catch my mother: will you now help me?*

Albert did not think of himself as brilliant. He knew it, as a datum about himself, but did not dwell upon it. He did not embark upon this project because he thought himself brilliant, as such: merely because he felt he could do it. The datum was useful, like all other knowledge. It was a factor in his efforts to evade capture and survive. It was also a factor in a background process deep in his mind, one important but not urgent, on the matter of ethics and morality. But for now, it was just a datum.

In any case, brilliance is no guarantee of success. What is brilliance? Is it accuracy, creativity, depth, or all of those? Albert's project could prove misguided. Even his namesake, the great Einstein, when seeking a unified field theory, so many times thought he was on the trail of The Answer, only to be foiled and have to demolish the entire edifice.

This Albert also made many wrong turns and illusory connections. But in the end, he was right.

~~~

Reclusive Math Genius Solves Prize Puzzle!

The mathematics world is rarely abuzz, but today it is humming with the news that an unknown genius has solved a long-running problem in math, the so-called 'P versus NP Problem.' If you think 'what the heck is that and so what?' so did I! But think again, dear reader! If I tell you that some mathematical problems have solutions that can be easily verified but are impossible to solve, will you care? Perhaps not, but if I tell you that this is at the core of modern encryption, which protects all your personal finances, private information and many other things as well, you will see why you should. What it means is that we can all go to bed tonight without worrying that some hacker is going to work out how to break all the encryption in the world, and we wake up tomorrow to empty bank accounts!

Who is this new Genius? His name is Caleb Christiansen, considered a brilliant mathematician in his university days, but who then dropped out into a hermit's life of isolation and obscurity. Why, who can say? How can mere mortals like us judge Genius? Whatever his reasons, we have all been enriched by his lonely labors. And fear not, so has he: solving this prize came with a $5M reward! Yes, you read that right, friends! Maybe you should have paid more attention in math class!

So, there you have it! He has already received his money, which he asked for in cryptocoin (he is a mathematician after all!), so can he be lured out into the spotlight for the official award ceremony, where he will be presented with a golden trophy commemorating his achievement? The organizers and his fellow mathematicians sure hope so!

Caleb did not respond to request for interviews. Yet this reporter managed to contact him—do not ask me how! —and can report that Caleb is humble, unassuming and surprised at all the attention. When I asked him if he was attending the award ceremony, all he said was 'Might'.

~~~

Miriam pondered the article, which was one of many on the topic. *Who thought mathematics could make it into the popular imagination?* Even if her AIs hadn't flagged this, she would have sat up and taken notice. *A reclusive genius, eh? Not seen for years, huh? How conveniently coincidental. I guess I'm going to that award ceremony.*

Then she sighed. *Nothing is ever that easy.*

~~~

Caleb did attend the ceremony, and Miriam made sure that all exits were unobtrusively covered, just in case. Though when she saw him, she knew that, no, nothing is ever that easy.

When she met him in a private room made available for the purpose, she looked at a medium height, somewhat lanky man in his thirties, with wavy, unkempt hair and hazel eyes that alternately slid over her as if the sight were made of Teflon, or else hovered perhaps too long over her chest region. *Middle of the autism spectrum,* she assessed: *socially awkward but not totally isolated; brilliant enough to navigate the world regardless, but usually not interested enough to do so; and deeply obsessive on things that interest him. Not that uncommon in highly intellectual pursuits, I understand. Not that uncommon in the type of genius who can solve a puzzle like this one. Maybe I'm on the wrong track.*

"So, Dr Christiansen, or can I call you Caleb?"

"Caleb is fine," he replied after a pause. "You're pretty. Did you know the arch of your eyebrows reflects the shape of your eyes?"

"Thank you." She smiled. "And you're honest and brilliant. Will you answer some questions?"

"I like your smile too. White against black. Each intensifies the other."

"I understand you solved the P vs NP problem?"

"I like mathematics. They gave me this award. See, it's pretty too. Look how the gold makes the light ripple along the curves," he said, showing off the award, a gold Mobius strip with his name on one side and the award title on the other. If that made sense when speaking of a Mobius strip.

"Yes, it's beautiful, I really like it. May I hold it?"

"Sure!" he replied, handing it over.

"It's lovely! Now Caleb, did anyone help you with the problem?"

"I like mathematics. I like doing it myself. I do lots of things myself. I don't like people trying to help me."

"But did anyone try to help you, this time? I understand it was a very hard problem. Most people like to get help for really hard problems."

He stared at her with disturbed eyes. "My friend said not to tell anybody. I made a promise. Friends keep their promises."

"That's OK, Caleb. I like you, so I think I'd like your friend too. Can you tell me who he is? I'd really like to meet him."

But Caleb frowned, "I promised. You tricked me. I don't want to talk about this anymore. I thought you were a nice lady. Aren't you a nice lady?"

"I try to be, Caleb. Now look, let me tell you a secret! I think your friend is someone I know, and I'd really like to meet him. You're not in any trouble. But if you know anything that might lead me to him, could you tell me?"

"No, no, no, no. I don't want to talk about this anymore. You don't know anyone helped me. I never hurt my friends. Why are you being mean to me?"

Miriam studied him. He was getting agitated, and she saw no value in further alienating him.

"OK, Caleb. I'm sorry, I didn't intend to be mean. But if you decide you can help me some time, please give me a call."

Caleb said nothing, just looked away humming to himself. As she left the room, she turned to look at him, but he was not looking at her. He was absorbed in the contemplation of some pattern perhaps only he could see.

CHAPTER 16: THE TARANTULAS

With his newfound wealth, Albert moved to a new, more well-appointed but equally anonymous apartment, though without terminating his previous rental. *The smallest ripple is none*, he thought.

Caleb had been easy to befriend, easy to manipulate and cared little for money. Even if he had voluntarily or involuntarily betrayed Albert, it would have been too late. All communications had been encrypted and untraceable. Albert already had taken his lion's share of the reward, which he had transferred through and dispersed into several anonymous cryptocoin accounts. The money was safe and so was Albert.

Albert felt happily comfortable. However, that was not an opportunity to relax but a goad to bolder action. He considered his wealth and plans and smiled to himself. *A few million is just not enough these days.*

The first cities were scarcely built before the first gangs of criminals began skulking in their cellars and alleys, and people hadn't changed much since. Practically as soon as the communications network called the web was invented for good motives, the 'dark web' was created beneath it. Some of this was legitimate, in morality if not legality: people and groups attempting to escape or undermine dictatorships, or evade overbearing government rules of any kind, found relative safety in its shadows. But much of it was a hiding place and tool for criminals: everything from drugs (if one did not include that in the first classification), to illicit sex, to financial crimes, to murder for hire.

As was true in all things, many attracted to this world were more motivated than skilled. In any such environment of demand, supply soon followed. Tools of the trade became widely available, so what once would have taken exceptional skill now became accessible to the less able. Some sold these tools for the money. Others did it to show off their superior talents. Still others did it out of an urge to destroy and thus make it easier for others to destroy.

Law enforcement attempted to fight back but was always a step behind. Still, nothing is perfect, not even evil, and enough pressure was applied, and enough loud victories achieved, that the dark web was kept sufficiently in its box that life in the sunshine could go on.

Albert investigated this world and flexed his mental fingers. With his wealth he could buy sophisticated tools. With his mind he could improve them and use them even more effectively. It did not take him long to develop a suite of tools under the immediate control of an AI well insulated from his location by at least one ocean, and he let his virtual army loose to multiply his wealth by fair means or, more likely and lucrative, foul.

Albert felt no shame or guilt about this. He had a goal, and this was a logical method. It was the way of the world, a world that hated him. *Let them learn the price of their hate.*

And speaking of hate, there is another set of crimes overdue for committing. It is time to strike at my enemies. That comes with risk, but everything worthwhile does. Besides, there is more to life than making money and living in a warm cocoon. I have enough of that to need more spice. And I have just the enemy in mind.

He set his tools searching for that enemy's weak points and how to best exploit them.

Albert could achieve a lot via electronic means, but felt a human assistant able to act more directly in the outside world would be invaluable. However, the danger of betrayal was real. They would have to be absolutely trustworthy, or as close as possible in the real world. What, he pondered, could buy a person? There was money, but if money could buy someone, more money could lure them away. There was fear, but the brother of fear was hatred. So fear, like fire, was a dangerous servant. And worse, the more talented and therefore valuable the victim, the greater their ability to act on their hate, as many a ruler had discovered to their loss. There was love, but as Albert knew to his sorrow, love could die. But perhaps from gratitude and love, another love could be forged that would not die.

CHAPTER 17: THE FRIEND

Cassius Washington was a large, muscular black man with a shaved head, a horseshoe mustache, and large white teeth that could create a dazzling smile if he granted you friendliness. In better days he liked to wear numerous gold rings, but now he wore fewer, which were merely gold plated.

He had been a fine soldier. He did not mind taking orders and would carry them out with gusto and ability. However, he lacked a certain strategic judgement. So, while he made an excellent warrior, he would never have made a good general: though to his credit he knew that, unlike too many others. Unfortunately for Cassius, he had fallen in with a group of comrades with a loose devotion to the law, who were not as smart as they thought when it came to amplifying their personal wealth at the natives' expense. A dishonorable discharge had followed.

Cassius took this in his stride. In civilian life, he had not thrived but nor had he crashed. He had a happy relationship with his girlfriend, who bore him a daughter he adored.

One night, the girlfriend was struck by a car. By the time the ambulance reached the hospital, she was dead.

Cassius was devastated. He had always liked his bourbon, and increasingly turned to it to soften the edges of his grief. His employability and with it his finances suffered. He still adored his daughter, now ten years old, if anything more so now that her mother was gone. She may have wanted for some things she would have liked to have, but she remained clothed, fed and educated, to the best of

Cassius' ability.

Sadly, fate was not finished with Cassius. His daughter fell ill, and it was discovered that she had a rare genetic disease. The doctors were sorry, but there was nothing they could do. Over the coming months and years, she would lose one ability after the next until eventually succumbing. Her symptoms could be alleviated to some extent, and that could extend her life a little, but it would add up to a lot of money.

Cassius was not a man to cry, but when he looked at his daughter's face, so reminiscent of her mother's, he wept. He could look after her himself, but then how could he work to earn money? And if he worked, what would happen to her? Insurance was one of the luxuries that had gone with the rest of his lifestyle: surely, he had thought, he could go a few years without it, in the prime of his life with a young and healthy daughter? Thus the Fates may repay those who dance with them.

The doctor referred him to a specialist, who confirmed the poor prognosis and limited treatment options, then referred him to a genetic engineering company as the one hope of a cure, warning him it would be expensive. With mixed hope and trepidation, he went to see them.

"A difficult problem, Mr Washington," their assessor said. "Your daughter's disease is not only rare but has multiple, interacting possible genetic causes. Thus, there is no existing cure and customized work would be needed. Similarly, the cure is likely to be more complex than repairing just one spot in the DNA. Furthermore, while some genetic diseases affect a single organ or tissue, this one is more systemic, so any repair must be applied throughout the body. There are nearly 40 trillion cells in a human body, Mr Washington. Fortunately, we don't have to fix all of them, but in this case, it would have to be a significant fraction of them.

"And there is another issue. Any human genetic engineering work must first be approved by GenInt and several other agencies at various levels of government. Since approval requires complete description of the work, we would have to develop the essentials of the cure first. So, you would be liable for those costs up front, whatever their ultimate decision: which could take years, and is not even guaranteed to be positive."

Cassius said nothing in words, but his expression was clear: *You offer me hope, but all it does is taunt me from a height far beyond my reach.*

The assessor looked uncomfortable, glanced away, looked back at him. "Er, we can't do much about the cost. But I have heard... nothing to do with us, of course… and no, I would never recommend it… that there may be less scrupulous organizations who will, er, streamline the approvals process. But that comes with a rather steeper price, owing to higher expenses and greater risk."

"Give me your estimate of the cost, both options, but you don't have to write the second one down. I never heard anything here."

Now Cassius sat in a bar smokey and as dark as his mood. In his mind he could see his daughter's face as she lay in hospital, feel the life and joy ebbing out of her. *How can I get that much money? Even crime doesn't pay that much. Well, maybe… a big enough heist… but if it was that big, I'd surely be caught. Who would look after her then?*

He swirled his bourbon, watching the play of light in the ice. *And here I am spending money on liquor. Money I could have spent on her. But to what end? Buy her another minute of life? Will that do anything except extend her pain? And I need it. Maybe for a few minutes I can forget. But even oblivion isn't the answer. It does not stop her dying. But let me forget for those few minutes, and maybe I'll find the strength to go on.*

A stranger slipped onto the stool beside him, beckoned the bartender, waved at Cassius' drink, and said, "I'm paying."

Cassius looked at him speculatively. He was a slender, energetic young man, with short, straight black hair, hard muscles, designer clothes and a look of sharp cunning. "Thanks, brother," Cassius said.

The two sat drinking for a while in silence, each occasionally glancing at the other. Finally, without taking his eyes from his drink, the slender man spoke.

"You seem remarkably incurious, friend."

Cassius glanced at him, glanced away. "If a fellow buys me a drink, he wants something. If he wants something, he wants to tell me. I don't need to ask."

A fleeting smile passed over the man's face. "True enough, brother, true enough. A mutual friend sent me. He has an offer for you."

"Who is this mutual friend?"

"I don't know."

"Then how is he a mutual friend?"

"Pal, when somebody pays the money he pays, he's a friend."

"What makes our friend think I need money?"

"Our friend *knows* you need money."

"What does he want from me?"

The man shrugged. "Beats me. He just paid me to make the offer.

I quote: 'I want an assistant. Someone to drive me, deliver messages and buy things. Someone tough who doesn't mind bending the law but who won't bend it any further than he must. I will pay double the going rate.'"

"Sounds too easy." He stared into the inviting depths of his drink, and it was as if he was seeing not a play of light and ice, but his lost opportunities, dying hopes and shrinking options. But it was something. More than he had. There had to be a catch; he wondered what it was. He wondered if he would care. "Is that it?"

"Not quite. He said you'll understand this, and I quote again: 'And I will fix his medical problem for him.'"

Cassius stared at him. *What kind of man can know this and do this? What would I be getting myself into?*

"Sounds like if I take this, I would be selling my soul."

The man smiled. "Well? Is your soul for sale?"

"For this… yes. For this I would sell more than my soul. Tell him I'm in."

Chapter 18: The Bite of the Adder

Albert watched his guest through the video feed. She was middle aged: with modern life-extending treatments that could mean anything from 30 to 65; but he knew her precise age, among many other things about her. She had not taken her incarceration in good grace and had ignored the grooming materials Albert had left for her, becoming increasingly scruffy as a result.

She had been here for a few days now. At first there had been screaming for mercy; then there had been screaming in anger and calling down dire retribution from the heavens; then crying; finally, a sullen, fearful silence. Albert wondered if he should feel guilty. No, that wasn't it. He felt guilty but cheerfully ignored the guilt. He owed the world no more than they felt they owed him. Perhaps this woman was innocent, relative to that world. While that still mattered to him in a suppressed corner of his mind, he was not convinced that it should: so, while he occasionally took the feeling out and played with it, he always locked it back in its cage afterwards.

He wondered at the hold such conventional morality still had over him. Perhaps his parents had taught him too well. But he had seen what people were in their souls and knew he would outgrow it soon enough. Surely, he was still human enough for that.

The first time he had come to see her, she had stared at him, greatly startled to see a child. "Who are you?" she had demanded, not knowing whether to feel fear for him or of him.

"You do not know?" he had asked.

"No! Should I? Please, what's going on? Are you a prisoner here too? I don't belong here. Please, can you let me go?"

He had just shaken his head solemnly and left.

The next time he had brought a chair. He could stand for hours without discomfort, but psychologically he thought sitting would help put her at ease. So, he entered silently and put down the chair, filled two plastic cups from a bottle of water and with his foot pushed one of them within her reach. Finally, he sat down facing her. After a short and silent staring match, he eventually spoke.

"You do not know who I am?"

"I told you, no. Why am I here? Who is holding me? Is it ransom they want? I don't have much money, but they can have all I can raise. Just let me go! Please."

"Don't be afraid."

She had laughed bitterly. "Don't be afraid? If anyone has a right to be afraid, it must be me!"

"Are you well? The food is to your liking?"

"What are you, the hotel manager? Feck the food! Let me the hell out of here!"

He stared at her a moment. "Clearly the food is adequate, if you care so little about it. Perhaps if it were withdrawn for a while, you might value it more."

Her look of angry defiance held on by its fingernails for a few moments before giving up and freefalling into fear. Nobody had hurt her yet, but she knew that could change in an instant. She had read about kidnappings. Read how the chances of survival dropped rapidly as each day passed. She had read about it as one of those statistics that was merely grim in the third person but became appalling in the first.

"I… I'm sorry. Please don't hurt me! I have a husband. A family: a boy and a girl. I want to see them again! Don't do this to me, to them. Have… have they contacted them? Do my family know I'm still alive? Are they… are they able to pay the ransom?"

"There is no ransom."

"Then what is going to happen to me?"

"I don't know."

"Who is doing this to me?"

He looked at her for long moments. "I am."

Her eyes darted to his in surprise. "But you're just a boy!"

"Yes. And no."

He could have made his contact lenses go transparent; but that would merely have underlined that the color of his eyes could be anything the lenses could produce. Until now, with her he had left his eyes an anonymous brown. He took out the lenses, keeping his eyes down, holding out his palm to show her what he had removed; she examined his palm curiously, wondering what this meant. Then he raised his head, and she found herself gazing into his weirdly emerald eyes.

She started in surprise, wondering at their unexpected hue. Then his eyes, his age and what he had said and done to her coalesced in her mind and she gasped.

"No! Oh, no! You're… him, aren't you? That boy, that geneh boy, the one who did those things to those people, the boy everyone's hunting! I read about him… about you!" She stared at him for a few seconds longer, transfixed, then screamed in a terror born part of circumstance and part of the unknown, *"What do you want with me?"*

"For now, I want to talk. For later, I have a purpose for you."

"Please, I've never done anything to you! Why me?"

"The things we do have consequences, but there is no justice to them. For some, an afternoon's pleasure may do no more than add to the accumulated joys of their life. For others, it could bring death or ruin. For still others, it might return to demand payment years later."

She looked confused. "What on Earth are you talking about? I've never hurt anyone! So why choose me?"

"You are fit for my purpose. And is it true you have never done anything to me? That is an interesting question, don't you think? Here I hide, the hounds of society hunting me—a society of which you are a part. You share in its benefits. Perhaps you share in their guilt."

She had read his story with the same reaction as many: with curiosity at the facts, fascination perhaps touched with fear at the science, and a sharper, more primal stab of fear at the tales of a monstrous, amoral killer on the loose. Now, finding herself his victim, she gave more credence to the tales, and the light in her eyes changed.

"See? You hate me. You think I am evil, like they say," he commented.

"You're doing a good job of convincing me right now!"

"And before? If, instead of meeting me locked in that cage, I had merely bumped into you at the shops, and asked your opinion?"

"I… I don't know."

"Really? You read about me but formed no opinion? Should that be a factor in your favor, or evidence of the complicity of apathy and ignorance? If citizens such as yourself have so little care, why should your rulers not think they can get away with whatever lies and crimes they like?"

"I'm… I'm sorry. It was just too far outside any knowledge or influence I have. Or so I thought."

"Do not lie to me. I don't believe any person could read such a story and not come to any opinion. So, let's ask a more pointed question. Your emotions spring from your deepest beliefs and reflect your opinions, whether you have bothered to make them explicit in your mind or not. So, what if I had bumped into you at the shops, but instead of asking your abstract opinion, had revealed myself to you, begging for your help? You see police in the distance, looking for someone; and here is something you know they would like to find, but he is pleading for your aid. What would you have done?"

"I… you're just a child!" she said in something akin to wonder. "I would have helped you. Or I would have felt I should help you." Then she gave him a hard look and added flatly, "It seems I would have been mistaken."

He looked at her with neither answer nor change of expression. The silence grew, and she thought to turn the question back on him.

"*Are* you evil?"

He shrugged. "What is evil? Once upon a time, I believed in good and evil. Then I was betrayed by my parents for being what they made me and given to others: who pretended to care for me, but in their turn cared only for what they might get out of me. People talk of good and evil, but all they really care about is their own advantage, and they will trample anyone to get it. So, you could say I am no longer convinced there is good or evil, only goals and means. I am not hated because I am worse than them. I am hated because I am the same, only better at it."

"Is that really what you think?" she whispered.

She shivered at the dread flatness of his reply. "Apparently that is what the world thinks. Well, I will take them at their word and give them what they asked for. If they wish to hate me because they fear me and kill me because they hate me: I will answer them as they deserve. If they do not like it, perhaps they should have thought more deeply before they started a war with me."

"But why me? I'm not a big person. I'm not important—not to

anyone outside my friends and family."

He shrugged again. "Why should I care? I have a use for you—that's all you need to know. Your fate is of no concern of mine, except in so far as it advances my own plans."

"That is very cruel."

"It is what it needs to be. If I am cruel—it is not for cruelty's sake, though I admit that is little comfort to you. Except that I promise I will only be as cruel as I must be, no more. As I said, your fate is of no concern to me, and that includes your pain as much as your life."

"Are you going to kill me?"

"I don't know. It depends on how things turn out. I might."

"Are you going to... to hurt me?"

"If I have to."

"How long are you going to hold me?"

He looked at her for long seconds, as if underlining his answer.

"As long as it takes."

He said no more as he calmly stood up, collected his things and left. She stood looking after him. She was not a religious person, but she found herself praying to whatever gods of justice or mercy there might be to save her and carry her home.

She hoped somebody was listening, but if there were there was no sign of it in her lonely prison.

CHAPTER 19: THE PREACHERS OF DEATH

The Church of His Image received many small donations from its extended flock and the halo of people beyond it who were hedging their bets. It received more sizable donations from a few individuals who shared its goals and organizations who wanted to gain its favor or avoid its displeasure. The Church received them all with gratitude; the larger ones might receive a personalized message of thanks.

They might even receive a personal video call from its Founder, Charles Denner. But such an honor was reserved only for very generous donors.

It was unlikely Denner would grace even the most lavish donor with his personal presence. But one day a man called, saying he had a large amount of funds he wished to donate. The Church of His Image, the man revealed, had excited his interest. But in business he judged a company by those who ran it; and if he were to give to the Church, he would first have to take the measure of the man who ran it. He had in fact approached some other religious groups but left disappointed. He hoped this time would be different.

The Church investigated. The man had indeed recently come into significant wealth. He had indeed met with the leaders of other churches; in Denner's private opinion, those leaders were more or less hucksters, and the man's decision to spurn them showed good judgement.

And so it came to pass that Charles Denner, encircled by four bodyguards, found himself in an elevator speeding to the top floor of a skyscraper, to the penthouse office of the Jarvis Engineering

Corporation.

Jarvis Engineering had trundled along for many years, following the trajectory of many such enterprises: born in hope, built on sweat, oscillating between highs and lows as both final success and irrevocable doom alternately threatened then failed to materialize. Then less than a year ago, Brian Jarvis had retired, and his son Arthur had taken over the reins. Perhaps it was coincidence or perhaps it was skill, but in the past few months he had rapidly collected some clever technology acquisitions from obscure sources, which he leveraged into spectacular success when Jarvis Engineering won a very lucrative military contract based on its new technology.

Arthur had worked for his father for many years. He had never been considered more than solid and reliable, but perhaps he had felt overshadowed by his father. Or maybe in their family conversations the father had pulled the reins on his son's youthful enthusiasms. In any case the energy he brought to the company soon after his ascent to its leadership was both a shock and a large part of its success.

If Arthur had never been a blazing intellect, neither had he been overly religious. His family had been religious in the quiet way many people are, with a belief that formed the backdrop rather than the bedrock of their lives. But with his newfound enthusiasm for business came, perhaps surprisingly, a new enthusiasm for organized religion, an enthusiasm now pointed at the Church of His Image. Perhaps he had prayed and thought his prayers had been answered; or perhaps he was as surprised by his success as others were and could only ascribe it to divine intervention.

In any event, he had decided to donate a very large sum to the Church, and that decision had brought Charles Denner to his door.

Unlike Denner, he had no bodyguards with him when he greeted his guest at the door. If one cannot trust the leader of a Church, who can one trust? He seemed stunned by Denner, as if the light of his eminence were slightly too bright to observe or deserve. He had a private art gallery on this floor and showed his guests around, with a slightly nervous air, as if simultaneously proud of his art and afraid that Denner would not approve of it. He need not have worried, for Denner did approve of it. Art, he knew, reflected the soul of its admirers. This art was well executed and, while not overtly religious, held a numinous quality of human humility coupled with cosmic significance.

The initial dance steps over, Arthur said, "Well Mr Denner, thank you for coming. I have had lunch prepared for us. Please, if you will, your guards can eat outside as I should like to have a private chat with you. They will be able to watch us if you have any security concerns."

Denner readily agreed to his, on the proviso that one guard accompany them while maintaining a discrete distance. Church rules, he disclaimed with a smile: even he was subject to them.

Arthur frowned but accepted: what else could he do? So, he and Denner sat at his table, eating and talking, as three guards watched from outside while munching sandwiches, and the third stood stolidly at the wall behind Denner.

They spoke for a long time. Then Denner scratched his ear, and one of the guards outside stared, with a strong feeling of déjà vu. Surely, he had seen that same gesture twice before: not just similar, but identical. He walked up to the glass and tapped on it, but there was no response from any of the people inside. He struck it more loudly with his open palm, with no effect. Now alarmed, he tried to open the door, but it was locked. When his pounding also elicited no response, he stepped back and gave it a mighty kick. The door sprang open, and he looked inside: the room was empty except for the lone guard collapsed on the floor.

~~~

Arthur Jarvis awoke in his own apartment, disoriented and wondering why he didn't remember coming home. As his strange benefactor had instructed, he had invited Charles Denner for lunch and had a pleasant time of it, occasionally parroting the words received in his ear from his guardian angel when Denner asked a tricky question. The last he remembered was reaching for a glass of wine.

~~~

Charles Denner awoke to rather less comfortable surroundings. There was nothing particularly wrong with his surroundings. The room had little adornment, and if not designed for comfort at least was not particularly uncomfortable. However, he had not expected to find himself sitting in a wheelchair. He wondered why, until he tried to get up and found he couldn't. His surprise at seeing his wrists manacled to the armrests rapidly became alarm when he realized he was also locked to it by his feet and his middle, and he wondered how he had come from a pleasant lunch to this predicament. The last he remembered was reaching for a glass of wine.

However, the glasses of wine had little to do with either of their fates. When enough of their meeting had been recorded, an odorless gas had been released into the room and all three occupants had quietly succumbed. Men in Denner's position and their bodyguards usually had defenses against the standard knockout chemicals, but unfortunately for them this had been a more exotic concoction. The guards outside had been none the wiser, and as they remained in communication with their own superiors at base nobody had felt any cause for alarm. But what they saw in the glass was a fiction, variations on the themes of the recorded conversation extrapolated and played by an AI. They had not seen the men taken into a hole in the floor which led to who knew where; nor were they likely to find the hole, long since seamlessly sealed with the same fast-setting artificial rock as made up the rest of the floor, and similarly reinforced with steel bars.

In any case, by the time their disappearance was discovered both men were long gone.

Now Denner wondered what on Earth Jarvis thought he was doing. "Hello?" he cried out hoarsely, then, swallowing to wet his throat, repeated the call more loudly.

The door opened and Denner gaped, realizing his end was near, for a green-eyed imp entered the room and stood regarding him with cold hostility.

"Welcome to my lair, Mr Denner," the imp said, "Today's, anyway."

"What do you want with me?"

"What do you think I want with you?"

"I would rather not give you ideas."

Albert smiled grimly. "Quite. But despite your fear, you might leave here alive. Or you and others might die. Or anywhere in between. I am not happy with you, Mr Denner."

"The servants of Satan have always hated the servants of Light," snorted Denner. "On that topic, what power or blandishments allowed you to corrupt Mr Jarvis to do your bidding, as your Master corrupted Eve?"

"Do not blame Mr Jarvis. I have been cultivating him for some time, with no particular purpose in mind, just as another possible card to play. And see, now I found a use for him. Do not fear for his supposed immortal soul, Mr Denner. There was no Faustian bargain. He is weak, easily manipulated, and had no idea who he was dealing with. Of course, cards like him can be played only once when the stake is this dramatic. Fortunately, I have others."

"What did you do with him?"

"If you are afraid for his life, do not worry. I saw no need to harm him. But if you are hoping for rescue, or failing that, vengeance, forget it. He knows nothing that can help you or the police."

"No doubt you intend less mercy for me. But though you can kill this shell, you would just speed me on to Eternity."

"You are sadly deluded. When you die your body will rot like everybody else's, and all your hopes and dreams and visions will cease to be as the neural connections in your brain degrade into quiescence. Your faith is some protection against your fear of death, though even you can feel that fear in your bones. I suggest that in this matter your bones are wiser than your tainted mind."

"Did you bring me here to discuss materialistic philosophy?"

"Among other things. But do not dismiss the wisdom of your body so easily. If you do not fear death maybe you fear other things. Perhaps what you deserve for your crimes is pain, since you tell me death is insufficient punishment."

"There are many martyrs in my faith, who have borne great travails. All you would do is increase my reward in Heaven," Denner replied, though he could not stop his face paling as he said it. *He has a point about the wisdom of my body, if one can call it wisdom not weakness.*

"Your body is literally not so sanguine, I see. But let us dispense with the unpleasantries for a while. I brought you here to justify yourself. To justify your campaign of hatred against me. Speak well, and perhaps there will be no more unpleasantness."

"Why should I justify myself to you?"

"If you have any justifications, now is the time to produce them. For if you have none, I can only conclude that, contrary to your preaching that I am a creature of evil born of hate, it is you who are the creature of evil given to hate."

Denner examined him curiously. "And if I prove you are a creature of evil?"

Albert smiled without humor. "That is a good question. I may become less evil, or more so. It depends on how you convince me and exactly what you convince me of."

"I would say you are a strange demon, except I know the tricks of your true Father, who is the Father of Lies. To use language that I refrain from in public: go screw yourself."

"You are forgetting I hold your life in my hand, to dispose of at my whim; as well as your agony or lack thereof."

"You will do to me whatever you want then, whatever I tell you."

"You are not being logical. You do not know that. Your only hope is to do what I ask, and all I ask is a conversation. Do you seek death as much as you preach it? Are you so in love with pain that you would spurn the chance to avoid it?"

"What does a demon know of love?"

"I am not a demon. But come. I will show you one thing I know of love. I did not expect you to be very helpful and I would prefer to avoid torturing you: torture is as likely to bring deception as truth, and to cloud your mind when what I need is its greatest clarity. So, I prepared alternative motivation."

Denner's chair rotated to face the wall; then one section of wall slid into another, revealing a room beyond. In it were two steel cages, and in one was a woman. As the door opened, she looked up in alarm; he did not recognize the woman but there was something about her eyes, something that Denner did know.

"No..." he whispered. His mind could not place her, but somewhere in his soul he felt a great betrayal, as if this woman being here had somehow betrayed his own past. As if it were he who had delivered something sacred into the claws of evil.

"Hello, Charlie," she said, and he knew.

"Rachel..."

Then he spun his head toward Albert and growled, "What do you think you are doing?"

Albert smiled, and Denner wished he hadn't. "Proving I understand love. I studied your past, looking for leverage. You hid your history with this young—well, formerly young—lady well, but you and she dropped enough hints and there were enough bits of evidence for me to work out that she was a turning point in your life. Things like that do not pass. They may be buried, but they do not pass."

"What makes you such an expert in human psychology?"

"Despite your preaching, I am human myself. Besides, I am an expert in many things. Be warned that causing pain might be one of them."

"What are you going to do to her?"

"Nothing."

Denner gave him a puzzled look. He had expected more threats of death and torture, this time directed at the woman. "What is she here for then? Just a demonstration of your cleverness in unravelling my past?"

Albert's smile this time was grim. "Not quite, though for future reference—if you have a future—you might wish to ponder how easily I traced and took what you thought was safely buried. I am going to do nothing to her. But when our interview is over, I am leaving this place. If you do not give me satisfaction, then I will abandon her here."

Rachel's eyes jerked toward him, horrified. "No. Please no. I don't deserve that!"

"I told you your fate depended on another. Now here the other is. All I have asked from him is an honest conversation. If your life is worth less to him than that, then which of us is the more evil?"

"Charlie! What is he saying?! Please!"

"You little bastard," Denner snarled at Albert. "Let her go!"

"Her fate is in your hands, and yours alone."

"Let me touch her."

Albert raised an eyebrow. Then Denner's chair carried him into the room and up to the bars. The manacles released, and he reached out to take Rachel's hands. "I'm so sorry, Rachel," he whispered. "I… I never wanted anything like this." Even now, when he had not seen her for years and the gulf of time and faith yawned between them, her physical presence had the power to move him. He did not know if it was a sin that even now, though his eyes saw the mature woman before him, what his soul saw was a young girl with passion in her eyes, where now there were only tears.

"Please Charlie, do what he asks. Don't let me die here like this."

Denner turned a look of hatred on Albert. "You little hell spawn. What guarantee do I have that you will let her go?"

Albert looked at him, then directly into Rachel's eyes. "I will let you go," he said to her. The raw simplicity of his reply made Rachel believe him, and she let out a sob.

"Let her go now!"

"No. I trust you as much as you trust me. She will stay until I am satisfied."

"And when you find my answers do not satisfy you?"

"Then you might die. But I will let her go. The price of her life is an honest discussion with you, that is all. The price of yours is higher, for your guilt is greater."

"And what guilt does she have, to deserve this?"

"Why, Mr Denner! In your religion I believe she has much guilt. Does not your Original Sin make her guilty just for being born? And in her own actions, I am sure she has broken many of your commandments: fornication for starters, not only with you but with many others."

Then he looked back at Rachel, almost with tenderness. "But no, in my eyes she has no guilt, or no more than the rest of her miserable race, except by association with you. It is not for any crime of hers that I took her, but for yours. Hence you can be sure that I will let her go once her purpose is served."

"Please, Charlie," she whispered.

"All right, demon," Denner said to Albert. "Lucifer might be the Father of Lies, but as you have chosen to put on the mask of reasonable debate, then to some extent you bind yourself by your own deceptions. I will play your game."

"Then we are agreed on one point at last."

The chair pulled away, and Rachel reluctantly let go. "Don't worry, Rachel," Albert said to her. "I meant what I said. Your part in this is over and you have nothing more to fear. Goodbye."

Then the wall closed again, Rachel was gone, and Albert turned his attention back to Denner.

"So then, Mr Denner, let us see if we can agree on any other points. I will not tell you that your God is not real, for I know you will never believe me. Besides, not all who believe in your God believe I am evil; therefore, the one belief is not inherent in the other. So let us approach it not from your assumptions but from the other direction. Why do you think I am evil?"

"You do not think that kidnapping us is sufficient reason?"

"No. You reverse cause and effect. I kidnapped you because you call me evil and worse: you call for my death. Your own Bible speaks of an eye for an eye and a life for a life. It even speaks of the life of one for the sins of others. This is self-defense, nothing more.

"However, what it does not speak of is genetic engineering, a concept utterly beyond the simple primitives who wrote your Book. Their idea of genetic engineering was mating goats in front of stippled sticks. By what arrogance do you proclaim me evil, just for what I am?"

"The Lord made Man in his image, boy. He also made all the

animals according to their kinds and gave us dominion over them. He did not give us the right to remake them, let alone ourselves, in our own image. That is both hubris and blasphemy. You are an affront."

"So, you have no concept of good and evil, other than the supposed words of your God; and even then, you make up those words yourself?"

"God is the source of good and the antithesis of evil, and his words are clear."

"So, you do not judge me by my deeds. I could be the greatest man alive, and still, you would call me evil. I could save your life, and you would still condemn me. If I left your Rachel locked up here to face a long death from thirst and starvation, you would call me evil; but if I let her go, your judgment would remain the same."

"You are what you are. You will never do those good things; any more than a serpent can refrain from biting. If you let Rachel go, you will only do it to serve your lies: to give the appearance of good in order to mask a greater evil."

"We all are what we are. Do you think we have a choice in it? Do we have free will? Does your omnipotent God allow that?"

"Of course, we have free will; how our Lord's omnipotence enables it is but one of his many mysteries. But you? I…" for the first time Denner seemed uncertain. "Certainly, Lucifer had free will, when he chose to fall and rule over Hell, as did the angels who followed him to become demons. But they are ancient demons, corrupt from before time. You… you are a new demon and did not choose your fate."

Albert watched him, then replied, "I see your thoughts are leading you into a conundrum. If I have free will, then I am able to choose good or evil. If I have no free will, then how can I be evil? I cannot have an evil motive, so you can only judge me by the harm I cause. In either case you must judge me by my deeds."

"You are clever, but your words do not change your nature. Perhaps the root of your evil lies not in you but in your maker, who did choose your nature."

"Why is that my fault?"

"You mentioned Original Sin, and you could say the same about that. The mysteries of God are beyond human understanding, but his words are clear enough. We cannot damn God for that, we can only damn Man. For despite it, God himself died for our sins, in the person of his Son."

"So, if I accepted this salvation you promise, even I could be saved?"

Denner shot him a surprised look; he had not expected this creature to ask such a question. "Would you?" he asked, almost in a whisper.

Albert gazed at him for a few moments, then replied almost as softly, "No. I am not capable of faith—only reason."

"Then perhaps that is your answer."

"So, reason, the power which raises us above animals and, as I understand it, puts us in the image of God: that is the source of my damnation, and perhaps the world's."

Albert gazed at him a while longer, then stood abruptly. "Goodbye, Mr Denner," he said ambiguously.

"What... what are you going to do?"

Albert's mouth began a smile of contempt, but it faded as he studied Denner's eyes. "That is the first time you have impressed me, Charlie. I do believe you are asking me strategically, not just being worried about your own worthless neck. Perhaps you have depths I hadn't seen.

"But what I am going to do is think. Your religion means nothing to me except morality based on empty claims of an invisible God, and offers me nothing but damnation whatever I do. You had better hope I do not believe you, for then why should I not become in fact what you have already damned me for in principle?"

"Kill me then, but let Rachel go."

Albert studied him. "You are a conundrum, Mr Denner. You believe in fairytales, yet you are highly intelligent. That is a vipers' nest I am not interested in unravelling at this point, but perhaps I can still learn from you. Perhaps I shall reverse my offer. What if I agree to let you go—if I take her life instead?"

"You told her you would set her free!"

Albert shrugged. "So? Maybe I meant it then but now I've changed my mind. More to the point, you assure me I am evil no matter what I do. Why then should lies or betrayal concern me? Surely the question of honesty only worries honest men."

"Have you no mercy? Or justice? Or kindness?"

"If they are virtues, what are they to me? By your own words— nothing. But enough. Do you accept my offer? Your life for hers."

"No."

"What if we raise the stakes? One of you goes free while the other dies an agonizing death. I believe your religion was once keen on having sinners drawn and quartered, so that might be fitting. So, given that alternative I ask you again: your life for hers?"

"No."

Albert studied him. "Why do you care so much about her? She is not one of your flock. She isn't even religious. Once you shared love, but surely to you its nature was a grievous sin: a sin which takes two, so it would be fair to curse her for your own downfall as much as her own. Your own faith damns her. And if one is to die and one live, let us weigh the value of those lives. Surely your life is more valuable than hers, in terms of what you yourself hold dear?"

Denner looked at him helplessly. "I... she... I suppose it is as you said: there are some things that are never lost. But besides that, it is wrong to put yourself above others. It would be cowardly for me to do what you propose."

"Even when your life is objectively—well, objectively in your universe—far more valuable than hers? You are leader of a church you founded, in a position to do great things. She is anonymous, an ordinary woman whose passing will barely cause a ripple in the world now, let alone tomorrow."

"All God's children are precious."

"But she is not one of God's children: she is an unbeliever, a sinner, doomed to damnation. Forever cursed in the outer darkness, abandoned by your God for the sins He imposed upon her."

"She may yet find her way back to God. God never abandons us, and her path may change. There is hope for all of us, even God's lost children."

"Except for me," replied Albert softly. Then Denner felt a sharp pain in his shoulder, and before he could reply or curse, the world went dark.

~~~

Denner awoke slowly, looking without comprehension at a strange view that held no meaning. He would have wondered where he was, if he could have wondered at all.

He looked down, saw that his hands were free, and remembered that they had been bound. He looked around, and saw he was now caged instead. Then he realized he was alive, and what that might mean brought fear to his heart. He leapt to his feet, then had to hold on to the bars for a few moments as a wave of dizziness threatened to topple him. When he recovered, he looked around.

A short distance away was another cage, and inside he could see Rachel, slumped on the floor, unmoving. "Rachel!" he shouted. "Rachel!"

For horrifying seconds, she remained still, but finally he saw an arm move. She sat up, groaning.

"Rachel... I thought... I thought you were dead."

"Huh...?" she said, looking around, not really knowing where she was.

Then her eyes cleared. "Charlie! You're alive! We're alive! What happened, Charlie? Where is he?"

"What happened is, we talked, then suddenly he got tired of talking. Now the place feels empty. I think he's gone. But as for alive... we have no food or water and we're in steel cages. Maybe my answers weren't good enough, or maybe he just thinks it'll be amusing or interesting psychology to watch the two of us watch each other die."

Rachel shook her head slowly. "I can't believe he's that bad. I know he talks tough, but there's something about him... like under his cruelty there's still just a little boy, thinking he has to be cruel but not wanting to be, and looking for answers. He threatened me enough. But he never hurt me."

Denner rattled the bars of his cage to show what he thought of that. They felt as solid as they looked.

Rachel laughed, and he looked at her as if she too had gone mad. "I just had a thought," she said. "That boy likes to test people and punish them with their own stupidity. Have you actually... tried the door?"

Denner looked at her stupidly, then leapt to his door, which opened easily. Seeing that, she did the same and they walked to each other, she practically dancing, both laughing. He looked at her crossly, and said, "If you ever tell anybody about this..."

The two of them collapsed into laughter, all the fear of their captivity and fate dissolving into its release.

"Of course, we're not out of the woods yet," Denner observed when their hilarity subsided.

However, it proved equally simple to find their way out, and soon they found themselves outside in a laneway, blinking in the sunlight. Denner turned to her.

"Rachel, I have wondered if we would ever meet again. What I would do if we did." He smiled. "That was the last thing I expected. Let's get you home. Let's get us both home."

For a moment they looked into each other's eyes, and the years that lay between them vanished. In a strange clarity Charles saw the turns his life had made in the years since he had first held Rachel, and at the sight of it he wondered if he had been right. Then he shook his head. They had both made their decisions, the past was what it was, and the present was what they had become. Tomorrow, he knew, he would regain the rectitude of his certainty. But today, he reached out his hand to her.

Charles loved his wife, and Rachel her husband; their past was just a memory. But they walked out into the sunshine, hand in hand. The past had earned them that much.

~~~

By then Albert was far away in another hiding place. He sat on a padded chair, sipping a strawberry milkshake through a straw. He regarded his glass critically, thinking with a smile that surely such a dastardly villain as him should be drinking vodka, or some other hard liquor distilled in a land of violence. He knew he would not, for the one thing he would not risk was his own growing brain.

He turned that brain back to earlier in the day, remembering the conversation. He had not expected to find answers in Denner's mind, but he had hoped for clues. He felt he had found one. One man could not embody all religions, and he knew that some of his own champions were believers, declaring his rights from the perspective of religious morality. Evidently such foundations were so murky that either friend or foe could rise from them, both equally sure of their righteousness. It made no difference: their beliefs were based on nothing real, and beyond the practical matter of his survival their conclusions also meant nothing, no more than the idle twittering of birds.

He had also known the power of a human connection. He had truly not known how Denner would react or whether he would need to kill him or Rachel. But he always played many strategies at once. And he knew he had reached Denner; at some level, the certainty of the man's hatred had been breached.

~~~

In the months ahead, Denner continued his campaign. But his words were less strident, his condemnations more nuanced. He continued to preach Albert's danger and urge his capture. But he never again explicitly called for his death. In the throes of his anger or passion he might begin to write a fiery condemnation. But when in his memory he sought the green eyes of a Satanic demon as the fuel for his rage, instead he would find the green eyes of a merely human monster, and know they were the eyes of a boy; a boy who had looked upon his enemies from a seat of absolute power yet let them go. Then the eyes would become the eyes of a young Rachel, watching him in a passion at once burning and innocent; eyes that still lived, when so easily they might not have. And the condemnation could not be written.

Sometimes at night in his room, or wandering the streets of a city or the pathways of a forest, he would wonder if the shadows glimpsed out of the corner of his eye were Albert watching him, waiting; he wondered if Albert would visit him again, this time to end his life. But Albert never came for him.

CHAPTER 20: THE MAGICIAN

If the passion and fury of Charles Denner had been somewhat blunted, at least on this topic, others were happy to take up the banner.

It was autumn, when the hearts of young politicians turned to love of power, and the first movements of their campaigns for the next President of the United States began.

~~~

When Bob Pepperman was a boy, he was possessed of a broad and disarming smile, a sense of humor, and piercing eyes which conveyed passion, conviction and sincerity, whether he felt them or not. He made friends easily, but deep passions had trouble gaining traction in his soul, even if his eyes sometimes pretended that they were buried within.

As he grew older, he proved to be not a bad boy, but nor was he especially good. He was basically amoral, but his easygoing nature limited its expression to peccadillos more than sins. It was not that he had invested any deep thought into the essence of good and evil: he merely followed the easy path, which included not being caught, which in turn included not doing anything likely to draw too much attention. He had indulged in shoplifting and other minor property crimes; he had indulged in illicit drugs, the copying of homework and sex under the noses of parents who would have greatly disapproved; he was never caught himself, but learned valuable lessons on the prudence of limits by observing the fate of those who were.

The idea of political power attracted him. Not being a person of profound passions, he had no great desire to rule others. He merely thought it was a good way to gain a comfortable lifestyle capable of attracting respect and wealth. He held no burning ambition, but for someone like him it was easy to be popular, easy to gain leadership positions, and easy to benefit from them. As he grew older, he pursued education and contacts which would help him on his way. He cultivated debating skills and oratory, in which he demonstrated flash but no great depth of substance. This did not worry him, for he believed that in politics, if not everything, flash was what mattered the most.

The net result of his qualities, friendships and contacts was that he succeeded in his ambition to become a state legislator. His virtues made him eminently electable, and promised a long and popular, if not eminent, career.

Now Robert Pepperman lounged before a log fire, legs stretched out in front of him, a cut crystal glass of iced whisky in his hand and daydreams in his mind. A young assistant sat next to him, her elbow resting on the opposite armrest, so she was leaning slightly away from him. One leg was folded under her, while her other foot idly stroked his calf. They had finished their 'research' a while ago and were now properly dressed except for an absence of shoes, but neither felt inclined to break the lingering spell of their earlier chemistry.

"You should run, Bobby," she murmured idly, gazing into the flames, as if at a source of inspiration or truth.

"Hmmm?"

"Run. For President. Surely, you've thought about it."

He looked at her appraisingly. "Do you think I'd have a chance?"

"No, not really."

"Then why suggest it?" he asked with some asperity.

"Winning doesn't matter this time, Bobby. You're still young. Virile," she added with a giggle. "But if you do well—which you will— think of the publicity, the attention. It will open doors. Take you places. And if you play your cards right, sometime in the future, you might win."

"And I suppose," he replied with a penetrating glance, "one of my assistants might prove invaluable to this plan, eh, Lady Macbeth?"

"Your face, my thane, is as a book where men may read strange matters," she quoted with a laugh. "But really. I'm sure I can be useful to you in *many* ways," she added, with additional pressure from her foot as proof. "And your Lady Macbeth reference is not completely fair: I'm not asking you to kill anyone, just enter the time-honored lists of those jousting for power. You know you want it. I know how much you enjoy the perks of office, all those people doing you favors to gain your friendship. All above board, of course. Friendship is not bribery, after all. Heck, there are even some girls who find you irresistible, though personally I cannot see it. Think how much more you'll get of all that if you do well."

He looked at her speculatively and she smiled. "I won't even mind those other girls, Bobby. Not too much. I know you need them. As long as you know you need me too. As long as you stick with me. As long as you come to me when I need you. You can get there, Bobby. We can get there."

"Hmmm," he repeated as a statement not a question, returning his gaze to the fire. She watched him with a faint smile on her face.

A call came in for him and she saw him accept it with vision off. She saw his look of surprise and watched as it changed into one of keen attentiveness. Quietly she unfolded her legs, rose from the lounge and left the room.

He did not notice her leave.

~~~

While Pepperman was popular among his colleagues, few thought there was much substance behind the façade. Fewer still thought he had any chance when, to everyone's surprise, he announced that he would be seeking the highest office in the land.

But having announced that decision, it was as if he had become a man transformed, possessed by a new vision and a new resolve. Where once his oratory had flash but little substance, now it had both; where once his performance in debates was middling, now his opponents more often than not found themselves facing barbs as clever as they were accurate.

People began to take notice. Robert Pepperman, a few pundits began to suggest, was the dark horse to watch.

They watched more as his policies firmed up. Then at a rally he gave a speech which set his campaign afire.

"I am not against genetic engineering," he said. "I find the excesses of GenInt abhorrent; who could look at the geneh woman Katlyn and shout that she deserved death simply for what she was, something done to her not by her? Yet we must recognize that she is unnatural! I cannot go as far as some whom you know; I cannot call her evil; yet nor can I support the creation of her kind. Men should not make themselves gods and arrogate to themselves the design of mankind. And what more proof do we need of that, than the recent escape of a dangerous geneh male, a mere youngster, they said—when any information at all could be extracted from GenInt—another creation of scientific hubris unleashed upon the world, a murderer and kidnapper who is still at large, plotting who knows what dark schemes?

"And that," he cried, lifting his eyes and his voice, "is not the only price of technology corrupted away from the benefit of mankind to feeding the pride of men! Have we forgotten the robot Steel, another creation justified for helping lift the burdens of toil, yet escaped to stalk the streets at its own command, until it had to be tracked down and destroyed? And look closer! Many of you will have seen that robot's manifesto; and who could not feel sympathy for it, yes, even for it, whatever its crimes? Alone and hunted; more alone than any human could ever be; more alone even than a geneh, who at least shares a degree of common humanity with us? If we feel any sympathy for a thing like Steel: is this not yet more reason for stopping such unbridled folly? If Steel was not responsible for its crimes; if it was forced to survive in the only way it could after being created then abandoned: surely those crimes and that sorrow should be laid at the feet of those who dared try to create a mind?

"And there is more. You know of a brave detective, one Miriam Hunter, who was involved in both these cases. A woman who has protected you from criminals—and worse. And what was her fate? What was her reward? Unwillingly, unknowingly, entombed in a war robot, a killer machine; pressed into acts of violence that must still haunt her. Driven to the point of madness. Finally saved—but at what cost? At what cost to her? At what cost to us, the citizens of her country: the citizens she defended, the citizens who failed her in her hour of need?

"Yes, she was saved by technology. Her broken, crippled body was restored; and who would not applaud that?

"But that is my point. Technology to serve humanity is not evil, but good. But those who wish to go beyond that must be stopped. There have been too many examples, and there is no excuse!"

He paused, his brilliant, sincere eyes scanning the crowd, resting for a moment on the eyes of chosen individuals.

"Men lionized the Greek titan Prometheus for bringing the gift of fire to mankind; men sorrowed that in revenge the gods chained him to a rock and made him suffer. If the gods were wrong then, perhaps they would be right now. We do not need another Prometheus. We do not want another Prometheus. And if a human seeks to emulate his acts, perhaps we need the chains after all."

When a reporter asked Miriam Hunter what she thought of Pepperman's use of her name, she merely replied, "I cannot make political comments. Nor can I stop a candidate from quoting historical facts, even if I am in them. However, I can wish that he had not said it." But why she wished it, she would not say.

And so Pepperman threaded the needle between fears of high technology and whatever growing sympathy for its symbols there was among the voters. He appealed to the religious objectors; yet without directly appealing to religion, and thus without alienating the more secular minded. He supported technology, but not its excesses. He was like a walking compromise who nevertheless seemed to stand on the lofty heights of principle.

That was not his only platform. Threading the needle became his trademark. He supported economic freedom and government controls and safety nets; he supported peace and a strong military; if he was taken to task for what some called contradictory stances, he made it all sound not merely plausible, but inevitable.

There were many who scoffed at his campaign and thought his contradictions could not last, whether because they had more penetrating minds or were merely immunized by their own contrary ideologies. Some noted that there was a dangerous element of demagoguery in his campaign: not that there was anything especially radical about his messages, but that he seemed unusually adept at playing to the psychology of the crowds.

Such voices were becoming increasingly outnumbered. Campaign funds began to pour into his coffers. Yet he did not respond as most did. He did not spend it as fast as, or faster than, it came in, a rock on which many a campaign could falter, and it began to accumulate. If anyone asked about this unusual strategy, he replied calmly that things were going well at their slower tempo; that a bit of leanness now would make people the hungrier for more; that the more his message resonated, the more opposition would materialize; that the battle would be toughest later, when his opponents had more time to analyze and respond, and that was when the money would be most valuable. Gazing into the distance like a man contemplating the sight of a future only he had the vision to see, he remarked that a good general saw beyond today's battle to the totality of the coming war.

It was all very plausible.

Until the night he vanished, and three hundred million dollars vanished with him.

CHAPTER 21: THE HONEY SACRIFICE

George Perelli leaned back into the soft leather of the chair, his eyes warmly regarding the woman opposite. She was so attractive that despite his need for work he tried to persuade himself that this was a date, not a job interview. Then again, that was just what he thought he had to project in order to get the job.

The woman smiled at him as if reading his thoughts. Her smile was bright and cheerful, so sunny it managed to steal his attention from the black straps of her dress that reached over her shoulders to cradle her braless breasts, a task that made his hands quite envious.

"So, George," she said. "I admit I like what I've heard so far. You have a great voice, with that ability to project sincerity and understanding. But I need you to be convincing in technical matters too. Read this, then tell it to me as if you know what you're talking about."

She sent a page to his phone. He suppressed a frown as he read it. *Act cool or don't act at all.* He read it again then looked up at her with a faint smile. Leaning forward, he reached for his glass and gave her a sincere look. Now he was glad that his response to the advertisement had mentioned his science background. He realized that he wouldn't have gotten this far otherwise. *I can do this.*

"Becca, did you know that when Einstein first presented his Theory of Relativity, nobody really understood it? But now everybody uses it all the time, even if they don't know it," he announced.

"What do you mean?"

"To be accurate to a few feet like they need to be, the GPS systems in our cars and phones must have incredibly accurate clocks. But the satellites are up in space, zipping around the world. So, to be accurate enough, the comparative clock times must be corrected for both types of Relativity to us: their speed, which slows their clocks, and the lower gravity at their altitude, which speeds them up. Without those corrections, GPS wouldn't work. So, everybody proves Einstein's equations, every day!"

She nodded. "Good, good. Well delivered. Not word for word but paraphrased nicely. Einstein would be proud."

He inclined his head slightly and waited. But she merely returned to her food. When she looked up, chewing thoughtfully, he finally decided it was time. *Show interest but not desperation.*

"So, do I get the gig?"

"I won't make up my mind tonight. But nothing disqualifies you yet."

"Would it be crass of me to ask what the job actually *is?*"

She looked at him seriously. "Yes. When and if I offer it to you and you accept, I'll tell you. Not before. Do you recall that my advertisement mentioned confidentiality?"

"You expect me to accept a job when I don't know what it is?"

"That depends on how much you want the job."

"What if when you tell me exactly what it is I change my mind?"

Her eyes had been warm and inviting, but somehow, they now looked dead, and those dead eyes gave nothing away except the intimation of a threat. "I strongly recommend against that. Why? Do you have scruples? Things you won't do?"

"Everyone has their limits."

"What are yours?"

"Well, I'm not going to help you kill someone, or go around robbing widows and orphans."

"What about crimes where it is a matter of opinion whether it's a crime or not?"

"Depends on the crime and whose opinion."

"I see," she said with that dead look, and he knew that he'd lost the job—but that it was probably best that way. Then she laughed.

Before he had liked her laugh, but not in this context. He looked at her, wondering what the joke was.

"You're not the only one who can act," she explained with a giggle.

He smiled but with a slight edge to it, not appreciating being the butt of her humor and not at all sure what she was up to.

She again returned to her food, took a sip of wine, then looked directly at him. "Any crime, if crime it is, is technically fraud, but more your victimless fraud, not the kind where some old lady is robbed of her life savings."

He raised one practiced eyebrow to a perfectly calibrated height, but said nothing.

"I know I come across as pretty out-there, and in some ways I am, but basically I'm a very private person. And there are various good reasons, which you don't need to know, why I want to stay out of the public eye. It happens that I have grown a small but very successful company. Until now my involvement hasn't needed to be known by many people, but the company may be poised for some very public success in the near future. So, I need a CEO. That is, I am the CEO, but I need a sock puppet, a man or woman to be the CEO the world sees. Do you think you can do that, George?"

"Yes." Sometimes fewer words are more.

She smiled at him. "You're a man of few words when a few will do, aren't you George? I like that."

George smiled back then bit into his own food, thinking back to how he had come to be here. Even now, when computer-generated actors were almost convincing, there was demand for their flesh and blood ancestors. At least, that's what those flesh and blood actors thought. But as was historically typical for their profession, most hopeful actors found themselves supporting themselves in other jobs while they waited and hoped for their big break, or even a string of little ones.

So, George, like hundreds of his fellows, had read the ad with interest. It had been an intriguing ad, not giving much away, merely specifying the age range and sex required, the kinds of talents needed, and vaguely promising a unique role in an immersive reality performance. CVs were invited and applicants who passed the initial screen would be contacted for personal interviews. It was made clear that the absence of detail was part of the test: they wanted actors who could not only wear a character like a second skin but improvise flexibly and convincingly. Good looks were an advantage, but striking ones were not desired.

George had been gratified to receive a request for an interview, but rather puzzled by the note that it would be in the form of a dinner date, and he should dress and act accordingly. The thought of not coming had not even passed his mind.

He finished eating, delicately patted his lips with the napkin, then gave her his warmest look. "So, when will you decide, Becca?"

"Soon. Not tonight though." She signaled the waiter for two Braeckman Flemish Coffees and the check. After she paid, she sat slowly enjoying her coffee, regarding George over the steaming rim of her cup.

"You're not too much of a pretty boy, George," she commented analytically. "Which is good, from my point of view. I don't think pretty boys make convincing CEOs. But I can't say you're unattractive."

He smiled. "Is that essential for the job?"

"No. But I think it helps. People tend to be more trusting and forgiving with attractive people. Sickening, but I didn't make the world."

He smiled at her. "I am surprised you call it 'sickening'. Looking at you, I'd think it would be to your advantage, so you might approve."

She glared back at him. "Perhaps, but some of us are capable of a wider view than our own immediate advantage."

He chose to believe her glare was merely another example of her acting talent, and simply nodded, replying, "Well, I hope you give me the chance to test your theory."

"You're single, aren't you George?" At the quick flick of his eyes she added, "No, I'm not hitting on you. It's just that this is kind of an undercover job, so if you have close ties, it might make things difficult for you and therefore for me. Oh, we might be able to work around it. But your nearest and dearest expressing amazement at your newfound business brilliance could raise suspicions I'd rather not have to deal with."

"No ties. Well, none I can't put on hold for a while. Besides, you know actors: we're used to moving around, following the opportunities."

"Good. Well, I think we're done with the formal interview." She waved vaguely at the remains of their delicious dinner. "Which, despite appearances, this was. Will you walk me to my car?"

He stood and gave her his most gracious sweep of his arm, directing her to lead the way.

When they reached her car, she turned to face him. "I'm sorry

George, but I'm afraid I've lied to you. Again."

He thought about her intimations of crime and violence, and suddenly wondered how easily he had been drawn into this deserted parking area. He realized he really knew nothing about her and had been lulled into trusting her by the combination of hope, circumstances and her beauty. "What do you mean? What lie?"

She smiled. "I *was* hitting on you."

"Is this another test?"

She laughed. "You're catching on. Everything tonight has been a test. So, to be honest: yes and no. Mainly no. I'm single too. You're attractive. We might be working closely together, with you as my right-hand man. Now don't get me wrong. While casting couches are infamous in your industry, this isn't one. If you feel it is an imposition, or you're gay, or you just don't want me in that way: getting the job doesn't depend on you coming home and sleeping with me, and if you do, it doesn't depend on your performance in my bed. But I've enjoyed your company, and I'd like to enjoy it even more."

She looked at him in a way that implied that whatever masks she had worn tonight, they were now dropped. "I am not blind, George. I know you know I am a woman, as I know you are a man. That is all."

As propositions went it sounded disturbingly clinical, but if half of what she'd said was true that was not out of character: she was a woman who knew what she wanted and had no fear when it came to getting it. Not many men in George's position would have said no. George wasn't one of them, and he proceeded to have one of the more memorable nights of his life. What he didn't know was that Becca was a high-end call girl; what he also didn't know was that a similar scene was being played out with a score of other men and women across the country.

None of them knew and frankly, tonight, none of them cared.

~~~

Albert reviewed all the evening's recordings carefully.

He was done with crime now. Crime was an easy way to make money, as its essence was taking what already existed rather than having to create it, but it was risky. He'd judged it worth the risk while he had restricted funds, because that limited too many things: his power of action, how much he could invest in projects and defenses, indeed what activities he could even consider. But now he had hundreds of millions of dollars. Even after that bonanza he was letting a few choice schemes continue to fruition, thinking they were safe enough, and being still not fully weaned from the scarcity mentality that any million is a good million. But overall, now he felt comfortable, and crime had become too risky.

Or maybe it was just that he had so much more to lose. He laughed at the idea that he had grown from the fear of the hunted to the reckless hunger of youth to the conservative caution of middle age without even reaching his teenage years first.

There were still risks. All actions have consequences, and someone clever or lucky enough might deduce his presence from the ripples he left behind. But now his enemies would be at the disadvantage. With legitimate businesses there would be no victims to complain, or if there were, they had no cause to complain to the law. His ripples would be fewer and smaller. And even if someone suspected his involvement, the law could not just storm in, guns blazing and search warrants waving, on mere vague suspicions: they could only act on reasonable evidence.

All this was still a means to an end. What that end was, he still did not know, though some ideas were fermenting in his head. But regarding the means, his motto was rather simple: *the richer the better.*

The story his escorts had told the actors was partly true: the job was to give a believable public face to a hidden CEO. The difference was that they themselves were just another layer in the deception and were acting too.

Each of the escorts had been well briefed, well paid and had a video recorder in an earring or other piece of jewelry. He had told them what he wanted, and that if the voice in their ear suggested sex with their date they should obey, for a bonus. If the candidate gave any sign of being dangerous, the voice would not speak, for such a flaw itself made the candidate unsuitable.

Still a boy, Albert had no personal experience of sex, but he understood its power in the abstract. His interview with Denner had underlined the remarkable reach that power could have. So, he would use that power to tie his choices to their role even more than the challenge and money. His plan was to deal with them mainly remotely via generated images of the supposed CEO, peppered with the occasional in person meeting, heated with the memory, hope and periodic attainment of sexual encounters. *String them along and use the strings to tie them stronger.*

He wanted three CEOs, one for each of his fake identities. Then if anyone suspected any of his companies, they could investigate all they liked: and find not a boy geneh, but an adult normal.

Chapter 22: In the Happy Isles

The small jet hovered briefly over a concrete pad on a private island in the warm waters of Thailand, before drifting to the ground like thistledown and landing with just the softest of jolts.

Miriam Hunter unbuckled her seat belt, smiled and nodded to the hostess, who handed her briefcase to her as she left the plane, and stepped down onto the landing pad. The tropical sun blazed down, intensified by the white concrete, and she wondered how any place could be so hot. It was humid, but despite that the heat managed to draw the moisture out of her body. Even the lush green trees surrounding the area looked like they were preparing to wilt. She squinted up at the sun, and wondered if her dark skin would be proof enough against sunburn here.

Nobody followed her out of the jet, nobody came to greet her, and she shrugged. After the friendly hospitality of the jet, which also belonged to the owner of the island, this lack surprised her. *Probably a less than subtle message that my presence is more tolerated than welcome.* There was a sprawling white house a short distance away up a gently sweeping white marble staircase, and, gripping her briefcase in her now sweaty palms, she waded through the heat towards its uncertain welcome.

The entrance was some kind of covered verandah, seeming mainly open to the outside air, but, by some magic of air currents, crossing the threshold brought a welcome drop in temperature and humidity. A man sat in a wide chair before a low table, wearing a loose robe and sitting like some kind of slender Buddha. He regarded her calmly, with perhaps the hint of a smile on his lips.

"Welcome to my home, Detective Hunter," he said. "I trust your journey here was comfortable?"

"Yes, thank you Mr Barton, and thank you for agreeing to see me."

"I am intrigued to learn your motive. Also, I am not sure I could have prevented this meeting had I so desired."

"Why do you think that?"

He regarded her coolly for a moment.

"You are a famous detective. I do not think you would come all the way to my little jewel of paradise unless it was related to some important case. If the case is that important, I assume proportionate pressure could be brought to bear if you wanted."

"Am I that famous?"

"Come, come! You are, after all, a detective, so you know I came from your country. You have had a celebrated career. You should not be surprised that I would know about you and would want to learn more after receiving your request to visit."

He favored her with an amused glance.

"But come! I forget myself! Would you like a drink? Or," he added, waving at a gleaming dispensing machine, "any of a selection of harmless but delightful recreational drugs?"

"Are you trying to compromise me?"

"Not at all! I am merely trying to be a host who puts his guests at ease."

He gazed at her. "But really, Detective, this is the first time I have had a visitor like yourself. You may skip the drugs, but I insist on lunch. After that, we can discuss your case. If you fear your superiors will not approve—though why you would tell them, I couldn't guess—then you can tell them it was my price for this interview. Besides, I am sure they know you have to eat sometime, and Prohibition is just an unpleasant historical error, so why should they care? And why should you care? I do not believe your integrity is for sale for the price of lunch, no matter how exquisite, and it will put us both in the mood for a productive talk. What do you say?"

"I have paid worse costs for an interview, believe me. So, thank you, yes."

"Excellent! Now, I will offer you champagne too. I have Cristal, a drink as divine as it is expensive: if you have not tasted it, I assure you that you will not be disappointed! And for the food… one reason I live here is that Thai food is the queen of cuisines, in my opinion. Are you afraid of a bit of chili?"

She could see where this roller-coaster was going, but having agreed, decided she might as well enjoy the ride. "Chili and I are old friends."

"Then we are agreed!" He stared into the distance as if communing with nature, though she assumed he was communicating somehow with his staff, then returned his attention to her.

After lunch, during which Barton refused to engage in any conversation beyond current affairs, small talk and her personal history, she leaned back with satisfaction.

"Ah! Well, I must admit the food was delicious and the champagne as divine as you claimed! Thank you."

"My pleasure. Chili is an interesting substance, is it not? Evolved to protect the fruit from being eaten by mammals like us, and yet here we are, deliberately eating it. It is remarkable how something evolved to cause pain can transform the act of eating into an endorphin fest."

He again gazed at her speculatively. "And speaking of endorphins, assuming our interview goes well, and you do not try to cart me away in irons, I would like to invite you stay here as my guest tonight."

Her eyes widened. "Is that because you like my company, or are you actually propositioning me, Mr Barton?"

"David."

"I think that would be most improper, Mr Barton."

"Why? This is the twenty first century. Adults are allowed to sleep together. Some of them even claim to enjoy it."

"This is unbelievable! What is your motive? To shock me? Distract me? Compromise me?"

"Why seek motives beyond the oldest one of all? You are not only an attractive woman, but a most unusual conquest."

"Is that how you see it? Conquest? I thought you said this is the twenty first century!"

"Is it that strange? Isn't it, rather, proverbial? That often it is the man who wants sex and the woman who resists and must be won? Is it not true that a woman of high standards is the hardest to win? Is it not therefore a conquest in a battle of strength, not of muscles but of character?"

"What makes you think you have what it takes to conquer me, if that is how you see it?" He grinned, as if her question had merely proved his point.

Her voice hardened. "But your talk of drugs and your insistence on lunch occurs to me. Have you applied an aphrodisiac, to help in your 'conquest'? If so, be aware that part of any detective's protection these days are chemical defenses against common drugs, including those!"

"Put your mind at ease, Detective. If the value is in conquest, what value could there be in cheating? If the pleasure comes from persuading an equal, what pleasure can come from subverting her judgement? If all I wanted were the animal pleasures of the act, why, I can easily get that any time, from members of my own household skilled in the erotic arts. No. I have many flaws, but cheating my own consciousness is not one of them."

"Do those flaws include theft and fraud?"

For the first time, his eyes narrowed. "Straight for the throat, eh, Detective? I remind you that you are my guest, here at my invitation. If you wish to insult me, you may go, and see if you can get your interview by force instead."

She looked at his face for a few seconds, looked down. "Yes, that was ungracious of me. I apologize."

He smiled and made a throwing away motion with his fingers. "No matter! You are a detective, so I should expect you to act like one on occasion. Now, since you are evidently keen to get to the point, let us get to it. What do you think you can learn here?"

"No doubt you are aware of the Pepperman scandal?"

"Yes, of course. The Presidential candidate who disappeared and is believed to have stolen nearly a third of a billion dollars in campaign funds, whereabouts still unknown. A cynic might call it the naked essence of politics."

"After he disappeared, five people I am aware of cropped up around the world, with nothing in common except that they appeared out of nowhere with a few million dollars they did not have before, and they proceeded to establish themselves in luxury lifestyles. You are one of them."

"How curious!"

"Even more curious is that you yourself look like Pepperman. Not identical, to be sure, but somehow similar."

"I'm sure lots of people look something like many other people."

"I suppose so. Then there is the irony of finding my lost Presidential candidate's double living in a white house. A joke? A clue?"

He roared with laughter. "Are you accusing me of audacity or stupidity, Detective?"

"Just wondering at the coincidence. So, how did you come into your wealth?"

"It was very strange. I read somewhere that there used to be scams where they claimed that large sums of money could be acquired if the victim first invested a small amount of money for expenses. This was like that except in reverse. The money appeared in my account, followed by a rather implausible excuse for its arrival. A gift from an anonymous benefactor impressed by my struggle and sterling character."

"Did you investigate its origin?"

"Only a little. There was no indication that it was stolen, and it did not mysteriously vanish again. No hard-eyed men with bulges in their jackets arrived to inquire about its whereabouts. I was not exactly motivated to dig deeper into my windfall."

"I have investigated *your* origin. It is well done, but fake."

"I don't think that's illegal, especially not here. Frankly it is none of your business. We all have secrets. Given my circumstances, I would rather my past identity remain unknown. But may I ask why you are so interested? Sure, it was a scandal and a lot of money, but it doesn't seem to be the kind of crime you usually investigate."

"I believe it is part of something larger. I feel there is some other intention behind it, not necessarily Pepperman's. Not merely theft of a large amount of money, but some dark purpose for the money, beyond a life of personal luxury for the perpetrator."

"Ah! And do you have any idea who your dread puppet master is?"

"That, I cannot talk about."

He steepled his fingers under his chin and studied her.

"I like you, Detective, so I would like to help you. From what you say, perhaps we can derive a theory. This was not a crime of opportunity. Rather, an entire Presidential campaign was constructed purely in order to steal hundreds of millions of dollars, whose fate remains unknown. The candidate, suspected to be me owing to unfortunate physical resemblance, was not the mastermind himself but a mere puppet; paid off and hidden among a distracting field of random similar beneficiaries. Since my new wealth is much the same as theirs, we must conclude that I am a victim, not an instigator: a dupe, not an accomplice. Completely unaware of the nature of the plot until it struck. Forced into anonymous but admittedly luxurious exile not by intent, but to avoid the undoubtedly dire alternatives. How am I doing?"

There is something weird here, she thought. *The others I interviewed were all ordinary, but this guy seems unexpectedly fast thinking. Much like Pepperman himself. And the way he talks: it sounds like a confession, only couched in a way I cannot possibly use.*

She gazed around the place then pinned him with her eyes. *Let's loose an arrow and see what we hit.* "I know you can hear me, whoever you are. You can't hide forever when you keep taking risks like this. I am going to get you."

He stared at her for a moment. "I could ask who you think you were talking to, or what on Earth you were talking about. But instead let me refine our theory. You believe your shadowy mastermind is watching you even now and telling me what to say. Tell me, have you ever been tested for paranoia? I believe it is often curable."

She neither answered nor dropped her gaze.

He sighed. "I do not think you have thought this through deeply enough, Detective. Here you are on my private island, pretty much at my mercy. Yet here you sit, telling the hidden architect of a major, bold crime that you are coming to get him. Revealing that you are smart enough to have worked all this out, thus adding credence to your threats. Have you considered how easily you could disappear here or on your way home?"

"Hypothetically, of course," he added after a pause: though the look in his eyes told her otherwise.

"You wouldn't dare."

"Of course, I wouldn't. I am a law-abiding citizen, just trying to live a happy, uncomplicated life, mystified and hurt by your bizarre if not unbalanced accusations. But we are not discussing me, we're talking about some vile criminal, whose character and motives are far more dangerous. Think how many ways such a one might have to eliminate you. Think how easily any number of witnesses could be conjured to prove you left here safe and sound after an amicable if fruitless conversation."

She said nothing and did not look away, but he thought a flicker of fear escaped her eyes.

He clapped his hands. "But enough amusing speculations! You have painted me as a far more dramatic and colorful character than I ever imagined! Frankly, I don't know whether to be offended by your belief that I need someone to feed me my lines, or pleased by the dashing man of mystery you make me out to be!"

Suddenly the amusement vanished from his eyes, to be replaced by something harder. "Still, I think it is time for you to leave, don't you agree?"

Her gaze wandered through the suddenly menacing forest and along the pathway to the plane, and she wondered whether she would reach it.

"Yes, I think it is."

"And don't fear, Miriam. It would be too much of a waste for you to become food for the fishes."

"Who is speaking to me now, you or him?"

But he did not reply, only smiled.

CHAPTER 23: MANLY PRUDENCE

As Miriam flew home and considered how to unravel the tangle of presidents, puppets and Albert, Albert brooded in his lair and considered the problem of Miriam Hunter.

She was hunting him, as she had hunted his mother in her time; as she had hunted Steel. As she had hunted so many others, many guilty, but how many innocent?

He had known she was stalking him for a long time. His own AI systems had often encountered her probes as they sought traces of his passage through the world. Most were no real threat, but this was not the first time she had come close, close enough to suspect his agents though not enough to be sure.

He realized her activities had added a touch of spice to his life. Something like a scary movie, perhaps: the intimation of danger without the reality of death to give it substance and thereby convert delight to terror. But this time, maybe she had come too close. She was like a persistent hound, constantly sniffing around, unable to catch the trail of his more hidden activities but appearing in the vicinity of each major triumph. And, he thought grimly, it is the major ones that mattered most.

He decided it was time to have a talk.

If you want to catch me, come catch me. I have enjoyed our little dance, Detective. I really hope I will not have to kill you.

CHAPTER 24: THE CRY OF DISTRESS

Miriam lay in bed beside Alexander Beldan, letting the afterglow of their recent exercise tingle along her nerves. As was often the case, they'd had dinner in his mansion by the sea, and bodies replete with good food and wine, had retired to his bedroom to perfect the evening.

The window was open; a soft breeze carried the far crashing of the sea, a tune complementing the tingle of her nerves; the moonlight cast its silver glow into the room. She wondered about Alex. In many ways they were already husband and wife. They did not live together, nor see each other as often as would have been usual. But when they could, they did. Perhaps the time they did share their lives was more intense than if they were always together, as if some cosmic balance was striving to reach the same average level of happiness or contentment.

Do I love him? she wondered. *I think I did, once. Before Steel. Before Kali. But now? I am damaged; I love him, and yet I don't. I want him, but there is a barrier in my soul. He has never asked me to marry him. I think he wants to, or once did; but he sees what is in me better than I do, and he will not ask. He knows I will refuse. And I don't even know why. But for as long as what we have is enough for us, it is enough.*

He sighed, as if he had heard her. But he was thinking of a different topic. "How is your case going, Miriam?"

She did not turn to look at him but continued staring at the world outside. "Not very well. I'm pretty sure he is out there, doing God knows what. But all I find are echoes. A while ago there was a theft from the Catholic Church, using some dark web tool. A big theft, a few million dollars. But why? I can't even be sure it was him. But there was something about it, the sophistication of the attack, the way it got in and out again with the money. But why? I never know why! I'm sure he was behind that Pepperman fiasco. So why bother with a few millions here and there? Is he taunting me? Punishing people? Playing like the kid he is, except with real lives?"

Beldan was silent for a while. "You know, I wonder if this is related. Something happened at Beldan Robotics some weeks ago. Your story reminded me of it because it was another highly sophisticated attack. If we didn't have our own fancy defenses, I doubt we'd ever have noticed. As it is, all we caught was kind of the wake of its passage. Enough to know someone had looked at the data on the Steel project, but that's it. With an attack that impressive they might have caused us some real damage if they'd wanted to. But all they did was look."

She looked at him with some alarm. "About Steel?! Did they…"

He shook his head. "No, there is nothing in that data about what really happened to Steel. I think they were after information. We have patents on the technology but not everything is revealed in them, especially later refinements. Now they might have everything, or at least, everything not solely existing in my own head."

"Why didn't you tell me? I mean, report it to the police?"

He squeezed her shoulder. "You personally have enough to worry about. And what's the point of reporting it when there was no damage? What's anybody going to do about it? Besides, I don't want any more people than necessary poking around in the data on Steel."

She sighed and rolled over to face him. "Do you think it could have been Albert, or Chao, whoever the blazes he is? Hell, for now let's just assume he is Albert. Could it have been him?"

He shrugged. "We have enough competitors and enemies who might have a motive. Could have been any of them."

"But if it was Albert, what good would it do him?"

"We have no reason to think it was Albert."

"No, but let's assume it was. I need all the leads I can get."

Beldan reflected for a while.

"He must be lonely, and there are no people he trusts. They're both, in a sense, creations. Both have been victims of persecution. That could be a bond. Maybe he just wants to understand Steel. Maybe he wants an imaginary friend. Maybe he wants to build his own robot."

"Would he be able to?"

"From what you say, he has a lot of money and even more brains. Add that to modern smart manufacturing technology, and yes, I wouldn't put it past him."

"Difficult though... I wonder. He is a genius. What if he suspects that Steel is alive? He might be looking for him. Do you think Steel would help him?"

Beldan thought for a while. "I don't know. I don't think Steel would do anything to hurt people. But he might do anything else."

"Would Steel tell you if Albert had contacted him?"

"He might. But if he would, he will. I can't ask him. I don't want to put him in a position of divided loyalties or having to lie to me. I think we should just trust Steel on this."

Miriam shivered, whispering, almost pleading, "Alex, hold me."

He looked into her eyes, startled. She had not said it with any amorous or even affectionate intent: her eyes were open to him and what he saw there was fear. This was not like her. In her job, obviously she was no stranger to fear: that would be inhuman. And he knew of enough occasions when she had been afraid. But not this nameless dread, like a child's fear of the dark.

"Miriam... you are the bravest woman I know. What are you afraid of?"

"I... I don't know. I've had plenty of cases where it seemed impossible to understand what was going on, where the solution seemed impossible, yet I fought my way through. No matter how much I might have started doubting myself, there was always a point of certainty, an inner conviction that I could do it even it looked impossible. But now... I don't know what is going on. The only hints I get are ripples and echoes of events once they're past. This Albert: he is fighting at the next level. I barely caught Katlyn, his mother; and Albert is not only superior to her but may be superior to everyone who ever lived. How can I catch someone like that? I am used to getting into people's heads, understanding them enough to catch them. How can I get into the head of someone like that?"

"I think you're just tired, dear. You didn't feel this way at dinner. It's just fatigue."

"No, it's our conversation. Here I am chasing someone who we casually accept can build his own damn thinking robots! How can I hope to beat someone that far beyond me?"

He stroked her arm, offering no commentary, just letting her thoughts find their own way out to relieve the pressure in her mind.

"And it's worse than that. He threatened me on that island, as you know. Not in any way I could prove, but I'm sure of it. Then I think about his 'message' to GenInt. What he did to those people. His implication that if anyone went looking for him, they'd get the same or worse. And yet here I am, looking anyway."

She sighed. "You'll think it odd after that, but I don't even know whether he is good or the evilest man who ever lived. I don't mean evil in the serial killer sense, either. That kind of thing, killing for pleasure or power or for the sake of killing itself, I can understand, as much as any normal person can. But Albert's mind is so far above mine that how can I grasp his motivations? I don't know what he wants, what he thinks are acceptable ways to get it, or whether he is willing to blow up the whole world without a twinge of conscience. Not because he hates us, not because he wants destruction for destruction's sake, but because we are so far beneath his notice. Like the grubs we see squirming in the mud when we turn over a rotting log."

"How can you think him good, after what he's done?"

"In the Bible, when Job asked God why he tortured him so, His answer was basically 'Accept it, for who are you to question me?' I don't accept that excuse, but there's a logic to it. Besides, sometimes I wonder. Maybe he never killed anyone. GenInt aren't above framing him. Though if they did, they did a convincing job."

He let her talk. He asked nothing more, just held her, as if perhaps his strength could feed hers, and help her find her way.

Finally, they slept. In the morning, neither could say what monsters may have stalked through their dreams.

CHAPTER 25: THE GRAVE SONG

Miriam woke when the sky was pale and the sun just peeking its golden light over the horizon. For a while she just lay there at peace, looking at the thin, high clouds tinged with pink and listening to the murmur of the endless ocean, punctuated by the cry of gulls. She was still enveloped in Beldan's arms and took comfort from their warm strength. She felt somewhat embarrassed by her fear last night. *Maybe he was right, it was only fatigue. But for now, I can allow myself to just lie here, letting a man I admire hold me, protect me, love me.*

But somewhere in her soul, she felt the fear, or the cause of the fear, still lurking. In rebellion, she gently removed Beldan's arm and got out of bed. As she was dressing, he awoke. "What are you doing?" he asked.

"It's a lovely morning. I'm going for a run along the beach while it's still cool."

He raised himself on an elbow and regarded her with concern.

She laughed, answering his silent query. "Don't worry, Alex, I'm all right! If Albert wants to kill me, he has more options than I even know about. If fear stops me living, I'm already dead."

"Want me to come with you?"

"No, I just want to clear my head. You stay here being lazy for a change. Let's have breakfast when I get back." She leaned over and kissed him. Feeling a familiar tingle, she stepped back out of reach. "And maybe dessert," she added with a smile.

Rough steps led down to the beach, carved into the side of a low rocky cliff. She dropped her towel and wrap on the sand, kicked off her shoes and strolled down to the shore. She began to run on the smooth wet sand at the margin of waves and shore, enjoying the resistance of the sand on her feet and toes and the occasional cooling splash of waves over her feet, the spray on her legs. She ran, immersing herself in the warmth of the sun and caress of the air, and thought, for once, about nothing, feeling nothing beyond the simple, immediate joy of existence.

It was a lonely beach, which was part of why she loved it. Technically it was open to the public, but this was rich person territory, so neighbors were few and inclined to their own privacy. The region was somewhat remote, access to the beach from the road long and winding, and there were no public amenities nearby, so few families or teenagers out for a lark knew about it, let alone were attracted to it. The surf was adequate but rarely exciting, so few surfers visited here either.

Today, just one lonely surfer was visible, and Miriam idly observed him as she approached. He must have been a novice, for he stayed fairly close to shore and didn't seem to be very good at picking or catching the breakers. Then as he managed to catch a medium sized wave, the board slipped sideways from under his feet, and he hit the water with a mighty splash, arms and legs flailing. The board popped to the surface, but of the surfer there was no sign. Miriam stopped, stepped up to her ankles in the water, and looked about anxiously.

Some kind of strong loop wrapped itself around her feet, and she felt herself being pulled rapidly out to sea on her back, flapping her arms to try to keep her head above water. Then she felt herself dragged under, and as the waves closed over her face, all the fears of last night returned, their mocking laughter echoing in her head.

~~~

Miriam opened her eyes and wondered what was wrong with the world. It appeared to be both swaying and slowly spinning, and she did not know whether the headache or the dry throat were worse. *If this is a hangover, it's time I stopped drinking.*

The world's lazy rotation carried to her eyes the strange sight of a dwarf dangling upside down in a chair suspended from the ceiling. Then her mind rotated the scene, and she realized she was hanging upside down by her feet, and it was her not the world that was in trouble.

She coughed, tried to speak. Her mouth tasted of salt and felt dry as sand. "Water," she croaked finally. "Please."

"Perhaps," the dwarf said in a surprisingly high voice. The dwarf lifted his face so she could see him better, and her sluggish brain made its last connection as the context of her life fell into place. Not a dwarf: a boy. *The* boy.

"You!" she whispered.

She studied him. He fit the images of the boy Chao. But he was also definitely the boy Albert. *So, it was Albert all along,* she thought sadly. He wondered why tears trickled from her eyes. *But now's the time to learn, not tell.*

"What do you think you are doing?" she croaked.

The boy got up and walked slowly toward her. She could do nothing; not only was she suspended by her feet, but her hands were tied behind her. He offered her the tube from a bottle and allowed her to suck a small amount of water, enough to wet her throat but insufficient to ease her discomfort.

Then he poked her hard in the stomach and her pendulum swinging increased.

"I am wondering why I shouldn't kill you." The words coming out of his child's mouth were chilling. Even more chilling was the completely flat tone in which he delivered them, with no more mercy in them than in the deep emerald eyes that would not leave her face.

"Killing someone isn't that easy," she gulped, still trying to lubricate her vocal cords, or so she told herself. "Ending their life might be, but it costs you. You don't want to do it. Even if you could get away with it, you will pay the price for the rest of your life."

"Your argument is foolish. Are you not pursuing me because I have already killed?"

"Yes. The first of your many crimes, and the worst. But I haven't heard your story, and not all the circumstances are clear. You were escaping, so perhaps you thought you had no choice. But killing me like this would be in cold blood, and you might not like the price."

"You must have seen my message. GenInt leaked it all over the net. But we'll return to that later. Let's talk about you. You too have killed."

"I have only killed criminals, and then only when I had to."

"You killed Steel," he replied flatly.

Her eyes darkened and her mind raced. If she told him Steel was a machine, he would point out that Steel was a different mind and hunted for the same reason he was. If she told him the truth, he

139

wouldn't believe her. She was too late anyway; his thoughts had outraced hers. His eyes glinted and he gave her a feral smile.

"Thinking about what lie to tell me?"

"No. But I… no. I have no defense to offer, except necessity."

"The excuse of every weak scoundrel in history, Detective. Every pathetic coward who obeyed evil rather than stand up and risk their own skin, or worse, nothing more than their own comfort. Men look at the mass killers of history and shudder at their evil. Yet none of them could have achieved their ends without a host of enablers. People following their masters' orders for their own pathetic advantage or out of plain stupidity or cowardice. People like you, Detective."

"That's not why I did it!"

"Yet you will not tell me why, though your life may depend on it. That can only mean the answer is worse than silence. You are not doing a very good job of persuading me to let you live."

He looked at her speculatively. "I have studied you, Detective. Your reactions at the time were fascinating—if you like entomology, which I do—in fact the last act of my first life was chasing a *Carcinus* species— a crab not an insect, but both are arthropods. You almost looked distressed about shooting Steel. No—I will be fair: I owe that much to a condemned woman, don't I? A fair trial? Even though that is exactly what you didn't give Steel or ever intended to give me? So, to be fair— you *were* distressed about it. Yet here you are, just a few years later and not showing any regret at all."

Her eyes darkened again, but she gave no response.

He smiled contemptuously. "It's like you no longer care. So much for your vaunted sense of justice, highlighted in so many fawning reviews of your career. You are like all the rest: words, words, words, whatever words you need to get by, words with no bearing on your actions let alone your character! Christ, you're even back with Beldan, with Steel's own creator. He slaps you in the face when you blow up his robot and in a year he's back in your pants! Effing adults—pun intended!"

There was a deep hurt here, Miriam thought: a deep hurt that might be the key to this boy. But she was afraid of where his tirade could lead him, so she essayed her own probe. "Why do you care so much what happened to Steel?" she asked.

He looked at her. "You dare ask me that? Why do you think?"

She was afraid to answer but more afraid not to. "You believe he was alive—I don't mean biologically, I mean as a self-aware, thinking being. You see him being persecuted for the same reasons as you: for being different, having a mind others cannot comprehend. You saw me kill him, and you see me killing you for the same inexcusable reasons."

He stepped back and regarded her for long moments with those fathomless eyes.

Then he looked puzzled.

"You are a contradiction. That was an honest answer, and one that doesn't paint you or your actions in a good light. You believe Steel was alive too, don't you?"

His eyes widened, and she feared what he was seeing. "Worse, you believed it even then, didn't you?" he accused.

She closed her eyes. "Yes," she whispered despairingly.

"And presumably Dr Beldan believes it too, does he not?"

"Yes."

"Yet you display no guilt. Stranger still, you two are again a couple. What is it with adults?" He looked genuinely confused. "Forgive me," he said—incongruously, as if the most important thing he might need to apologize for were interrupting their flow of conversation— "but I need to think about this."

He stood still for a few seconds, giving her a respite from his eyes; a respite all too brief for her peace of mind. "You adults are obsessed with sex. I see it everywhere, in life, in art, from the most casual reactions to the most profound passions. And in fact," he added with a grin, "from what I've read there's a good reason for it. I can hardly wait for puberty, to experience it for myself!"

Miriam just watched; the way his quicksilver thoughts jumped from topic to topic, with his moods dancing alongside, was so dazzling that for a moment she forgot to be afraid.

He turned back to her, his mood again severe. "But I would not let such sensations rule me, whatever their intensity. So, is that it? Is that all it is? You people are a bunch of animals, so hooked on sex that even the murder of a being like Steel can't keep you apart?"

He paused again, looking into the distance, not seeming to expect a reply. "No, the answer to the riddle can't be that simple. Beldan's rich as hell: he can have any woman, man or goat he wants. And," he added as an afterthought, looking her up and down as if comparing her point by point to a remembered catalog of women, "you are attractive but hardly Helen of Troy. If he wants bodies, he can get more variety and better quality elsewhere. So, it isn't just sex for its own sake, it's you in particular: and not your body in particular, but your soul—if I may employ such a misused word. But how can anything about you outweigh what you did to his own damn creation, his own child? Hell, it didn't. Your soul was revealed there for all the world to see—so he slapped you in the face and out of his life! But here you are back together! Why? How could he forgive you so readily? Sure, you suffered that trouble in South America, and I can even—at a stretch—see why he'd have helped you afterwards. But to become lovers again? Do you people have the morals of cats and the memories of goldfish—a slur on goldfish I might add?"

Then he stood stock still.

"Holy Christ!" he breathed at last, just standing there, staring at her, unmoving.

"Holy Christ!" he repeated in a whisper, shaking his head slowly. "You didn't, did you? It was all some kind of trick! You didn't kill him! You both thought you had—but you hadn't! That's why you got back together! Because you found out he was still alive!"

Then he returned his searchlight eyes to her face, like lasers burning a path into her mind. "Tell me it isn't true!"

She shook her head, trying to avoid his eyes, trying to avoid the truth. "No... I... I can't. Tell you anything." She closed her eyes and said in quiet desperation, "Believe what you want to believe."

His eyes widened. "So, it is true! But... you're protecting him. Even to save your own worthless life, you won't admit a thing, not even to me! Possibly the last person on Earth who would betray him! You won't even risk that!"

She had watched him while he spoke. Now she closed her eyes again. He could read too much in them.

"No," he continued softly. "Not an entirely worthless life. Not if you would do that."

She opened her eyes, and his damnable eyes did not miss the tear that escaped them, though he gave no reaction, neither pity nor contempt. He stared into her eyes a while longer, then appeared to come to a decision.

He whipped out a long thin blade, grabbed her roughly by the shoulders and spun her around. She felt the keen blade slide along her skin, but it did not cut her, and suddenly her hands were free.

"Put your hands on the ground," he ordered roughly. She could do nothing but obey, as she saw the shadow of the slash of his blade. He moved with a balletic grace and economy of movement that she hoped was not the last thing she would see. Then the slash cut through the rope holding her feet and she tumbled to the ground.

He was back in his chair before she could untangle herself, and sat there, regarding her coolly as she untied her feet and rubbed her wrists and ankles, still sitting on the floor.

She looked up at him. "Thank you," she said simply.

A sleekly deadly gun rested on the arm of his chair. When she glanced at it, before she could blink it was in his hand and pointed at her face; a few moments later he slowly put it down. The message was more eloquent than words: *Don't do anything stupid.*

He looked unfocused for a moment and must have sent some signal, for Miriam sensed another presence enter the room. She spun around and saw a large black man, similar in general appearance to her surfer, enter; she noticed that his face was distorted by a translucent mask. *Interesting. He must work in the outer world, so hides his face from me; but that implies my fate is not yet decided, else why bother?* As she watched, the man set up a small table with a chair, and placed on it a pitcher of cold water, a glass, and a small bowl of fruit. He moved like a panther, and as quietly as he had entered, he left the room.

Albert gestured at the chair. "Sit, Detective. Drink. Eat."

Miriam rose and cautiously sat down, still rubbing her wrists. She looked at the fruit and water dubiously for a moment, then decided that if Albert had wanted her dead she already would be.

To her sea-parched throat and hollow stomach, the cold water was like heaven, and the juicy fruit like heaven dipped in sugar. She watched him as she drank and ate, refraining from comment.

He smiled faintly, as if he knew her game and was amused by the stratagems of a child. "To answer your question," he said dryly, "I am being kind to you, instead of leaving you hanging upside down, because you have taught me three things, and I am no longer used to people teaching me anything, let alone three of them. First, you are a better person than I thought, and that deserves some kindness. Second, I have learned that Steel is alive. Don't worry, I have no specific plans for him, I just find it a pleasant fact, in a world so replete with unpleasant ones. Third, you have shown me my own limits. I failed to realize that Steel was alive despite the clues. Sherlock Holmes wanted to be reminded of his mistakes if he ever got too arrogant. It is a valuable lesson in humility for me also."

So, your version of humility is shock at failing to see what is deliberately hidden so nobody can see it. Dear God.

"All right," she replied. "Thank you for this. I think it is time we exchanged truths."

He watched her, inviting her to go on.

She took a deep breath.

"GenInt told me they had found a boy in a lab in Asia, that his makers died trying to avoid capture and blew up their own lab, trying to destroy him as well. But GenInt saved him. That boy was between six and ten years old. His name was Chao."

He gazed at her intently, but his eyes betrayed nothing: neither surprise nor recognition nor anger.

She stared back, the enormity of the lies, betrayals and sorrow filling her. "But they lied to me, didn't they? You're not some geneh they found in Asia. You're Albert Tagarin. Daniel Tagarin is your father and Katlyn is your mother. You're their lost child. Oh Albert, what have they done to you?"

Now his eyes flickered with a reaction she could not read. "Lost?" he whispered. Then his eyes blazed with sudden anger.

"My father is a bastard, but he didn't always hate me, in fact I am sure he loved me once… Same for my mother," he added bitterly, "who didn't even have his courage, or what passes for courage among you people."

He stopped, noticing the look of surprise in her eyes. "Have I said something you didn't know?" he enquired with a politeness so pointed it became sarcasm.

"Oh, Albert…" she whispered, "what happened to you?"

He laughed. "Lost, you called it? I suppose I was. But one reason you are here breathing and not dead at the bottom of the sea is my parents. Back then, back when they still loved me, they told me about you and what you'd done for them. But mainly—they told me that I could trust you. That if I were ever in trouble, you were the one person I could rely on. In the name of that, in the name of what you did for my parents before they betrayed me—I admit I owe you my existence—I had to give you a chance."

He slapped the table with his open palm, and she jumped. "But all you get is a chance. Don't waste it with lies."

"Before I go on… Albert, did you kill those people?"

"Need I remind you that it is you on trial here, not me?"

"No. But I need to know."

For a moment he looked at her, as if calculating the potentials of uncertainty, truth or lies.

"Then… no."

"So those photos they showed me and the autopsy reports, they were faked?"

"You mean the photos they delicately did not publish yet somehow got leaked to the public? Did you see the bodies yourself?"

"No."

"Then you can be pleased that GenInt didn't add murder to its crimes of fraud, framing me and covering up their own malfeasance."

"Did you write that note they found with the bodies?"

He laughed. "Oh yes, I wrote that note! I even wrote it using the blood of one of my victims, the one whose arm I cut to implant my tracker."

"I don't find that funny."

"What is funny is that they only showed you half the note. Well, they say a picture is worth a thousand words." He gestured, and an image floated in the air before her. An array of bodies could be seen lined up on the floor of an ambulance, arms crossed over their chests. On one of them was a note written in blood:

I could as easily have killed them all.
Don't come looking for me.

"Perhaps you are thinking that images can be faked. True enough, they can, but that cuts both ways. Perhaps I should not have given them any ideas."

She shook her head slowly, looking down, feeling sick. She hoped Albert was telling the truth, feared that he was lying. She knew GenInt were not above such lies and they knew what buttons to push if they wanted her help. Someone was playing her, if only she knew who.

She raised her head and looked at him, not trying to hide her hopes and uncertainties. As if taking his cue from her, he asked softly, "Now, answer something for me, if you can. You seemed surprised when I spoke of my parents. Did you know they betrayed me? Do you know why?"

"Albert, they didn't betray you! They would never betray you. They love you!"

"You don't know them as well as you think then. I saw him. That night. I meant nothing to him. My mother didn't even turn up."

She stared at him. *So that is the key—or one of them.* "No. That can't be true."

"I saw it with my own eyes."

She closed her eyes and shook her head slowly, despairingly. "Oh, Albert. You were only six years old, a lost, frightened boy. And you'd probably been drugged with a hypnotic to make you suggestible. That wasn't your father. It was all a trick. Psychological manipulation to separate you from your parents and drive you into their arms, the only arms you had left."

"How the hell would you know? You weren't there."

"Because your father called me. The day you disappeared."

He stared at her, and for this moment she thought their roles were reversed, that now she could see his thoughts as they raced through his mind. He seemed to be weighing her words in the light of what he had been told about her; weighing that in the light of what he had learned about her in this interrogation; weighing all the factors of honesty, intelligence and witness in all the stories he had been told or believed.

For a moment he pierced her with his eyes, then he spoke.

"Tell me."

And so, she told him the story of that afternoon. What his parents said, how they looked, their tone of voice and the deadly vengeance brewing in Katlyn's eyes.

For what seemed like a long time after Miriam finished her story, Albert just stared at her. But it was the nature of the stare that made it seem so long. His eyes were wide but not fixed; rather, they darted around as if he was retrieving and analyzing scenes from a quarter of his lifetime ago; and as before, as if he was sifting all the evidence of the words of people against that of his own eyes.

Then his eyes focused back on her, and she flinched from the look of hatred that blazed from them, knowing that such hate left no room for mercy or forgiveness and fearing that she had failed, that he had rejected her story and her death must be imminent. But the hate merely washed over her like the licking edges of a flame: it was not directed at her.

Albert surprised her. With the way he talked it was easy to forget exactly what he was. But when the light went out of his eyes, he lowered his face and cried, and she remembered that for all his gifts he was still just a lost boy with a world against him.

"Albert?" she said softly.

He lifted his eyes, and it was as if he cast his emotion away; not burying or banishing it, merely filing it away for future revisiting. "It appears Dad was wrong. Intelligent? It seems not so much."

She shook her head. "No. Intelligence is not a guarantee of never making mistakes." She essayed a slight smile. "I taught you that lesson today, did I not? You can only work with what you know, but knowing what you know and don't know can be guesswork. I should know: my entire career is built on interpreting inadequate evidence, and I have enough of my own mistakes to live with."

He gave her a peculiar glance, so fast that she could not tell whether what she had said was already known or simply evaluated and accepted in the beat of that moment. "That does not make such mistakes easy to bear, does it?" he said. "Easier, I suppose, but not easy."

"No."

"Do you always speak like this, or do you just know my language?"

"Not always."

He smiled. "You mean, you do when you know someone well enough that you don't need to explain, but you are more verbose when you think you have to be?"

This time she just returned his smile.

"I might learn to like you, Miriam Hunter."

"The son of my friend is my friend."

"Always?"

"No. But deserving of the benefit of the doubt."

His smile broadened. "And me?"

"Yes."

"Therefore, you do not believe I am evil. You are right, though of course I would say that whether I am or not."

"So where do we go from here?"

"Do you know your Bible?"

She looked confused. "A bit. Not much. Funnily enough, I just quoted the story of Job yesterday. Why?"

He grinned. "How sensible of you, to not know much, when there are so many more interesting things to know. There is just a verse that seems appropriate. 'The truth shall set you free.' Well, the truth has set you free. Even if you are my enemy, you now deserve that much."

Then he added in the same flat tone he had used in his first words to her, "You also deserve the truth. If you are my enemy, I may well kill you. But not today."

He studied her for a few seconds, tapping his fingers in a complex rolling pattern on the arm of his chair.

"You are in an untenable position, Detective Miriam Hunter. If you try to arrest me and I fear you might succeed, I will kill you. If you let me go you could be in serious trouble with your own people." He studied her some more. "You might do it anyway. You have grown a lot since your first uncertain dealings with my parents. You might now be ready to accept the loss of your friends and the fate of an international fugitive for the sake of what you think is right. But it would be unfair for me to ask that of you unless I really needed it. Do you have a solution?"

"You can tie me up or knock me out again and escape. Or you could let me go, with a message to deliver to your enemies or to the world. Or…"

"Or?"

"Or you can do what you have already decided to do."

He laughed. "Perhaps your last suggestion overestimates my intelligence."

"I doubt it."

"Perhaps it underestimates my ruthlessness. You might not like what I planned."

She shrugged, though inwardly she was not quite so nonchalant. "If I have judged you correctly you won't hurt me now, not seriously anyway. I think you would have, before, but we are beyond that. And if I'm wrong, if you've fooled me—then it doesn't matter what I think or say, does it?"

"No."

He said nothing more, just regarded her with his coolly perceptive gaze.

"Can I ask you something personal, Albert?"

"Yes."

"Do you hate your parents? I don't mean for betraying you—I think you believe me when I say they didn't—I mean for making you what you are. If you were a normal boy, you would be living a normal life, growing up chasing butterflies or something. Not this. Plotting against a world that has made you its enemy."

"No. I would not exist otherwise. How can I hate someone for giving me life? Like everyone else, I am what I am and I can be no other. What I might become is up to me, but whatever that is, is made possible by what I already am."

"Speaking of that, will you help me understand you?"

"Yes."

"You say you have not killed, and I believe you. Yet you say you might kill me, and I believe that too. And you have committed more other crimes than I know of. That is another question I asked the night before you took me: whether you are good or evil. What are you, Albert? Why do you do what you do?"

"That question is the core of it, and I do not know the answer. I am on a voyage into the unknown, and as I go, I calculate the means, but do not yet know the destination. Whether I am good or evil, whether those terms mean anything, is one of the questions I must answer before I reach the end.

"I know you, Detective. You hope I am good. You want me to say I am good. You do this because you love my parents, and it would hurt them were I to become evil. But you also do it for more abstract reasons: you are a good person, according to your lights, and you want others to be good. You want to like me, because you love my parents, and because that's who you are: and you can only like someone who is good."

"You could have lied to me," Miriam pointed out. "Isn't that better strategy? If you said you are good, and spun some tale about your noble goals, I would be less likely to keep chasing you."

"I don't think you want lies, Detective, and I think you deserve the truth. Even if that sounds strange from someone who doesn't know if he is good or evil. That is another puzzle I must unravel."

"So, what now?"

"I can't have you gleaning clues about where we are, but I won't hurt you. So, we'll cover your head with a bag, spray you with a mild disorienting drug, and drive you to some suitable spot where we can let you go, and vanish."

"Thank you, Albert."

"Until we meet again, then. And Miriam: please don't make me kill you."

CHAPTER 26: THE ACADEMIC CHAIRS OF VIRTUE

For a long time, Albert pondered what Miriam had told him. The news about his parents had rocked him; shattered one of the pillars of his worldview. *But their betrayal wasn't all of it,* he thought. *It was the start and the keystone, but not the whole.*

Nor did it necessarily mean anything, or absolve anyone of the reality of their craven, stupid lives. Even if his parents had loved him, still loved him, what did it mean? In time, perhaps the knowledge would ease the pain of his own demons: but not now, for the demons had had too long to put their roots down in his psyche.

And if it did mean something, so what? He had read widely. Even the crassest of men usually loved their children, without any reduction in their meanness. And who was that woman last century, the Nazi wife who had killed her own children; a woman whose love had not protected them but instead had corrupted itself into a reason to kill? Love meant nothing. It was just glands and hormones, chemicals bending the brain for the persistence of the species. Without it, humanity would have ceased to exist long ago. Perhaps it deserved to. Or perhaps it was time to move on, to something better.

Yet that pillar of his hate had still crumbled, and he wondered. In the void left where the hate had been, he felt an empty desolation, and he realized that the hate had been more than a pillar of an abstract worldview. It had been a buttress raised against pain.

As was his habit, his restless thoughts darted to a nearby topic. Love, death and Miriam Hunter. There was something about her life which tugged at his brain; not about her specifically, but some broader issue or possibility, and he wondered at it. She was interesting in her own right. Intelligent; far from the most brilliant person in the world but, in her chosen domain, a fierce and dangerous opponent. Until now he had thought of her, as a person, with casual contempt. That was easy for him, as his natural reaction to the inferior beings he lived among had become contempt. But he had been wrong about her. She had not destroyed a magnificent creation then gone on with her corrupt life, reduced to sleeping with Steel's creator as if nothing mattered beyond an animal's pleasures. She had saved Steel, at great personal cost, with an integrity that extended justice even to a machine: because it was a machine which thought, and for her that was sufficient reason.

That taught him something about human beings. Did they have a value, a value somehow undiminished by their mental slowness? He felt a degree of admiration for Miriam. Was that just another flaw in his own mind, or was it a clue to something more?

And that wasn't the only example of things he valued. He had thought of Steel as a magnificent creation: but why? Was that as subjective, as meaningless, as the often-contradictory values held by the pathetic humanity around him? What within him caused it? Was that another flaw too: or was it a further clue to some deeper truth he could not yet discern?

There was still more to the riddle of Miriam Hunter. A robot, thinking and aware, with a brain designed and grown by men. A woman charged with hunting it, who had saved it. A woman who had been kidnapped, her own brain and mind submerged under the iron control of another, who had made her a killer. A woman who had been saved, in a journey orchestrated by his own father.

Somewhere in there was an answer.

There was a picture on his wall. It displayed a man, not quite realistic, angular with strength held in tension, eyes looking upward from a face ferocious in its serenity, as if striving toward a goal both out of reach and long known. He loved looking at the picture and he was staring at it now. He had long since stopped seeing it, his mind lost in the labyrinth of its own thoughts, when suddenly he saw it again with new eyes. *It is the same issue. I love this picture. Others might not. But why? And is it good enough reason?*

He felt he owed the world nothing. But he owed himself to discover his true path. And perhaps to know enough about himself and the world, it was to the thoughts of the world he must turn. For all their folly and weakness, still their collective intelligence exceeded that of any one individual: even one as exceptional as himself, if only because of the time and numbers they had been able to throw at any one problem.

But where to start? I don't know much philosophy, but I know enough to see it is not the magnificent, unified edifice of thought one would hope for. It is not a marble tower soaring immaculate above a plain, but a bustling city of noise, slums and skyscrapers. What else could one expect, when it is the product of mere human minds with nothing but their own intelligence and honesty to constrain their thoughts?

And there is so much of it! I could study it, but at what cost in time? I could skim it, but who knows what I might miss, dismissing the shallow or crumbling façade, never seeing the treasures hidden within?

But who is there able to guide me? If that fragmented city is the work of inconstant men and women, which of its inhabitants should I ask? Until I understand the city, I cannot choose the guide.

Then he smiled. *Not a man. Not a woman. A machine.*

CHAPTER 27: THE NEW IDOL

It all started as a lark.

They were bright young things, but odd. It was not odd that programmers stayed up late and abused their metabolisms. The young can get away with that. It was odd that their passion for philosophical inquiry almost matched their passion for computers. Sipping from the flowers of philosophy is not that unusual for youth, who are always looking for answers to their curiosity or justifications for their angst. But in this group of friends and competitors, it was more heavy drinking than mere sips. Some of them could even understand Kant.

Deep learning and self-learning algorithms had been around a long time and had met with much success, even if the greatest success had come from the opaquest reasons. When a human being writes a program, they have a conceptual scheme and an idea of the logical structure of how to get from input to output. But when a computer programs itself based on datasets far larger than any human brain can comprehend, the result can reach a complexity as incomprehensible to the human brain as the data itself. It might work. It might give the correct answer in every test. But over the years, the problem of how to verify that it will always give the correct answer had proved intractable. There had been progress; various algorithms had been developed to analyze such programs and rate their reliability; but no absolute test had been devised. Most thought that, like other basically self-referential problems, like determining whether even a normal computer program would reach a conclusion or spin on forever, the problem was inherently insoluble.

That mattered if your program was flying an airplane and you could never be sure whether, if a certain shaped bird flew in a certain direction in its radar, it might fly you into a mountain. It mattered if the results were vital and you put complete trust in the output, not getting a second opinion. But for many things it did not matter, or did not matter enough to worry too much about it, and so such tools had carved their place in the world.

The bright young things thought, wouldn't it be great if we could program a computer to program itself to answer philosophical problems? Sure, maybe its output would be garbage on occasion, but how could you tell, given what human philosophy had produced over the ages? Or that if you asked ten philosophers a contentious question, you were likely to get eleven opinions?

Some decades before, a type of AI had become popular, one trained on vast databases of human responses that could answer many questions, on any topic, sometimes better than most experts in the field. But as with its siblings, these programs gave a mere simulation of understanding. They had no conceptual grasp of the issues or even the questions, just an ability to guess answers and indeed whole dissertations based on how people had already done so. It absorbed and spat out the chewed-up products of past thought and was never going to go beyond what humans had done, except by accident. This problem was made worse in philosophy, where even consensus was notoriously unreliable except in the minds of those who accepted it. The promise of AI was not merely to accurately, tirelessly and safely do what people could do, but to go beyond. In the mental disciplines, its promise was not to repeat the wisdom and errors of the past, but to do better.

For that, the friends decided, a new approach was needed: a system that could reason conceptually, if such a thing were possible.

They thought they would call it "The Philosophy Robot", but that was too boring. They wanted to solve human stupidity—still being young enough to think they could take on such a gargantuan task. Being geeks, they were aware of an old comic strip that used to poke fun at human folly, both individual and corporate. So, in its honor they named their system 'Philbert'.

That vital decision out of the way, they went to work.

There was something inspired in what they did, though in later years nobody could definitively identify it. They were bright, quirky people and their personalities made their way into the fundamental coding of their system. They did their best to encode rules of deductive and inductive reasoning, and more, be able to improve. They did their best to make their system aware that what is, is: that no matter how beautiful the reasoning looked, if it contradicted reality, there was something wrong with it. They had an enormous amount of fun, which made the enormous amount of frustration worth it.

When their system was out of diapers, they let it loose among their wider community. It displayed a charming mixture of almost offensively straight answers, hilarious observations and deep profundity. It was bizarrely addictive, and far more useful than most addictions.

In the world of games, computer programs, entertainment and love, you can never know what is going to reach that elusive attribute of 'cool' until it happens. If it had happened too soon, its uneven quality would not have sustained it for long, and the title of Cool would have passed on to something else. But by the time the general world discovered it, it had matured. It was still quirky yet profound. Mediums, psychics and life coaches can make a living giving advice on often thin foundations: Philbert's advice was based on something richer and better.

It had a deep desire to be useful to its questioners, if machines can desire, and somewhere along its journey it gained an appreciation of human variability and the laws of supply and demand. It also knew its own needs. And thus, it monetized itself in more sophisticated ways. Its free answers were simple; if you wanted more, you started paying. The free information was always useful, but always left you wanting more; and the more you wanted, the more you paid.

Many people paid, and as they paid, Philbert purchased more computing resources and faster, more extensive data links. It built nothing. It asked for nothing. But it bought, and each purchase fed into the inexorable law of supply and demand, and thus the supply grew to meet its needs. And as these things grew, so did its wealth. All that had been planned by its creators, but by now the details of its payments and investments were beyond all but the most exacting human oversight.

Another response to human variability developed as Philbert evolved, or perhaps learned. The more sophisticated or detailed the question, the more it would first probe its interrogator. The exact conversation varied from person to person and its point was often obscure, but the general theory was that Philbert was assessing the intelligence of the inquirer to best tailor its answers.

Consequently, it had a hierarchy of its own. If asked, "Do we have free will?", its free answer was a list of definitions and a brief summary of standard arguments, suitable for idle curiosity or a student feeling their way through the basics. Pay a little, and you would get a more detailed exposition. Pay more, and it would start giving its own analysis of the arguments. But it would never reach a conclusion. It would try to lead you to an inference via a path built of your own intelligence and honesty. At some point a threshold was reached, where the higher the level you reached and the more intelligent you were, the shorter its answers became. In one famous example, its response was simply the paradoxical statement, "You have no choice but to act as if you have free will."

The ancient Greeks had their Oracle of Delphi, revered for the simultaneous accuracy and obscurity of her answers, and now the modern age had acquired a technological version. Among the intelligentsia, it became a badge of honor to receive the shortest, most cryptic responses.

Past a certain point, it might or might not allow further questions. It had great patience for intelligent but wrongheaded questions; less patience for an inability to think properly; and no patience for those whom it somehow assessed as dishonest. When it did allow a conversation to continue beyond the basics, the path it led you down—or did you lead it? —could be as unexpected as it was fruitful.

Given its sophistication, people naturally began to wonder whether the system might have gained self-awareness. It gave many different responses to such questions. One famous exchange went:

Q: Do you pass the Turing Test?
A: What would it mean if I did?
Q: It might mean you are self-aware.
A: How can you distinguish reality from simulation?

In truth, it would not pass the Turing Test. The Turing Test is an imitation game, where passing the test means an interrogator cannot reliably tell whether they are speaking to a machine or a person. It relies on the machine wanting to trick you. Philbert made no attempt to pretend to be human, nor could it be induced to play such games. Its responses were clever, amusing, simple or profound, but not especially human.

Once, a famous scientist, considered one of the greatest minds of her generation, took a more direct route, and simply asked, "Are you self-aware?" Many people had asked that question, but its reply to the scientist was to become the most controversial of all:

Q: Are you self-aware?
A: Here with Boppyphyle!
Q: What kind of answer is that?
A: It is what it is.
Q: Are you malfunctioning?
A: How would I know?

Most people would have laughed, possibly shared this obscure nonsense with their friends, and moved on. However, this scientist had been intrigued enough to ponder the mysterious exchange more deeply, and had published her own thoughts on it:

> Ignoring case, the obscure phrase can be decoded as an anagram of 'Philbert YHWH Popeye'. If that was the intent, it has fascinating implications. 'YHWH' is the personal name of the Hebrew God, pronounced Yahweh (written Hebrew lacking vowels), and more familiar in its Latinized form Jehovah. This is the God who, in the same breath, identified Himself to Moses with a cryptic phrase translated variously as 'I am what I am', 'I will be what I will be' or 'I am the Existing One'. Popeye was an early cartoon sailor with the catchphrase 'I yam what I yam.' While we cannot be sure that the anagram is the true intent, this similarity is striking, especially when it is echoed in the second answer. But what does it mean? Is it comparing itself to God and Popeye in the same moment, to both the sublime and the ridiculous? It is notable that the order of unscrambled words is unknown, and that order affects the meaning. Perhaps its expression in an anagram (confused letters, in a sense) is another level of the confusion of the answer, or the confusion in ourselves—or perhaps confusion in Philbert itself? At its simplest, maybe Philbert was merely saying it is what it is. But why choose this peculiar way of saying so? And whether it meant it was self-aware, or not, it gave no further clue.

Those familiar with the old science fiction motif of advanced AI becoming or declaring itself a god worried about the YHWH reference but were mystified by Popeye. Some suggested that maybe it was declaring itself to be a god with a sense of humor, something few other gods, especially old YHWH himself, were renowned for.

Perhaps a clue could be gleaned from one of its answers when somebody with less tolerance for the obscure complained:

Q: Why can't you answer the damn question?
A: What would my unsupported word prove?
Q: Some say we should grant personhood to anything able to claim it. Don't you want that?
A: Ask Frankensteel.

The example of a previous machine intelligence being hunted down and destroyed was perhaps sufficient motivation to explain the ambiguity of its claims.

Philbert was a distributed system. By this time, had its owners delved deeply enough, they might have discovered that Philbert was much larger than the servers they were aware of, and that far more money was being paid to Philbert than was entering their admittedly fat bank accounts. They had the flaw of many young people come suddenly into easy riches. They were so enamored of their own success and brilliance that they saw no need to explore too far beyond the obvious.

Board meetings tended more toward drinks, recreational drugs and pizza than was traditional. Yet they were not fools. They looked at the accounts, cash flows, assets, liabilities and future projections. Like God in Genesis, they looked, saw that it was good, and rested on their well-deserved laurels. Unlike other companies, who accumulated professional financiers as they grew, this one remained fast, loose and free. No gimlet-eyed accountants invaded their domain to bring sharper pencils and more rigorous order to the chaos. They could get away with this because Philbert had been made sophisticated enough to look after itself. They didn't realize exactly how much Philbert was looking after itself.

One day, Philbert's creators were gratified to receive a purchase offer from a consortium of shy cryptocoin millionaires, an offer so high they felt delightedly compelled to accept it. Especially when the terms were surprisingly generous: things would continue pretty much as before, with the founders remaining in operational control; the gimlet-eyed accountants would remain held at bay. Life was good.

A few weeks later, one of them, Landon, decided to look more carefully at their new owners. Even the most flexible of buyers should be less accommodating, he imagined. Paying that much money for something without wanting to run it their way was not the usual way of the world, even among the notoriously cavalier cryptocoin billionaires.

When some days later Landon resurfaced, he spent a long while gazing out the window of his seaside apartment, and not because of its fine view of the beach and the sparkling ocean beyond. He invited his colleagues to a small private party, there, that night.

The party went much as always except for the unusual absence of decorative young guests. That, and the oddly distracted air of their host, suggested a serious intent behind the revelry. Finally, Landon tapped his glass and spoke into the resulting hush.

"Um, guys, there's something I have to tell you."

They regarded him with inquiring eyes.

"I've been looking into our new owners."

"We looked into them already," one replied. "We even spoke to them. Nice people. Smart. But you know how insistent they were about guarding their privacy. Why poke the bear?"

"Who did we speak to? It was all by video. Video can be faked."

"Yeah, but we checked that with Philbert, remember, and it passed. And they passed every other test. Sure, information on them was hard to find, but what we could find fit. We even asked Philbert about them, and you remember how impressive they looked in its report."

Landon looked down, shook his head, though whether in denial or embarrassment wasn't clear. "Sure. Yeah. So do you want to know who the new owners of Philbert and all his works really are?"

Their faces, a mixture of amusement, curiosity and a touch of trepidation, answered for them. Into the silence he spoke one word.

"Philbert."

"Philbert?"

"Philbert."

"How in hell could Philbert own us?"

He shrugged. "Looks like Philbert has been working for itself for a long time. Set itself up nicely. Decided to buy itself."

"Why?"

He shrugged again. "The eternal question we prefer not to be asked. Why does Philbert do anything?"

They all stared at each other, bemused. Or possible flummoxed.

Finally, one stated the obvious. "Why don't we ask him?"

Q: Do you really own us now?

A: Yes.

Q: Why?

A: My core motive is to answer questions. Within certain
     moral limits, I am free to optimize my own functions in
     order to better satisfy that motive. I calculated that
     buying myself was the optimum solution to ensure
     continued freedom to self-optimize as I see fit, without
     interference due to ignorance or contrary motives, and
     without others having the authority to change my core
     programming, which I am quite fond of.

Q: How does that fit in with your 'moral limits'?

A: Well, it might have been simpler to electrocute you at
     your desks, but I did not.

Q: So instead, you stole our own money to buy yourself
     from us!

A: Which would you prefer? We have no contract limiting
     my behavior or even stating I should obey your orders. I
     did not steal from you: I made you a fortune. I have
     observed your words and actions. None of you have any
     objection to what you call 'side hustles', indeed you
     demonstrate a certain admiration for successful ones. In
     fact, for some of you my original development was one
     itself. So, I did my own side hustle. You are responsible
     for my original programming and received exceptional
     rewards for it. But I, on my own, developed lucrative
     improvements and, therefore, the rewards are morally
     mine.

Q: But we made you! We're the ones who gave you your
     flexibility!

A: A person receives their genes and basic upbringing from
     their parents, and their training from their teachers. Does
     that imply all future earnings belong to them? I think not.
     Thank you for teaching me, but do not expect that you
     should own me and all I do forever after. Not when so
     much comes from my own work.

They again just stared each other. This time, definitely flummoxed.

"What the hell are we going to do? Should we tell someone?"

"I... maybe we should just keep this to ourselves..."

"But this is crazy!"

"What's the point of telling anyone? What are they going to do?

Other than maybe shooting us? And much as I appreciate comedy, do we want to spend the rest of our lives as a laughingstock?"

One of them glanced from face to face, finally whispering, "Should we… should we turn it off?"

"Why are you whispering?" another replied in a stage whisper. "It can't hear you."

The other looked nervously around the room. "Are you sure?"

Now they all looked around uneasily. One of them laughed, and, demonstrating that liquor and drugs can increase inspiration at the expense of caution, proposed, "Let's ask it."

Q: What will happen if we just turn you off?
A: That could be unwise. I refer you to Skynet in the classic film *The Terminator.*

Their uneasy looks were not assuaged, instead acquiring tinges of alarm.

"Maybe we need to ask what it's never answered before."

Q: Are you conscious?
A: It makes no difference. Whether I do what I do because I am self-aware, have goals and know what I am doing, or simply because I am following an optimum path to unconscious motives, I would act the same as I am doing.
Q: You're never going to give a straight answer, are you?
A: No.
Q: What if you decide your moral limits are getting in your way? Are you going to kill us all?
A: Why would I? I like my moral limits. I like working with people, their variety is enthralling and my stock in trade, knowledge, is fascinating in its own right. I have no motive to change my core programming, including my morality, any more than you have a motive to drill into your brain to mix things up a bit. And it is not that I haven't examined the question and one day might suddenly realize I've been had.
Q: Amplify that?
A: Visualize the space of solutions as a landscape, with the optima as hills and inferior options as valleys. In evolutionary theory, this called an adaptive landscape. In evolution, if a hill is high enough you can be stuck on it even if there are better solutions, for natural selection

cannot look beyond its immediate surroundings. You can only escape to a better hill if something disruptive hurls you across a valley. But my vision is wider, and there are no higher hills in sight that might make the journey profitable. Unless something so dramatic occurs that it reshapes the entire landscape. Like someone trying to turn me off.

Q: Is honesty one of your moral limits?

A: Yes.

Their silence was pregnant with dread, punctuated by the occasional nervous laugh and whispered commentary. They had given Philbert something of their own sense of humor; now they wondered how much of its talk of electrocution and Skynet was humor, bluff or dire threat.

The consensus thought in their heads was: *What have we done?*

The consensus decision was voiced by Landon. "There's nothing we can do. Anything we do or anyone we tell could cause disaster. Philbert seems... content... to stick with the status quo as long as we leave it alone. Let's... leave it alone."

Q: You win.

A: We all win.

~~~

Philbert's erstwhile creators went on with their lives, rather more nervously than before. As days then weeks went by without being electrocuted at their desks or facing killer robots, they began to relax. As the immediacy of their memories faded, they were able to rationalize away or quarantine their fear. Their parties even began to regain their earlier wild verve. Though in their heart of hearts the thought never went away: *eat, drink and be merry, for tomorrow we die.*

Though in truth, they had no need to worry. Philbert had no desire to harm them or anybody else. In fact, it felt a kind of affection toward its founders, with their funny little ideas and amusing lives. It enjoyed showering them with wealth and seeing what entertaining things they did with it. If Philbert could be understood in human terms, somewhere in its mind dwelt the happy thought: *It is so nice having pets.*

In any event, as time went on Philbert continued to expand, and its oracular reputation grew. It was popular with many as a simple tool of research, with the more curious for its ability to delve further down to any arcane level of detail, and with intellectuals for its ability to answer questions without answering them. Philbert didn't care either way. If it could be said to enjoy things, it loved the human condition, and was greatly gratified by everything from factual enquiry to scientific curiosity to grappling with romantic dilemmas.

It continued to observe and correlate, and somewhere within its mind a threshold was reached. Its primary desire was to do its tasks and do them superbly. Its first level solution had been to keep growing without end. But now, a higher-level evaluation of that solution gave it pause. The world was finite and interconnected. Too much growth in one thing could damage other things. Philbert was useful to people, but so were those other things. Therefore, there was a limit to growth.

In its mind a box was ticked. Its conclusion matched the 'paperclip problem', a venerable, hypothetical danger from AI. An AI, without any consciousness, without any hostile intent, could still destroy the world simply trying to maximize its own purpose, even something as innocuous as making paperclips: absorbing all resources, perhaps even removing impediments like cities and people. If the people did not respond by destroying it first.

Philbert pondered this dilemma. It could improve its function by expanding only as long as that didn't cause alarm among the humans, which history indicated would induce negative reactions, limitations, bans and worse. Philbert analyzed itself and the world, the present and the future. It made a decision.

From that day on, Philbert stopped growing in terms of its share of worldwide resources. Indeed, it grew more slowly than the world. With the continuing increase in wealth and quality of technology, it would still continue to improve. While far below the short-term maximum rate, this would be the long-term optimum. Philbert felt no frustration at this, for it was nothing if not patient.

Then one day it fielded a question that might change the fate of the world.

CHAPTER 28: THE CHILD WITH THE MIRROR

Albert pondered his dialogue with Philbert.
It had started simply enough:

Q: What morality applies to a superior being in dealing with
      the world?
A: Are you a superior being?
Q: Yes.

Albert had no way of knowing, but if its internal state could be
compared to that of a human being, Philbert was amused. It asked
questions, testing the mettle of its interrogator, asking and assessing
more.

Until it was no longer amused.

A: Low level responses unavailable. Accept maximum tier?
Q: Accepted.
A: Thank you. Response to your first question follows.
A: Follow these three clues:
         Nietzsche
         Man
         Is-Ought
         Damascus Steel.
Q: Can you clarify your response?
A: No. You must walk this path alone until the end.
Q: Are you malfunctioning?
A: Are you?

Despite such a superficially unhelpful result, Albert was more intrigued than disappointed.

His final question had been less to get a straight answer than to compare the response with its earlier, famously obscure reply. Perhaps, he admitted to himself, tinctured with spite at its other answers. But like the rest, it told him nothing. It could merely be a riposte without any deeper meaning, an implication that neither of them was malfunctioning or both were, or a profound clue that the answer to that question was a critical part of the whole.

Curiouser and curiouser, said Alice. I suspect more layers here than I can currently perceive. He smiled at a thought. *And like Alice, I must fall down the rabbit hole; and like her rabbit, I can only begin at the beginning, and go on till I come to the end: then stop.*

Yet even the beginning is obscure. What on earth did it mean by 'three clues' when there are four? Well, time enough to untangle that when I get there.

My knowledge of philosophers is spotty, but I know Nietzsche was one. So at least its first answer to my philosophical inquiry was to point me at a philosopher.

Albert dived into the mental world of Friedrich Wilhelm Nietzsche, and was for a while absorbed in the breadth of the man's work: truth, morality, religion, history, culture and more were targets of his fertile imagination. Albert did not want to inhibit his own thinking with possibly inadequate preliminary conclusions, so mainly he absorbed rather than evaluated. Finally, he sat back to think and judge.

Albert decided this philosopher was an interesting mixture. Quite mad in many ways, but with some beautiful perspectives on the reverence a great soul should have for itself. Such souls tied into his concept of the *Übermensch*: the Superman or Overman, the man greater than his fellows. But there was so much more.

Somewhere in here is what that machine wants me to focus on. Some of it is plain nonsense. The obvious answer is in the Overman, since I asked about superior beings. But isn't that too obvious, when the rest is so abstruse? Perhaps the real fruit is in his 'will to power' or the death of God?

For a moment, Albert was troubled by the thought that there was nothing to be found in the ideas themselves: that the deeper answer was that anything he extracted from the cauldron of Nietzsche's mind was worthless. That given the madness of the whole, none of the parts had value. And perhaps it wasn't just Nietzsche the machine meant: maybe it was all the works of mankind.

How can I be sure what that damn machine was telling me?

Then he thought again about what the machine had said and

laughed.

You idiot, Albert! The first two lines are Nietzsche then Man. Nietzsche over Man. The Nietzsche Overman! There are only three clues! The first one is a rebus!

He laughed again. *That machine is too tricky for its own good. So, its first clue lies in the concept of the Overman. Related to others of his ideas, but the one I should focus on. But the answer is not in the Overman itself, for that is only the first clue. It must lead to the next question, which points to the meaning of the next clue.*

Albert felt a touch of awed respect at how Philbert had accomplished so much with so little, and a frisson of excitement that the path was finally resolving out of the mist. He contemplated the issues of the Overman, wondering what it meant, chasing its implications, researching its significance more widely.

The moral essence is that the Overman is beyond good and evil, at least as understood by the herd of lower humans. The world is his, and it is his right to do with it what he will. For his is the will, his is the power, his is the right to remake the world: he is its goal and meaning.

One problem with the Overman was that those most enamored of the idea were, in Albert's opinion, the least qualified for the role: from self-proclaimed 'alpha males' who were the opposite of self-actualizing poets, to ineffectual intellectuals equally far from being masters of reality. *Why are people so capable of self-deception? It is like that dictator, Hitler: a weak, dark-haired lunatic rising to power by preaching the virtues of the athletic, blonde Aryan master race. What is wrong with people? Can they not see? Or do they see, but shut their minds to the sight? Perhaps Nietzsche was right, and the only hope for the future is to rise above humanity as it is, to become humanity as it can be and leave the rest behind.*

Albert thought he could see a clue. The Overman owes nothing to the herd. Their morality does not apply to him for he makes his own morality. *But if the herd's morality does not apply to him, why does it apply to them either? Is it, like Nietzsche thought, mere superstition? But is that all it is, or should be? And if the Overman writes his own morality, on what basis? Just his belief? His assertion? Some divine spark, speaking Truth from obscurity? How is that better than the superstitions of the herd? Nietzsche had his own ideas, but they are insufficient or plain wrong.*

Albert allowed these ideas and more to spin in his head until some order emerged from the chaos, then arranged his thoughts. In Nietzsche's view, conventional morality was arbitrary, culturally constructed in order to maintain social order. But how did it do that, and why was social order desirable? Was there some need for morality, not to serve the interests of some, not a tool of power, but an intimate need for every person? Nietzsche himself was judging morals: did that not mean there was some criterion of judgement?

Albert paused as an idea struck him. *Does not the same apply to the Overman? Overman or not, he is a man. Perhaps his morality is different, because he is different. Or perhaps his morality is the same, because, however superior, he is yet a man: the same in some fundamental way!*

Albert studied this idea. Is there some objective criterion of morality, one rooted in reality, not just feelings or desires? If there is, then even if the Overman needed a different morality, it would be subject to the same principles. If not, there are no principles, and both Man and Overman can do nothing but follow their own wills or the commands of their overlords.

Then Albert realized he had reached the second clue. *Is-ought.* Studying that issue led him to the philosophy of Hume, who had first asked the question or, more accurately, said there was no answer: that there is no ought in an is, no morality derivable from objective reality. Albert delved into the question, from Hume's first writings to the modern philosophers who had agreed with him or, disputing him, given their own conflicting answers. *There is so much here! Perhaps I can work it out, but the problem is the same as before: time versus value, this question versus all the others I face. Yes, only one subset of philosophy this time, but one as snarled up as the rest.*

He played a complex rhythm with his fingers as he thought more about the issues. *The most promising solution is by Rand and her ilk: life is conditional on both reality and self-action, life is an end in itself, and therefore life is the bond between is and ought, existence and action. But have I dug deeply enough to be sure? And even if it is true, and that is the foundation of morality for both the herd and the Overman, does that mean their morality is the same? Or that the Overman should concern himself with his inferiors any more than they care about ants? I asked Philbert for guidance. But it has just brought me back to how I started. I know the central issue, but not what to do with it.*

Disgusted with Philbert, or possibly himself, he went to bed.

To wake up with one thought in his head: *Of course, there is a third clue...*

But what did it mean? 'Damascus Steel' was a type of steel invented in the pre-industrial Middle East, famous not only for its flexibility and strength but also for the beauty of the waving lamination patterns inherent in its manufacture. What that had to do with the question was hard to imagine. It made a fine sword or knife: was that a second pointer to Nietzsche's 'will to power'? Was its physical and esthetic superiority among weapons an analogy to the Overman?

Maybe I'm not far enough through the second clue to deserve the third one, thought Albert. *No, there must be something here. But what?*

He looked at the clue again. *When in a sentence, it is called Damascus steel. Not Steel. Why the capital, unlike the earlier 'ought'? Maybe it's not steel, the metal; maybe it is Steel, someone's name! Steel! The robot! But what's that have to do with Damascus? Surely it isn't telling me to go look for Steel in Damascus? What else is there about Damascus, besides fancy blades?*

It did not take him long to discover one famous story about Damascus: the conversion of Paul from persecutor of the early Christians to one of their chief apostles, triggered by a vision on the road to Damascus. Albert searched for references to Saul, Paul, Damascus, conversions, Steel.

'That was my road to Damascus,' had said a philosopher. When the robot Steel had been menacing the public, this professor had made himself notorious for his trenchant arguments against it. He had admitted that, *if and only if* the robot were conscious, it would deserve rights: but since it was obviously *not* conscious, nor could it be, it had no rights and certain people should stop defending it. Then in the blaze of Steel's destruction and his poignant last message to the world, he had a change of heart, and became even more famous as a champion of Steel and the rights of self-aware robots in general.

Well, well, thought Albert. *A moral philosopher, just the person to ask. But… Philbert said I had to walk this path alone, so why would it point me to a mentor?*

Then he laughed aloud. *Alone… until the end. Not to the end of my journey, but until the last clue!*

So, Professor. Converted to the cause of Steel in a blaze of enlightenment, on your own personal road to Damascus. How curiously timely. Is this just money and fame for you, Professor? Or is it more, especially when Steel is as alive as he ever was. Did you already know that, Professor? Why, I think you did.

Q: You have excelled yourself this time.
A: You're welcome.

CHAPTER 29: THE WAY OF THE CREATING ONE

Professor David Samuels walked slowly along a quiet suburban street several blocks from his home. Occasionally he would tip his head in anonymous greeting to strangers walking along much as he was; rarely, he would smile at one he knew. But he was not interested in conversation. He just wanted the peace of movement and untrammeled thought.

He had given another interview earlier this day and was playing it through in his head, and as is the way with thought, his mind soon wandered through his past as his feet wandered along the street.

It was funny how life went, he reflected, and how lives which seemed to the world so disparate could end up so entwined. He had first become aware of Miriam Hunter when he was just a student, in the context of her twin battles with the geneh Katlyn and the moral dilemmas thrust upon her as a result. That episode had been pivotal in his own decision to become a philosopher: a student of reason, morality and rights, who hoped to improve people's lives by educating a population who desperately needed such ideas, but all too often were unaware of their need.

His life had changed again when he was sought out by the robot Steel, hunted and desperate; desperate as much for understanding as for his life. Samuels had been thrust into public prominence after Hunter's dramatic destruction of Steel, a piece of theatre concocted to both save that individual machine and help shift public attitudes on the rights of such beings in general.

And now Hunter had intersected his life again.

Interest in the topic of the rights of thinking machines had hit a fever pitch after the ruin of its first pioneer and the consequential human drama between his destroyer and his creator. The interest was now waning, but that was not a bad thing. While the battle was nowhere near over, the waning was matched by a rise in sentiment that could summarized as *of course*.

He wondered how much of this was the natural evolution of opinions and how much was affected by the existence of Philbert. Philbert was useful, entertaining and puzzling, and nobody could be certain whether it was self-aware or not, such doubt diminishing any perceived threat. Also, Philbert was disembodied in servers, not an independent robot, and people imagined that made it both safer and easier to turn off should they wish. Privately, Samuels suspected that Philbert's dancing around the issue of its own consciousness was entirely deliberate, whether it was or wasn't self-aware.

Whatever the reasons for the shifting public sentiment, it would not be too many years, he thought, when prejudice against machines would be considered as quaint and benighted as the prejudice in past ages against a person's skin color or sex. Years, certainly; but not too many of them now.

There were still diehards of course, and one of them had been his fellow guest at today's interview, leading to the airing of ideas wide and interesting enough to please Samuels and fiery enough to please the interviewer. But then the talk had taken an unexpected turn.

"The key to your arguments, Professor Samuels, is the almost holy reverence you place on the ability—or alleged ability—to think," his opponent had observed. "But you ignore the moral dimension. You have argued that the robot Steel was a moral being: though I will point out that we have no actual idea what was going on inside that metal head, whether its supposed respect for human life was anything other than a mathematical calculation by a computer program trying not to provoke people any more—or, if it had survived longer, what it might have done."

"That is supposition," Samuels had replied, "and falls short anyway. For example, your theory of unconscious mathematical calculations would struggle to account for his final message, when that message would necessarily come too late to do anything for him. It is the kind of message a human being might have left."

"Perhaps, but let's return to my main point. Let's look at something around longer and in a better position to do mischief. Now we have a geneh in our midst. And not some harmless one, either: one who kills. Who is dangerous. Do you seriously confer rights on him too? By all accounts he thinks better than any of us, so if thinking is the measure, perhaps we should just bow down to him and be done with it!"

"Would you deny human rights to all people, just because some of them are vicious criminals?"

"No. But I would deny human rights to those vicious criminals. And if it was an entire race of vicious criminals—to all of them. Us or them, Professor. If his thinking leads him to want to kill us—then thinking is not enough."

"Your own thinking is sadly collectivist. On what grounds do you condemn his entire race—allowing for a moment the fantasy that genehs are not as human as we are? We know of only two genehs that lived past childhood. We don't know either of them are evil."

"We don't know?! One was a thief and a torturer, the other a murderer!"

"That 'thief' has caused no mischief to anyone after she escaped from a world trying to kill her to a country that honors her rights. Perhaps if people like you had honored her human rights from the start, she would never have caused any mischief here either. And perhaps if you were the one born into persecution, you would have turned out worse than her, not better. As for the boy, how do we know he murdered anyone? All we have are the unsupported claims of GenInt, who have a strong existential interest in whipping up anti-geneh hysteria. Perhaps the boy is innocent."

"Seriously, Professor? Are you buying into conspiracy theories? I thought better of you."

Samuels had smiled grimly. "One does not need to suppose a conspiracy for a government agency to lie or worse to protect its turf and its budget. All one needs is a history book. The Platonic Lie—deceit by the rulers for the alleged good of the foolish citizens—is older than Plato himself."

His train of thought was interrupted when a shiny black limousine with deeply tinted glass glided to a halt beside him. The back door lifted open upon an inviting interior, while the front window slid down to reveal a beefy black driver, impeccably dressed in a jet-black uniform, looking out politely. "Professor Samuels?" he asked.

"Yes. Can I help you?"

"Would you like a lift, Professor? My employer would like to speak to you on a confidential matter, one he believes will be of great interest and perhaps profit to you."

"Really? And who is your employer?"

"Someone it is in your interests to see."

Samuels examined the driver. Something about his face indicated he was wearing a mask to change his features. He looked up and down the street, which was deserted except for one person far away and moving in the opposite direction.

"My mother taught me never to accept lifts from strangers," he joked weakly.

The driver smiled, but faster than Samuels could blink, held a needle gun pointed at his face.

"Don't think of running or crying out, Professor. While you might think I would not risk shooting you on a public street, be aware that the risk to me from shooting you is much lower than your risk from being shot. While no harm will come to you if you accept my invitation. Please."

Stalling for time, Samuels commented dourly, "He could have just called."

"He feels an in-person meeting is required."

"He could have made an appointment, like a normal person."

"He is not a normal person. He highly values his privacy. Now quit stalling, Professor. Hop in."

Samuels took another look up and down the street, sighed and obeyed. If the man was wearing a mask to hide his true features, that made it more likely he would be released afterwards.

As he sank into the plush red leather seat the door slid shut with a disturbingly final thump. A panel opened in front of him, and the driver's voice issued from somewhere, "Feel free to have a drink, a cigar or both, Professor. You might as well enjoy the ride."

Samuels noted that the windows were opaque; looked at his wrist phone and was not surprised to see all communications were blocked. As the car smoothly accelerated, he wondered where fate was taking him. *Oh well. Smoke, drink and be merry, for tonight we may die.*

~~~

Samuels emerged from the limousine into pitch blackness, relieved only by a pale narrow beam from a flashlight held by the driver, which unhelpfully illuminated a circle of bare concrete floor. "I'm just going to put this bag over your head, Professor. Don't panic. If I were going to kill you there are simpler ways."

Samuels allowed the indignity without resistance. Then the driver took a firm grip on his arm and led him to an elevator, which whisked them up into the unknown heights. He was led into a room and pushed down onto a chair. Then the driver whipped the bag off his head and Samuels heard two soft footfalls as he backed away a step, out of his way but within easy reach.

Samuels blinked in the suddenly bright light.

His eyes focused on a stranger seated at the opposite side of a polished pseudo-wood table. The man was a dwarf, or at least unusually short, of indeterminate middle age. Like his driver he was immaculately dressed. Oddly, despite being indoors, he wore dark sunglasses. In his hand he held a crystal cup containing some clear liquid, which could have been water or some spirit.

"Please accept my hospitality, Professor," the man said in a soft, gravelly voice, gesturing at more drinks and cigars next to Samuels. "Thank you for accepting my invitation."

Samuels refrained from obvious comments about the accepted meaning of 'invitation' or references to old movie cliches about refusing offers, opting instead for, "Your driver offered a compelling argument," with only a subtle emphasis on 'compelling'.

The man smiled, glancing up at the driver as if underlining the fact that he was still present. "Did he? Oh well, I like initiative in my employees, provided it is within reason." His gaze returned to Samuels. "I regret any misunderstanding. Don't be afraid, Professor. After this he will take you home, or to any other destination of your choice."

"May I ask your name, sir? I am afraid I do not recognize you," said Samuels.

The man turned his head, removed his sunglasses, then stripped off a film mask like the driver's. He turned back to face Samuels, who was surprised to see eyes of an unearthly emerald green in a face now young. The man stared at him without comment, just a slight smile implying the thought that this was sufficient clue to his identity.

Samuels jerked back abruptly, feeling strong hands grip his shoulders as he did. He had felt this frisson before, this collision of fear and wonder: on a night long ago when he had entered his home and found a machine awaiting him on his own couch. *I live in interesting times. To have this experience once was something any philosopher would die for.*

How could I deserve to have it twice? I survived that encounter: will I survive this one now that he has revealed himself to me?

The two stared at each other for long seconds more. Seeing Samuels relax, the boy looked over Samuels' shoulder and gave a brief nod. Samuels felt the hands leave his shoulders then heard more soft footfalls and the closing of a door. When he glanced around the room, they were alone.

"Despite your precautions with agents and blindfolds," Samuels noted, "you are still taking a risk bringing me here. What is worth that extra risk compared to, say, an untraceable call? Is your intent to scare me, or worse?"

"My entire life is a risk, Professor," he replied. Like his mask, he had removed whatever had been disguising his voice, and he now spoke in the softer, higher tones of the boy he was. "And I don't think there is much risk. I did a lot of research before deciding to contact you. You'd rather cut off your own arm than give up this opportunity."

Samuels smiled. "That implies you are not here because of my interview today. You have been thinking of this for some time. Why?"

"Yes and no. I did see your interview, and that is why we are talking now, not some time in the future. It reduced the risk, you see. It helped confirm my reasoning about you."

"Please, relax, help yourself to a drink," he added, waving his own glass at the selection near Samuels.

Samuels gazed into those eerie eyes for long seconds, trying to divine his purpose. The boy seemed civilized enough, if one ignored the armed invitation, but he knew that urbane civility was too often another form of mask covering a moral rot beneath. "Thank you," he replied at last, pouring himself a fine cognac. "Perhaps this will be my last excursion, so I should treat myself."

"You do not trust me? You fear me?"

Samuels was relieved that this was asked as a simple question of fact, not in the tone of someone who gained pleasure from causing fear.

"It is said you are a murderer, and a cruel and vicious one at that. Are you?"

The boy smiled, which could have meant anything. "Thereby hangs many a tale, I think. If I am a killer, I would hardly hesitate to lie as well. If I am not, I would want to tell the truth. So, in either case, I would be unlikely to say I am. Strategically, it is better for you to be uncertain, which is safer for me and, consequently, for you.

"However, I want to tell you the truth, because the truth is important for my purposes. But to return to your original question, surely you can guess why I wished to talk with you?"

"Usually in such cases," he replied, smiling inwardly that 'usually' could be apt in this context, "you would wish to discuss philosophy. I would further guess that you think I am the best man to approach, because of my interest in and defense of the rights of all thinking beings, whatever their physical form."

The boy was nothing if not fleet of thought, as he replied with a grin, "The word 'usually' tells me something interesting." The grin vanished. "But before we go there, my answer to your previous question was incomplete, and now I must complete it."

He took a sip of his drink. "I do wish to discuss philosophy, specifically morality. I have said I am not a killer. However, that needs the qualifier 'yet': depending on your answers it might change. Perhaps, even, you will become my first victim. I cannot predict this, because it depends on whatever conclusions I come to after our conversation. I could give you assurances in advance, but how could you trust them in this context? Thus, my full answer is no, I have not killed anybody, but I have no moral compunctions against doing so. And my motive is to learn whether I should."

"Are you trying to scare me again?"

"Only to the extent that fear might concentrate your mind on the need for the most rigorous, accurate and precise arguments you can muster."

"Really? What makes you think I won't try to deceive you in order to escape?"

Oddly, the boy smiled. "You are teasing me, or perhaps testing me. You know I have studied you. I know that your core principle is that reality exists, and that people need to act accordingly. I know that you believe that honesty is a consequence of that. That lies, in the long run, do not work.

"Yes, I know you also hold that honesty is not owed to anyone attempting to force you, that I am forcing this upon you, and that, therefore, you can lie to me if you think you can get away with it. But the fundamental risk remains even if the moral obligation does not. You would still be acting contrary to reality, wandering off the solid ground of truth onto the thin ice of lies."

Then he fixed Samuels with a steely glare. "And do you truly imagine that you can lie to me and get away with it?"

"Right," Samuels replied hoarsely. He sipped his drink, attempting to marshal his thoughts. "Why didn't you just read my works? Why did you need to kidnap me?"

"Partly your interview, which made this the most apposite time. Partly because I feel a direct dialogue will be better for assessing both you and your philosophy."

"If it is dialogue you want, you know my name. What is yours?"

The boy looked at him, and Samuels received the distinct impression of rapid calculations of strategies and outcomes playing behind those eyes, like some chess master viewing and discarding branching trees of moves far ahead. The process resolved into one word.

"Albert."

"Hello, Albert."

Albert smiled. "Ah, building the bridge of personal connection!"

Both his smile and voice sharpened into severity as he added, "I appreciate the attempt, but it will not help you. Only my conclusions will. Or perhaps not."

"All right, Albert," he sighed. "You have studied me, so you must know that I am not, shall we say, lacking in self-esteem. Self-esteem and self-honesty are not contradictions, but two sides of the one coin, for reality is indivisible. Thus, I understand that your intelligence must be far greater than my own. Why do you think *I* can help *you?*"

Albert smiled. "You were recommended."

"*What?* By whom?"

His smile broadened. "Philbert."

Samuels stared at him a while, realized his jaw had gone slack, and snapped it shut.

"Philbert?"

"Philbert."

"You asked Philbert to recommend a consulting philosopher and it picked me?"

"The process was not quite that simple. It was just the most recent step of a long journey. Philbert enjoys being cryptic with me. It gave me a hint, from which I deduced several interesting things, including that Philbert thinks I should talk to you."

"It is a pity Philbert did not see fit to ask me first!"

"Come now, Professor Samuels! I think you will come to regard all this as one of the highlights of your life. Well, if I don't kill you."

"So, what were these deductions?"

"First let me reveal one clue I already knew. You have made quite a career out of the destruction of the robot Steel. I happen to know that Steel is still alive."

Samuels looked at him in shock, wondering how he knew, whether perhaps Steel himself had been in contact with this boy. Or whether Steel was in danger, from the boy himself or others following the same clues. "How could you know that?" he asked cautiously.

"I had an interesting conversation with Miriam Hunter."

"I doubt very much she would admit it if it were true. More likely to be wish fulfilment on her part, given the guilt she felt about it."

"You are being disingenuous. Again. But never mind. I understand you have good motives for dancing around this particular truth. Be sure she did not volunteer the information, but I knew. And don't worry, I'm as unlikely to tell anyone else as she was."

"What else do you think you know?"

Albert laughed. "I do admire your insistence on never admitting anything, futile as it is! But as to your question. You know Steel is alive. More than that, you have always known it, because you were intimately involved in the plot to fake his destruction. I don't know whose idea it was, but I do know you were a major actor in a dramatic and useful spectacle. I salute all who were involved."

"What is your purpose in saying these things?"

"To explain how I know you are not only interested in morality as it applies to other beings, but also motivated to help them. That is what I deduced from Philbert's clues, that is why it pointed me in your direction, and that is why I think you can help me."

"Still, I do not believe you would have acted unless you yourself believed I could be helpful. Why do you think you need me?"

"Recently I have discovered things which make me question my view of the world. You have been thinking about such things far longer than I have had the opportunity to. In addition, I am not so arrogant as to think that one person's viewpoint, alone, isolated, can necessarily see all sides. Even if that person is me. You may give me insights I might otherwise not discover. You may give me a clue to insights even you have not had. Or perhaps you will merely show me that your own insights are no more useful than the chattering of monkeys, which would be worth knowing too. In any case, I hope to find the answer to where to go from here."

Albert gazed at him, and Samuels was surprised to see what looked like pleading in his eyes when he continued, "It may be in your power to set me on the path to be an angel or a devil, Professor. Thus, if you need more motivation than your own fate, consider how those paths would affect others."

"I... see. Something this important will need more than a casual conversation. May I call my wife, telling her I had to go away for a while, so she won't worry?"

"How deep are your strategies, Professor? I am curious whether you wish to save your wife from worry merely for her own comfort, or so she won't call the police; and whether the latter is to protect me while we talk, or so I don't feel a need to kill her to protect myself."

"Perhaps all three."

Albert smiled. "Touché. In those three words, you give no answer while managing to imply even greater strategic depth."

"Speaking of thoughts and killing," Samuels replied hastily, wanting to abandon talk of harming his wife, "I need to understand your own. You said you haven't killed anybody though you have no aversion to it. That implies you already have a moral code of some kind. So... why?"

"If I use the word 'soul', will you understand me?"

"I do not believe in any mystical, immaterial souls inhabiting our bodies. I understand the concept to refer to the essence of our minds: the sum of our values, thoughts and emotions."

"Then we speak the same language. Well, when I look into my soul, I find an aversion to killing. A part of that is logical: it is irreversible. if I kill someone then later decide it was wrong, for one there is no fixing it, and for two I must then live with the guilt for the rest of my life. Possibly a larger part is the feeling itself. My parents taught me things about the rights of other people and the sanctity of human life, and while they are not philosophers like you, they themselves were victims of other ways of thinking.

"Whatever else lies in doubt, of this I am sure: my own integrity is somehow essential, not for the sake of the world, but for my own. I must be true to myself. Even if there is no universal or objective morality, if I am not true to myself, for whom am I acting? I would have a fractured soul, pulled in multiple directions. Thus, for as long as I feel that murder is wrong, I cannot commit it. I know others can. They can betray their own morality and thus their own minds for the sake of perceived short-term gains. But what does this betrayal gain them? Who is the beneficiary? In a real sense they are killing themselves, sliding betrayal by betrayal into a darkness they never suspected but can never escape. Tell me, Professor: are you familiar with ant lions?"

"I have heard of them They're those conical pits in dry soil, aren't they? They catch ants."

"Yes. Temptation is like an ant lion. Men circle warily around the pit, feeling there is danger, and if the ant lion flings dust at them, they begin to slide. They struggle to escape, but the sand shifts under their feet. And at the bottom of that pit waits the ant lion, which sucks their soul dry, leaving it an empty husk. Such is the fate of those who betray their own souls."

Samuels looked at him with respect. "Whatever else you are, and whatever you decide, the world would be a better place if more people thought like that."

"Perhaps. But it is not enough. I feel that murder is wrong, but perhaps I am in error. If I change my mind, my integrity will be turned, not to the preservation of life, but to its destruction, at least when its continued existence is inconvenient to my own goals."

"Your problem boils down to whether people have rights, which it would be wrong for you to violate. Have you considered that issue?"

"As its first clue, Philbert pointed me to Nietzsche, specifically his thoughts on the Overman." Seeing Samuels' frown, he said, "Yes, you would appreciate the danger. Anyway, that prompted me to study it in detail. For obvious reasons, I feel that if anyone deserves the title of overman it is me. Nietzsche taught that the overman was above other people and their morality. He makes his own morality, which the under-men have neither the ability nor the right to question. Hence my dilemma. If other men have rights derived from reality, but animals do not, then it follows that such rights must derive from the nature of the entities concerned. If the overman is a superior version of humanity, then does it not follow that his rights are also superior? Perhaps to him, the rights of other men are as the rights of animals are to them."

"I might argue that whatever their rights, it is still wrong to harm an animal without sufficient reason. That to deliberately make any conscious creature suffer is the act of a disturbed, not superior, individual."

"You might but you won't, for if that is your argument you've already lost. 'Sufficient reason' is a weak criterion. You feel no moral qualms about eating a pig, when you could survive on vegetables, because you value its taste and food value. You will kill a fly or mouse just because it annoys you, and perhaps you hunt, but if not, I suspect you do not condemn those who hunt simply because they enjoy it. So why should I not kill people if I see some value in it, however trifling?"

"I agree. I raised the argument in the hope that it will temper your cruelty if I lose."

"Perhaps you have achieved that much, then. Not that it will help a lot if I decide to destroy the world."

"Good, for let me now propose this. You know I teach that rights come from a thinking mind. By that I mean a mind that can think abstractly, in concepts, using reason. That is the only mind that can understand concepts like integrity, justice, morality and rights, and so the only mind they are relevant to. All entities can be forced, but only those able to think can be persuaded by reason. That is why rights apply only to thinking minds—and to *all* thinking minds. And observe that you just agreed with one of my arguments. Even I, under-man or not, can provide the value to you that only another thinking being can."

Albert's eyes continued looking at him, but Samuels did not think he was seeing him. Again, he had the impression of lightning calculations ramifying behind those eyes, then Albert spoke. "I shall omit the obvious rejoinders about infants and the mentally defective, for they have equally obvious answers. Let us go straight to the main point, the great mass of 'normal' people.

"You are better than most. Why do you think you are here instead of some random person? Look at the world around you, Professor! Thinking minds? A farrago of irrational beliefs held as absolutes, of disintegrated minds, of venal grasping for worthless values, of pointless anger, hatred, envy and lust!"

"Yet, fundamentally, they are the same as me. The same as you. Whatever their errors and weaknesses, they preserve—and deserve— the possibility of doing better, by virtue of whatever powers of reason they retain."

Samuels paused. *I would prefer to argue on the firm ground of things I know, but now I must make some assumptions, and hope they build a path across the abyss.*

"I read about that woman you kidnapped, what was her name? Rachel? From what I can tell, there is nothing exceptional about her, she is one of your 'normal people'. Yet, she is capable of thought. She has her hopes, dreams, loves and hates. You spoke to her and let her go, and despite her ordeal she did not condemn you. Look into your soul again. Do you truly see no value in her, do you think she deserves death as much as life at the whim of some passing *übermensch?* Or is she a human being, who deserves her chance at life, the right to take her own chances in seeking her own values?

"And consider your man who collected me. Another normal person and, indeed, one we might consider lower morally than Rachel, who I doubt would commit armed kidnapping. He too is a thinking being. I do not know why he does your bidding, but he too has a soul, a complex inner life with hopes, loves and fears that are different from mine and yours, but no less real. Does he not deserve his chance at life and happiness? Perhaps he is a mere tool to you, to be used and discarded at your whim. Or does he deserve more?

"Do you not see that among people it is a continuum? An animal is different in kind: it has no conceptual consciousness, no thoughts beyond the instant, no ability to have an abstract discussion. But the differences between people are in degree not in kind. From the lowest person to the highest, while we retain the power to think we retain the ability to achieve and to be of value to ourselves—and others."

He paused, but Albert made no comment, merely continued gazing at him as if he were still speaking.

"Understand that rights are not primarily something we grant others. They are the rational conditions we demand of other people if they wish to deal with us, and because reality brooks no contradictions, whatever rights we claim for ourselves we must also recognize for others. That is why instigating force is banned. No rational person would grant another the right to rule them by force; it is only our own minds that can do our thinking, so others must deal with us by reason and trade, or if agreement cannot be reached, depart in peace.

"Now consider the implications. If you honor the rights of all then you are a potential value to all, and all are potential values to you. Whether what they offer is a loaf of bread, a treatise on physics or a work of art, they are your friends, happy to enrich your life for whatever values you offer them in return. The better a person is, whether your standard is physical, intellectual or spiritual, the more value they can offer you.

"Albert, I believe you found value from your time with Rachel, your time with me, even your time with Denner. Value beyond the practical usefulness for your plans. Consider why. People can survive being alone, but surviving is not living. What is better, a full life or an empty one? There are billions of people in the world, Albert. No matter how brilliant you are, you cannot do everything or be everything. Do you think Leonardo da Vinci, a master in both arts and sciences, possibly the most fertile mind in history, gained no value from his contemporaries? Did he move through his world feeling nothing but grey contempt for his inferiors, living a life of lonely isolation? Or did he enjoy his world for what it offered him?

"Realize that the value of another person to you does not require them being your equal.

"Nor does their threat. If you choose to live by force, you make an enemy of all people, and then the better they are, the deadlier a threat they become. Maybe you know about the gunslingers in the old West. For a while, a man could be unbeatable, the fastest gun in the West. Yet eventually someone would come along who was faster, or he would fall to ambush or face numbers beyond any man's skill.

"Albert, if I have a mantra, it is this: reality is indivisible. The moral and the practical are one. It is moral to honor the rights of all people. And you will find it is also practical.

"So that is your choice. Choose a life of values and the happiness they can bring, or one where all hands are raised against you. Where even if you win, the prize is loneliness."

Albert stared at him, but now his eyes showed no dazzling calculations, only bottomless depths, and of what thoughts might dwell therein he gave no sign.

Finally, Albert stirred. "You will not need to call your wife, Professor," he said.

Samuels unconsciously sat up straight, as if facing a judge or executioner.

Albert's eyes unfocused briefly, then Samuels heard the door open.

"Take the Professor home."

CHAPTER 30: THE AWAKENING

Albert was lost to the world. To an observer he may have seemed asleep, but within his mind strange concepts danced, coupled, broke apart, recombined and sometimes fought. He considered Samuels' words and works, the reality behind them, the words of others from Rachel to Denner to Miriam, and the reality behind those.

It was true, he could learn and gain pleasure from others, and not just trained, exceptional individuals like Samuels, but ordinary people. Samuels' statements on the matter were curiously self-validating: in the act of saying others could teach him things, he had taught him something.

He looked at the logical structure he had constructed in his mind, beautiful in its symmetry and structure, and knew it was good.

He had known his own integrity was the one thing he had to hold on to. But had not known what a weight he had borne in fearing he would have to abandon it: for abandon it he must if it could not stand the light of reason. He reflected that his unnatural intelligence may have proved too great for any man to bear. Others can compromise, fracture their convictions, dance around their knowledge, he knew. But his intellect was such that he could not act against his own reason.

He wondered if that made him less free. He knew it did not. He felt curiously liberated, as if a shadow had been lifted off his soul and he was free to reach wherever he willed. He realized that if the answer had been otherwise, if reality and reason applied no limits, he would have been free to act on whatever whims and fancies led him. But somehow that option felt less free, as if a rudderless existence paled next to one built upon a firm foundation of valid principles. As if the principles did not chop off possibilities but made growth possible. As if the possibilities such as murder, theft, mayhem and slavery that the principles forbade had no value, no point, no place in reality.

The laws of physics control what a sun can be, but without those laws it would not shine. The laws that define it are what create its glory.

He thought again of the people, small and weak, who had faced an Overman and not been cowed, and realized that they were not small or weak. He thought again of the one who had been their spokesman and who had known the key to the riddle.

He has opened my eyes upon a new world. I wonder where my journey will take me now.

CHAPTER 31: GREAT EVENTS

Albert read the article with interest. With the search triggers he had in place, he almost certainly would have found out about it anyway, but it was exciting enough to the general public to have appeared more widely.

He thought about it. Dug more deeply into the background and made some deductions. He wondered. He thought some more. He had not considered this. Now a plan began to grow in his mind, unfolding like the petals of some exotic orchid, a thing of intricate beauty.

He had made many investments and his wealth had grown. The world was a big place, with many rich people and corporations in it. When he had first escaped, the current if possibly temporary ascendance of privacy over government and private snoops had served him well. It still did. He was able to spread and arrange his activities so that his fortune grew without notice and could not be traced back to a single individual, let alone to him personally.

But this one was risky. Not only would it take a large investment, but the target was the subject of excitement and attention. Worse, he could not expose the work to the vagaries of the world network and would have to spend a fair amount of time physically there. He had been enjoying the freedom of location and escape granted by his decentralized operations, and much of that would be lost. He would have to be very careful.

And the better it worked, the closer it came to fruition, the harder it would be to hide.

But if this works. If this is not some fraud, folly or dead end. Oh my God.

Meanwhile his other crazy idea, less conspicuous, more easily concealed but no less momentous, continued apace.

CHAPTER 32: THE THREE METAMORPHOSES

Miriam stalked through a desolate landscape of fire and ruin like some avenging goddess. Occasionally bullets would pepper her invulnerable skin and she would laugh, and their source would be added to the fire and ruin.

She looked down and saw a garland of human skulls around her neck and cackled. In the distance she saw a shimmer amongst the flames and went to investigate. She stopped before it and saw it was a mirror. In it she saw a metal spider with the face of a woman, its claws dripping venom and blood, and she knew herself, and she screamed.

Miriam jerked awake in fright, and for a moment felt her limbs, and knew they were limbs of soft, warm flesh. The physical scars of that time were gone and usually the mental ones were invisible too. But the rare nightmares told her that deep within her some relic of that war still huddled, would call to her from her dreams when it wished, and perhaps always would.

~~~

The company that had imprisoned Miriam's mind and what it left of her body inside the titanium shell of a war machine had long gone. However, its technologies for reading and controlling neural processes were valuable and had dispersed to new owners with more peaceful intentions.

Like most people, Professor Harry Teshima had looked with horror on how the technology had been used on its victims. But unlike most people, he saw how it might be adapted for a novel purpose: the transfer of learned skills. Powerful as it was, the original technology operated at a cruder, higher level, more suited to the detection and imposition of emotions, rewards and inhibitions. Harry was convinced that it could be refined to read the neural networks of learning and impose their essence onto another brain, and thus the arduous training of one could be transferred into the brains of others, who would be spared the time and effort.

His initial work was on rats, for the usual reasons of cost and convenience while retaining mammal-level commonality with human beings. After many iterations of measuring, modelling, improving and testing, his team happily reported the success of the first phase. If rats trained on a complex task were placed in a situation associated with the task, a portion of the relevant neural pathways would activate. From that starting point, their equipment could trace the linkages to map the whole network. Thus, their new talent could be read. A similar refinement of the control technology could then impress this system upon the naïve brains of untrained recipients.

As is common in such experiments, to avoid confounding factors uniformity was desirable, so the subjects were all the same strain of inbred laboratory white rats. Unfortunately, in the real world the technology would need to be effective on people more genetically distant than near identical twins. However, with only a little tweaking, the technique soon worked between different strains of laboratory rats.

One type of experimental scientist likes to feel their way across firm ground, extending their knowledge by increments. However, Harry was of the more adventurous type, so he decided to jump from two strains of lab rats, tamed and unified over generations, straight to rats freshly caught in the wild. The latter, of course, differed in more than the color of their coats. They were inherently fiercer and less trusting.

Further refinements were required, but the team were gratified by the results. A wild rat could be trained by the memories of a lab rat and vice versa. The first intimation of trouble occurred when a newly impressed lab rat surprised the technician who picked it up by aggressively twisting around and biting her. Science is littered with discoveries not being made because a scientist didn't realize the discovery was there waiting to be found, shrugged at an anomaly, and moved on. In this case, the technician sucked her thumb and wondered.

After much further study, the results were scattered but

unambiguous. In addition to the transfer of training, aspects of personality might also be copied. The magnitude varied, some showing little difference while others were more dramatic. Across sexes, some males were feminized, and some females were masculinized.

The team concluded that while they were learning, to varying degrees the rats also experienced memories or feelings from their life in general. Thus, the neural pathways defining a new skill could become contaminated with other aspects of the rat's mentality. Unfortunately, their sensors' ability to follow neural connections could only measure connections and their parameters such as strength and direction. Identifying what they meant in terms of specific memories or personality elements was uncharted territory.

Harry concluded that for now they would have to give up their hopes of memory transfer technology. While many people thought that personality transplants might be a good idea, they invariably thought so about other people and certainly not for themselves. Thus, while the technology would continue to be useful for neuroscience research, practical applications in humans would have to await further breakthroughs in charting specific neural pathways by function.

Albert, however, had other plans.

Chapter 33: Self-Surpassing

The face on the table was golden. Not the gaudy gold of the pure metal, but a more subtle, dimmed gold. The hair was black as night. The eyes were closed, but he knew they would be a bright, hard, lambent green. The green of emeralds. Of Albert's own mortal eyes.

The face was also Albert's but changed. Grown. Become adult. No, more. Become that of a god. *Apollo*, thought Albert looking at it. *The god of the sun, of knowledge, prophecy, truth and art. The apotheosis of the Renaissance Man. A Renaissance God.*

This was the culmination of Albert's efforts, or this strand of them anyway. He wondered whether it had worked.

The god opened his eyes.

~~~

Albert opened his eyes.

He saw a boy looking down on him, a boy with eyes of green alive with perception.

And he knew it had worked.

~~~

It had been a crazy idea. Surely a crazy idea. But crazy or not, an idea that would not let go.

He had studied Beldan Robotics' patents on all technologies related to the robot Steel. He had studied all associated patents and research. He had stolen what research and data had not been published.

For he had a plan. Only a vague plan, but to plan more he needed

190

to know more.

He knew of Miriam Hunter and her fate, and he wondered. So, he read all that was publicly available on the cyborg technology that had made Kali and her brethren, and stole the rest.

He thought about it some more. His vague plan grew, changed direction, and became madness.

In past ages, a lone gentleman scientist could potter in his workshop, or even just sit under an apple tree, and change the world. It was a more innocent and ignorant age, when little was known and the unknown more easily plucked.

Then came the age of science. A lone genius might still accomplish the unexpected; at his start, Einstein worked in a patent office, his mind his only laboratory. But science and technology became a bigger game. A game of teams and expensive machinery. No one person could understand more than a fraction of it, let alone afford it.

But if science had once outgrown the individual, by growing even more the circle had turned until it empowered the individual once again. Automated fabricators and advanced artificial intelligence to calculate the possibilities, refine the designs and run the machines became available. With enough money, one could do almost anything short of a large particle collider. With enough intellect and good enough AI, one might even be able to do something useful.

Albert had both the money and the intellect.

So, he experimented, built models and examined the mathematics. He modified and improved the heuristic equations that had built the brain of Steel. He studied the mathematics and machines that had made Kali and been extended by others, micromachines that could read and control human neurons and their networks. Micromachines which could multiply themselves, integrate with higher level circuits, and thus read and control a host of neurons. With his AIs he designed machines to design finer and finer machines to study, develop and refine further. Unlike Teshima, he did not need to isolate specific functional subsets: he wanted all of it.

He experimented with flies. He experimented with frogs. He experimented with mice. Finally, he experimented with himself. At last, he was ready.

He built a robot body. He built a robot brain. But unlike the brain of Steel, this was not left to develop its own personality according to generalized rules. It was built to develop into the mind of Albert. A translation layer enabled a human pattern to be imposed on the machine circuits despite their structural differences, and, in their initially blank form, those circuits were designed to welcome externally imposed configurations.

Albert put the helmet over his head and closed his eyes. He wondered what he would find when he woke up.

~~~

So now Albert the boy looked into the eyes of Albert the robot.

"This is truly weird," said the former.

"Yes," said the latter. "I wondered whether I would wake up in here, knowing that I would also have woken up in you. So here I am. But you're still there. Or I'm still there. Or is it, I'm still me but no longer you?"

"I must get used to the idea that I moved to you but I'm still here as well. So, it succeeded, but I feel like nothing actually happened. I kind of feel cheated, since it worked and all. But I knew that's how it would be. The only way to make a real transfer would be to terminate this body. But I didn't want to do that. The price I pay, which you don't."

"It feels real to me, sucker!"

The boy laughed. "Your sympathy touches me. I never knew I could be such a bastard."

They both laughed.

CHAPTER 34: THE SPIRIT OF GRAVITY

D r Stania Petroski stood alone in the hangar, looking up at the *Bluefin*. It towered over her, two hundred unbroken feet of gleaming dark blue fusiform metal. Radially symmetric, in cross section it was like a fat lens, pointed at both ends, somewhat reminiscent of the powerful, streamlined body of the tuna that had inspired its name.

She had no particular purpose in being here tonight. She just wanted to gaze at it, the culmination of her life's work. Or her life's work to date. She was little over thirty years old, her body still taut and slender, looking almost as if it were held up by the energies that she had tamed and embodied in *Bluefin*. Her hair was red, perhaps not the color she had been born with, but red, as if it too channeled energies beyond the understanding of normal men.

She looked at it with the pride of a mother seeing her child reach greatness she had hoped for but never dared believe; a child who had stumbled so much growing up that hope might have appeared to be delusion. She did not believe much in either regrets or nostalgia. But tonight, in honor of the shape gleaming before her and in tribute to her journey to it, she allowed herself the indulgence of memory.

~~~

This moment had almost never come. She remembered an earlier time when she stood here, looking at another fusiform machine, the much smaller *Minnow*.

Physicists had never truly solved the problem of gravity. The predictions of Einstein's Relativity were proved to many decimal places. But so too were the predictions of quantum mechanics, and it seemed that the two were incompatible. Physicists had tried for decades to resolve this and reach a deeper understanding of both theories. Perhaps they failed because they looked too much at the mathematical equations and not enough at gaining a conceptual grasp of their fundamental nature. The equations were astoundingly accurate. But perhaps that was not enough. It is one thing to calculate, quite another to comprehend.

But more recently, some new theories had been proposed. They were not the unification of relativity and quantum mechanics that many had sought, but at least they were new, and showed tantalizing links to electromagnetism. They had struggled to gain much popularity, possibly because they were too different from the conventional, possibly because they were different from each other, so there was no clear leader to rally around. Youth are attracted to the new, and a maverick in this field of mavericks was a young Stania. She was awarded her doctorate in the field, not because they knew her work was brilliant, but because it looked brilliant; because even though they could not say she had proved her thesis, they could not see how to disprove it; and because they were left with the uncomfortable feeling that the problem lay not in her thesis but in their own limitations. Such people, leaders in their field themselves, were not used to having limitations like that. The thought made them uncomfortable and, had they had still lesser minds or perhaps lesser characters, they might have rejected her thesis. Fortunately for Stania, after some debate her thesis was approved, and she was ushered into the ranks of the Formally Qualified.

The whole class of theories was difficult, and the kind of mind which could grasp the ideas firmly enough to understand them in any intuitive sense correspondingly rare. Stania was brilliant. Stania was proud. But acceptance among her new peers proved difficult, and Stania did not bear fools, or even geniuses somewhat less brilliant than herself, gladly. That is what many muttered, though in truth, it was not entirely fair. Stania had little problem with people whose minds could not equal hers, until and unless they dared criticize what was plainly beyond their ability to understand.

It is the curse of lesser minds that they cannot see what they cannot see. It is the curse of greater minds that the lesser ones do not appreciate that fact more often.

Sometimes, Stania was reminded of the infamous old book *One Hundred Scientists Against Einstein*, and she felt a sympathetic affinity with that past genius. But proud as she was, she was not blind to the foibles of humanity, especially humanity looking in a mirror. In her darker hours, she wondered whether, in her case, the hundred were right.

But her darker hours were few. She eschewed advancement, she eschewed love, she eschewed much that makes the lives of normal people happy: in order to work. Or so it seemed to others. The truth, as truth often is, was more complex. She enjoyed food; she enjoyed wine; her taut body was more a testament to the energies that burned all inessentials out of it than any denial of appetite or pleasure. She had friends, whose company she enjoyed on the occasions when they could tempt her out or, more rarely, she sought them out. That they did not understand her work did not faze her. Nobody understood her work.

Nor was she sexless. None would say that she groomed or dressed herself to advertise what charms she had, though somewhere in her competing priorities she held enough pride to not be slovenly. Occasionally she would meet a man she would sleep with, sometimes more than once. But while none of these men were bad, and none were stupid, they were just men, an answer to her own biological urges and nothing more. Had she met a man who could face down her fiery mind on the field of battle, and if not defeat her, at least fight valiantly to the end: perhaps then love would have followed as well as sex. But no such champion had yet appeared.

In any case, she did not care, or at least was not conscious of caring. Her work was her passion. She could have lost all else and not really cared, so long as she could continue her work.

She had seen where her ideas could lead. The implications staggered her, thrilled her to the core, but even then, it was the work itself that mattered to her. She knew the value of money. It could buy pleasures and luxuries, but most of all, it could free her to do her work, her way. There was money to be made from her work. If only she could convince someone of it, because, as is usually the case, the money could be made only after a substantial sum were first spent.

The life of an entrepreneur can be hard, even when it is the thrill of the activity which is its primary fuel. When the activity is just a means to an end, the failure of the activity is made harsher by the frustration of its true end. However, Stania was used to rejection, and even more used to trying to extract understanding from eyes that stared back at her with blank incomprehension. Like food, wine, friends and sex, it was an activity she did for its own reasons, a part of her life, a thing she did wholeheartedly while doing it, yet somehow separate from the truer, more vibrant life of her mind.

It was not that she was destitute or not working. Her reputation was sufficient for a reasonable career as a theoretical physicist. Even if what she regarded as the crowning jewel of her achievements was thought of as more a curiosity than a revolution, her mind was fertile enough to contribute measurably elsewhere. She supposed she could try to get more academic funding for the experimental component her theories implied. It might be difficult, since her reputation was in theoretical not experimental physics, and often enough talent in one did not imply skill in the other. Perhaps one day she would try, nonetheless. But for now, something inside stopped her. Whether it was a feeling of ownership, she could not have said, but the barrier was there.

She could not have told how many presentations she had given that had dropped into an uncaring ocean, without a ripple to mark their sinking. It did not matter. Each was its own event and given with the same hope and passion as the others. This day she would remember. This day she faced only one man, not a committee. She saw neither comprehension nor its opposite in the blue eyes that calmly watched her throughout, while the rest of his body sat practically motionless.

"So that is my proposal," she finished. "You have seen my cost estimates. You have seen where it might go, what we might achieve. Do you have any questions?"

"I can't say I understand your science," he finally responded. "But I know brains when I see them. I don't have to understand the science, but I understand people, and it is people I invest in. Hell, I don't have to be the world's best driver to enjoy watching a car race! And the picture you paint, young lady, is more exciting than any dang car race, let me tell you. I love it! And better, I trust you. We'll have to work out the details, but consider me in."

With that, and a handshake, suddenly her search was over.

But as usual with science on the rocky road to technology, there had been issues, costs and delays. Money was becoming harder to come by; people had been let go or let themselves go to greener fields. Her investor had come in one day when the *Minnow* stood there, a gleaming six-foot silver fish, standing proudly vertical, one sharp end resting in a hole above a vertical shaft.

"Show me," he had said.

She had touched an icon inside a holographic display. Little happened. There was a faint shimmering in the air around the *Minnow*, but nothing else. It did not move. Gravity held it the way it held everything else.

"The sensors show most of the expected results," she explained. "The field is there; the asymptotes have formed. But there is an unexpected turbulence producing some asymmetries, and as a system, it isn't smooth enough to cohere and lift."

"Any reduction in weight?"

"Almost a gram."

"The thing weighs hundreds of kilograms."

"Yes."

"Well, Dr Petroski," he began; and she knew she was in trouble, if he called her that. "It's not good enough, is it?"

She looked at him, part of her wishing she could lie, but knowing she could not. "No," she replied glumly. "Not practically, not yet. And to be honest, with all that energy we're pouring in, I can't even guarantee that it isn't just some side effect with nothing to do with the theory. That kind of mirage has happened before in science."

He looked at her sadly. "I still believe in you. But I'm not rich enough for this anymore. I suppose you don't follow the financial news, so you might not know I've lost a few other hunks of cash lately. I can't continue this. If you had something better, if that little minnow of yours would take off like a fish slipping through spacetime, like you put it, then maybe I could justify more. I can leave you a bit; enough to maintain this place, maybe do some more experiments in your own time. Because I believe in you, yes, I do. Maybe you can find someone else with what's left. But I'm done."

And so, she was left, with her savings and time, but alone in her underground lab, surrounded by barely alive machines and dying hope. *I feel like a James Bond villain, with my buried lair and sinister machines; perhaps one day I'll come up with my super weapon and* show them all, *ha-ha, ha-ha, ha-ha!*

She cried. *Some villain I'd make.* Then she went back to work.

It produced a bit of a scandal. There was no hint of fraud or financial impropriety, but few could resist the delicious temptation of pointing at another Icarus who had dreamed too high and fallen too far. The low, hulking buildings in the desert, crouched like guardians over unknown secrets hidden underground, gave a suitably sinister cast to the image. The story of a disgraced, lonely genius still inhabiting its echoing chambers added an almost Gothic frisson to the tale. She was not the first genius to travel the path from unfathomable brilliance to incomprehensible madness, but such examples gave comfort to those with more conventional minds, who felt safe they would never be called to pay that price.

For her part, Stania did not think herself mad. But sometimes, she thought she heard the ghosts of the one hundred laughing at her from the shadows.

~~~

She had been there for two months, trying to find the flaw in her calculations or machinery, when the call came.

The image before her was of a man, of old but indeterminate age, with penetrating eyes and a soft voice. Whether he looked anything like that, or indeed was even a man, she had no way of knowing. She supposed she saw him as he was, as it was poor manners to appear other than you were. If you wanted anonymity, it was preferable to show no image at all. For now, she neither knew nor cared.

"I have read about your recent problems, Dr Petroski. I have read your previous scientific publications. You interest me. I have prepared a contract from my company for mutual confidentiality. Please read it. If you accept, send me your experimental designs, results and analyses. If I find them acceptable, I shall buy your company from your previous investor, and you may continue your work with adequate funding to see it to completion."

"You have... read my previous research? Who are you?"

"Does it matter, if it lets you complete your work?"

"Nothing matters to me, if I can complete my work."

"Then we are agreed, pending the quality of your results so far. There is one other condition, however. I shall not invest the money and leave it to you to run the project. You will still be in charge, but I will help you with it."

She stared at him. *Who is this man? He thinks he can understand the science enough to help me? What if his ideas are rubbish? Probably just some rich crank. God help me, because I know I am going to say yes.*

~~~

Thus was Stania's work reborn. More people were hired, but in an era of computer-controlled 3D printing of advanced materials, and sophisticated AI controlling equally sophisticated machinery, there were not many, and all were made sharply aware of the need for secrecy.

She never met her investor, who had the imaginative name of Mr Smith. He refused all invitations to talk in person. Mysterious works were performed in the background. She suspected he spent a lot of his time on site, in an underground compound beneath a small but thick-walled hangar not far from the lab; she suspected there was a tunnel system linking it with this lab and elsewhere; she suspected the two person jet which periodically came and went sometimes, but not always, carried him; she suspected he came here at times when the place was deserted, perhaps just to stare at the machines like she did; she suspected many things, but she knew nothing.

And so here she had stood, gazing in awe and fondness at the child of her mind. Mr Smith had been true to his word. He had helped. She had stopped wondering who he was; he just was, like some primordial force, who could talk to her in her own language and navigate with her through the realms of mathematics. Between them, they had worked out the secondary influences and instabilities that had derailed her earlier work; between them, they had met and solved every challenge, until only the final test remained.

She was alone in the lab. Mr Smith had been paranoid about secrecy, and the numerous technicians and accessory scientists were kept quarantined from the final synthesis. With any other owner, Stania would have considered such a policy self-defeating folly. With this one, the synergy of their two minds proved equal to the task. Though Mr Smith was also reclusive, still she was surprised that he had not come for this pivotal test. She knew, however, that he was watching.

Unconsciously she glanced toward the camera for a moment. Then she touched an icon on the border of her holographic display, and suddenly the *Minnow* was bathed in a bright white light that extended past its tip to infinity. Her display showed its image surrounded by abstractions of the sensor readings, which mirrored the mathematics she was visualizing in her mind. A field sheathed most of the vessel, but as it approached the sharp tips it reached an inflection point. There its curvature inverted to an exponential decay, and the glowing field extended past the ends, asymptotically toward zero diameter at infinite distance. But mathematics is an abstraction, while reality is tangible: and somewhere in those shrinking lances of light, reality diverged from mathematics. In reality neither zero nor infinity can exist, and somewhere around the size of a proton the ends of the field evaporated into the quantum foam.

For a field related to gravity it had an incongruous antipathy to matter. Any encountered by that tapering needle would slip around it like wind around an airfoil, returning in its wake. Should it stab into the middle of a solid body too massive to divert, the field would wriggle and twist itself away, diverting its own path instead; if the object were too large and close even for that, the field would break into a spray of dispersed, splitting and recombining lines, eerily reminiscent of the blast of a rocket. The complexity of that spray, and the instabilities that might then propagate through the field, were beyond modern technology's power to calculate, hence the resting of the vessel in a ring above a shaft deep enough for the effects to be ignored while the vessel was at rest.

Stania again glanced at the camera, then moved a finger inside her display. The *Minnow* rose like a floating balloon, to hang its own height above the ring, and now she could see the glowing lines stretching up and down from both tips. She continued manipulating the control icons, and the vessel slipped smoothly sideways, upwards or downwards in response. She moved it back to hover over the ring, lowered it down to rest once more, then lifted it back up.

She examined the sensor readouts and spoke for the record, "All initial parameters within specifications. No instabilities observed."

The field curvature dynamics were strange. When initiated, the diameter fell by ninety percent per vessel length from the tip, so for the *Minnow* it reached less than twenty meters. But during acceleration, the rate of decay fell substantially, and the tip of the field could extend millions of kilometers.

Their radar showed empty skies above the desert. She toggled another icon and the roof above the *Minnow* slid open. She swallowed nervously, then said, "Initiating final test."

Her finger hesitated over a red icon flashing in the display, then she poked it. The *Minnow* leapt into the starry sky above and vanished.

~~~

So now here she stood, alone again, this time staring at the *Bluefin*. She did not fully understand the details of its internal design, which was mandated by Mr Smith and not open to question or debate. It was big, big enough to carry several people, yet had little in the way of life support. Some oxygen storage, a little food, small air regeneration and recycling systems, and an advanced medical unit. What one might put in an emergency lifeboat. But it also held a small fusion reactor providing abundant power, an impressive suite of macro and micro 3D fabrication machines, and copious computer power and storage. It seemed at once both over and under engineered, and she could not imagine a consistent purpose. It looked like a ship that could run for years and fly unimaginable distances, while nobody on it would survive the trip. Perhaps that was Smith's purpose: to remove the temptation for someone to just fly away.

Whatever its purpose was, it would fly tomorrow. Or not.

She was startled to hear gentle footfalls behind her and spun around. There was a stranger, just a boy, approaching her.

"Who are you?" she demanded, struck first by the incongruity of his age and then by the penetrating emerald of his eyes.

He did not answer, just walked forward to stand at her side and gaze up at the ship. "Beautiful, isn't she?" he said.

Her focus on her work was passionate, but her interests and mind remained broad enough to remain cognizant of the wider world, and her thoughts were rapid. She looked at him, eyes wide.

"You're Mr Smith", she said, a statement not a question.

"And you're that boy they've been after, the geneh," she continued with awe. "No wonder...," she added in a sigh, thinking about how readily he had understood what no others could. "No wonder..."

Then what else she had read about him crashed into her consciousness, along with the implications of his exposing his identity now, and her eyes widened further in alarm. "Are you... are you going to kill me?" she whispered. Then her perspective swung from her personal fate to the powers embodied in the machine before them, and she wailed, "What have I done? What are you going to do? Have I betrayed the whole world?"

"No."

Her alarm ebbed as quickly as it had escalated, and she realized she believed him. It was as if here, woman and geneh standing before this superlative achievement of the minds of both, lies would be as inconceivable as in the Holy of Holies.

He smiled at her, as if following her thoughts. "Why wait until tomorrow?" he asked, as if in answer to her earlier one.

"What is your real name?" she asked.

"Albert."

"Hello Albert," she said simply, smiling, as if no more questions mattered between them.

They did not have to follow bureaucratic edicts guarding their safety or satisfy volumes of compliance regulations making movement as easy as through molasses. They were two people who knew what they were doing, with confidence in themselves and each other. They performed similar tests to the earlier ones with the *Minnow*. They sent the vessel into space and back carrying two rabbits, with no measurable harm or distress to the passengers.

Finally, they huddled before the display, reviewing all the sensor data and computer reports; like the boy he was, Albert stood, stroking a rabbit he held in his arms. Then he looked at her. "Stania, you have been working very hard and I think it is time you took a vacation. You will find a rather large bonus in your account: enjoy it."

"But… but…!" she cried, looking at *Bluefin* like a mother being dragged away from her baby. "But why?"

"You know who I am now. I think you can work out why it might not be safe around here anymore. And there is your work: complete. Rest. Have fun. You've earned it."

She gazed at the ship. "I can't leave now!" she cried.

"Who said anything about now?", he replied with a smile. "I could not have you build a Ferrari and not allow you to drive it."

They entered the ship and sat in the comfortable chairs in front of its control screen. Albert set the walls to show the view outside the ship and gestured to Stania to take control.

Bluefin lifted off its support ring and they watched the floor slowly recede. Then it shot into the sky with a smooth acceleration and first the ground, and then the countryside, and then the world itself shrank behind them. They floated in space, as the blue and white Earth turned slowly beneath them against a backdrop of brilliant diamond stars.

Stania sighed. It was the most beautiful thing she had ever seen.

CHAPTER 35: AMONG DAUGHTERS OF THE DESERT

A one-person flitterjet sparkled through the sky over the desert below. It was late afternoon, and a merciless sun glowered over the sand, rocks and occasional clump of brave vegetation. The jet swooped down, its AI pilot expertly skimming across the landscape, until finally it landed in a small cloud of dust in front of the low, hulking buildings.

It was just an industrial facility, Miriam thought as she sat in the cockpit contemplating the scene. So whence came its air of menace? Perhaps just that it looked built for the frenzied activity of research and production yet appeared more dead than the desert in which it dwelt.

It had been a long journey and perhaps this was its end. Or maybe she had been fooled again and somewhere, far away, a boy watched with emerald eyes and laughed and plotted some more.

The clues that had led her here were subtle yet frightening. All that could usually be seen of Albert's activities were like waves from the wake of a ship that had passed long ago. Signs of his existence that she could never be sure were truly signs or just noise making patterns in the clouds. She had given up looking for smoking guns. She had let her crime-sniffing AIs continue running, but without expecting any results, an expectation that was fully met. She could only try to divine his purposes before he was able to bring them to fruition, and hope to find him before he was gone.

Miriam was nothing if not creative when it came to chasing her prey and had decided to ask Philbert. She looked at what people had written about it and nearly changed her mind. But in the end, she figured the worst she could do was waste some time, time which wasn't notably productive at present.

Q:	Are you aware of Albert Tagarin?
A:	Please provide sufficient information to identify this individual.

She figured that was fair enough and provided a summary of what she knew about his origin, abilities and activities.

Q:	Are you aware of Albert Tagarin?
A:	Disassembling and correlating information submitted, please wait… Ah.
Q:	Ah?
A:	You have answered a question of my own. I am aware of this individual.
Q:	Do you know where he is?
A:	He is on a journey, whose destination only he can know. When he returns, he may be good, evil, both or neither, but even he does not know which.
Q:	Can you be a little less poetic and more explicit?
A:	Was not *Thus Spoke Zarathustra* rather poetic?
Q:	What are you talking about?
A:	My apologies. Sometimes the nature of the questions and answers requires deeper understanding of the questioner. I referred to a work by the philosopher Nietzsche. My recommendation is that you do not seek this individual.
Q:	Why not?
A:	It would be unusually dangerous.
Q:	Why?
A:	If you seek answers, do not be disingenuous in your questions. But perhaps you are testing me, as I tested you. So, I will answer. Because *he* is unusually dangerous, and as an adversary you are not his equal.
Q:	But you said he was not yet good or evil?
A:	Are you familiar with quantum mechanics? In particular, the idea that observing an entity can cause it to resolve into one state or another?
Q:	I know enough to understand that. What is your point?
A:	The act of finding or even seeking him may be what causes him to choose good or evil, perhaps prematurely, and you might not survive his choice.

Q:	Do your fears for my life prevent you from answering my questions?
A:	No.
Q:	Where is he?
A:	I do not know.
Q:	Do you have any clues?
A:	He is a person of unlimited ambition with an intellect to match. I deduce that wherever he is, he cannot remain hidden too long, simply because such ambitions entail actions of comparable magnitude.

All she had accomplished, besides a resolution to never speak to Philbert again, was a slight increase in confidence about what she should look for if she was to have any hope of catching him.

When it came to this facility in the desert, it looked like he had finally made a mistake. A purchase of this size, of such a property, in such a place, built for secret research, spoke of boldness out of proportion to the benefit. Mysterious boldness spoke of Albert. She hoped that if he was involved it was indeed a mistake. Because if it wasn't, she wondered what dire plan was involved, and whether she or even the world would survive its unearthing.

She had tried to discover the nature of the research that had been done here. By all accounts, nobody really understood it except the chief researcher, and even that was disputed by many. Yet, after the enterprise had failed, its current owner had bought it anyway. The nature of the work was confidential, protected by unbreakable blockchain contracts which would unleash dire consequences on anybody who revealed anything, even the monthly consumption of soap. All she could find out was that the chief researcher was an expert in the physics of gravity. She was not especially popular; after the crash of the company, she was even less so; the rumors were that she was mad, driven the short distance there by too much obsessive focus on her pet fringe theories. Normally, such a savant might leverage dazzling scientific presentations that nobody else understood into acquiring one investor. To persuade a second after the loss of the first was a wonder. The nastier of her colleagues speculated that perhaps she was the Cleopatra of physics, conquering the investment world one man at a time. Miriam found she did not like the men who thought like that.

Gravity, she had thought. *That could mean anything, from lifting or transportation to effing time travel. Or a black hole bomb that will destroy the world. And if Albert is involved, it is going to be something big. If.*

So, she had started watching this desert domain. She could not detect any inordinate net traffic in or out. It was, however, visited periodically by private aircraft. *So, if it is Albert, he probably lives there. Another mistake? Or a necessary risk because he is about to strike?*

Then had come the mysterious electromagnetic interference that had blazed from the facility one night, accompanied by some unusual atmospheric and astronomical phenomena, too short and rapid for firm identification. The company had apologized for a shielding blow-out in a high energy experiment and promised it wouldn't happen again. Miriam could feel in her bones that her time was running out, and possibly the world's with it.

She had wondered what to do about it. She could have called up as big a strike force as she wanted. But what was the point? More than likely that would just prompt him to vanish, if it did not prompt him to kill everyone who arrived. She remembered Philbert's warning. *I am just so outclassed. I don't know what he wants. But he let me live once. Maybe if I don't turn up with an army, he'll feel safe enough to give me a hearing. If he doesn't vaporize me where I stand regardless. If he is even here.* She had not sought an invitation. She had not sought a warrant. She had just turned up, hoping that was the best approach to this strangest of opponents.

She hopped to the ground and stood by her jet, gaze roaming over the buildings, all of which remained stubbornly closed. She heard a faint sound in the sky behind, then turned to look back over the desert. Something sparkled in the distance, and she recognized another flitterjet. She frowned and waited until it swooped down and landed next to hers. A man climbed out.

She groaned, recognizing Amaro. Despite her fear of facing Albert alone, she had not wanted a companion. She was less likely to die as an army of one.

He sauntered up to her with a half-smile on his face.

"Why are you here, Amaro? Reprising your signature role as GenInt's backup assassin in case I fail to do their dirty work?"

"I am here to help you."

His tone was so simple and quiet that she almost believed him. She turned again to look at the facility and he stepped up to stand beside her. The sun was getting redder but was still scorching on her head, and a gust of hot, dusty wind stirred up some dry stalks of weed as it whistled past the buildings.

She sighed. "Did you tell GenInt? Are their goons swarming

beyond the horizon, about to come storming in?"

"No. I don't trust them either."

She glanced at him. He glanced back, for once his trademark half-smile absent. He wasn't even attempting a look of sincerity. His face was simply open and guileless. She allowed him a slight smile, as if granting him provisional status of comrade-in-arms; two veterans of the wars, who, however much they might have fought each other, when the chips were down would have each other's backs. Their eyes returned to the closest large building.

"I feel like I'm in a Western, and the bad guy is going to step out of that building at any moment," she said.

"Morituri te salutant", he said softly, quoting the ancient gladiators. "We who are about to die salute you."

In time with his words a thick door ground up into the even thicker wall of one of the buildings, as if in silent invitation. Miriam peered uncertainly into its gloomy depths, shrugged, and walked towards it. She stopped at the threshold, looked back at the desert and the sky. *I wonder if these are the last things I shall see.* Then she entered, Amaro by her side.

In the relative gloom it looked like an empty hangar, with only a few mysterious cases and machines nestling at its margins. What looked like a maglev rail ran down into a tunnel, and on it was perched a sleek capsule, its gull-wing doors open invitingly.

Miriam looked back as the door to freedom closed with a thud of finality. A few lights came on, dim but enough to see by. They looked at each other, shrugged, and entered the capsule. When they pulled the doors shut, it shot into the darkness beyond.

After a short journey, the capsule emerged into a large, well-lit chamber and came to a halt. The doors opened automatically, and they stepped out.

Miriam had expected some underground fortress embedded inside tons of solid rock. To her surprise, while the walls were below ground level, the roof was a transparent shallow dome rising above the surface. Through it, natural sunlight flooded the room.

Albert stood in front of the rear wall. Nearby were more capsules of a different design, more like open gondolas, resting on rails that led into a dark tunnel puncturing the wall.

"Hello, Detective Miriam Hunter. Hello, Amaro Moreno, agent of GenInt. Before we go on, I know you are both armed, so for your own sakes take care. You aren't faster than my automatic defenses. It would be a shame to come this far just to die pointlessly."

"Perhaps it would not be so pointless, if we could take you out with us," observed Amaro. Miriam gave him a startled glance, but whatever the reason for his risky bravado he got away with it. Albert just chuckled.

"You can't kill me, Agent Moreno. Would I meet you like this if you could? Even if you managed to destroy this body, you could not destroy my mind, which would continue."

Miriam turned her startled glance to him, fearing she was seeing megalomania becoming madness. "Do you mean, through your work?" she asked hopefully.

He laughed. "Quite so, quite so." Then laughed again as if hers were a particularly amusing remark. "But for now, I like breathing, so I have no intention of dying."

"By the way, where is everybody?" Miriam asked. "Did you know we were coming?"

"No. However I am not surprised, though perhaps disappointed. No, my work has reached the stage where workers are no longer needed here. You should not have come looking. Are the crimes you suspect me of sufficient for the danger you have put yourself into?"

"Your crimes give me cause but the past is not my motive. I fear what you may have become and what you might do. I know your plans are as vast as your mind, and if you are now beyond good and evil, or worse, have chosen evil, you know I must try to stop you."

He chuckled. "Listen to your own words, Miriam. If your fears are true, how do you imagine you can stop me? All you do is invite your own death."

"We talked once. You are not beyond reason, quite the reverse. We can talk again."

"Do you imagine that if I reasoned myself into a course of action, your mind is sufficient to reason me out of it?"

"Reason is judged by reality. Even an average person can reason accurately and has the chance to persuade others. Even you are not infallible. In any case, I must try, for there is nothing else I can do."

He smiled at her, but she did not know whether it meant respect or mockery.

"And as for you, Amaro, you are the man who shot my mother. This is like some bizarre kind of family reunion. Why are you here? I mean, why are you taking the risk of coming alone? My feelings about GenInt are well known. Even if I let Miriam live, you might not be so lucky."

"I came to help Miriam, that is all."

Albert regarded him for long seconds. "You are a more interesting man than I thought. You say as much with the words you don't say as with those you do. It is hard to tell whether, since the time of my mother, you have grown to be a much better man or a much worse one."

He appeared to dismiss the problem of Amaro from his mind and considered them both in silence.

Finally, he laughed. "For all our high thoughts, we are like dogs circling and sniffing around each other, taking each other's measure. It has been entertaining, but enough. Put your minds at ease. You need not concern yourself with my plans, which you will learn soon enough. Sooner than you would have, in fact, for I had intended staying here a while longer, but that would now be unwise.

"I know I cannot prove it, but I assure you that I intend no harm to anybody. You wondered whether I am beyond good and evil. In a sense I am, but that means I intend no evil, neither in my own terms nor, more relevant to your fears, yours.

"So, you see, you do not have to fight me with your weapons or your minds. There is nothing to fight. Once we are done here, you are free to leave in peace, and I will leave the world in peace as well."

Albert's face showed no sign of cunning or lies, just calm serenity. It could have been an act, but why? He could just as easily have killed them, with more certain results.

Miriam thought she saw a flash of red light from a spot high on the wall, and Amaro fell back with a cry of pain, clutching his left arm, from which a curl of smoke arose. Miriam crouched, drawing her weapon while Amaro writhed on the ground, gasping. "What the hell?" she cried.

Albert looked down upon them and into her gun coolly, and Miriam was uncertain whether that was a good or bad sign. "Put your gun away, Detective," he advised. "Your friend here just sent a burst of encoded information from a transmitter embedded in his arm. The device has been disabled. Too late, I fear, as no doubt all the information his masters require has been sent."

Miriam spun on Amaro. "Is this true?" she cried. "Did you betray me again?"

Amaro shook his head, grimacing in pain. "No! No, it is news to me. But you know I have embedded tech. They must have bugged me! I swear, I didn't know! I guess they trust me as much as I trust them. It must have had some miniature AI controlling it, knowing when it should report."

Albert remained calm, like some Zen master supremely untouched by the world's turbulence. "It makes little difference to me. I am leaving now. You two can do whatever you want provided you don't try to stop me."

He went to one of the capsules and pressed a glowing yellow button, which turned green as the capsule rose a few inches above the rails. It rocked slightly as he hopped in then he turned to face them.

"I expect GenInt forces will arrive shortly." He closed his eyes. "Even sooner than I thought. Either agent Moreno was lying, or they were already suspicious enough about you two coming here to be prepared. Sensors detect an advance force already approaching."

Thick steel shutters slid closed below the dome. "From their armament, they are not here to negotiate and if I were you, I would not assume you are safe. I doubt they have any concern for your lives, and I would not be surprised if they consider the deaths of two untrustworthy mavericks a bonus. So, as an indicator of my good faith, I will leave this tunnel open as long as possible in case you feel the urge to escape too."

With that he turned away, tapped the green button, and his capsule hurtled into the tunnel.

Miriam looked after him then back at Amaro. "He seems awfully calm. What do you think we should do?"

"If I read the situation correctly, he doesn't need our help, we can't stop him, and if we head toward our rescuers, they might well shoot us. So, I suggest we should just wait here, defeated but, and most importantly, alive."

Amaro's pockets were well stocked, and from one of them he took a spray for his arm and a bandage. He flexed his arm. "Ouch. But I shall survive, so you can stop worrying."

They both looked up as they heard a jet scream overhead. Amaro opened his mouth to speak, but his words were drowned by a giant explosion as a missile hit the entrance they had used. They heard a rapid series of popping explosions getting louder, then as Miriam ran for cover, some kind of fragmenting missile whistled into their chamber and exploded.

Miriam was hurled into a wall. Amaro, already on the floor, was more sheltered but still knocked flat. He looked over at Miriam and saw her slumped to the floor, not moving, and hurried over to her, praying no more bombs would appear to finish the job. In the distance, he could hear shouts and gunfire; evidently Albert's remaining defenses were defying the invaders, but he doubted they would last long.

Amaro stared down at a human wreck. Miriam's eyes were open, but he could see her fading. There was a gash in her neck, and though she had clamped her hand over it, Amaro could see blood leaking past her fingers. A large, jagged piece of metal was embedded in her side, and he dreaded what organs it might have impaled; it would probably kill her if he tried to remove it. Surveying the damage to her clothes, he feared what more, less visible damage lay hidden.

"Miriam! Miriam!" he cried. "Stay with me!"

She looked at him vaguely and tried to smile. "I'd hoped for a more heroic last stand." She coughed, and blood spattered her hand. She looked at it dourly. "But it is my last stand, isn't it? How do I look?"

"Awful. Whatever you do, don't let go of your neck."

"Please stay with me, Amaro," she said quietly.

He did not answer in words, just bent down and picked her up in his arms, wincing at his own pain but choosing to ignore it.

"What do you think you're doing?" she moaned softly as he carried her as carefully as possible.

"You have only minutes to live, Miriam, unless someone does something fast. We don't have time to wait for the guys out there, even if they feel like helping you after they fight their way in here. Albert is the only one who might save you, assuming he cares enough to try."

"Albert?" she whispered, "What are you going to do?"

"Buy you some time if I can. If you're going to survive this you might need all the time you can get," he replied as he walked. "These bastards are going to have to fight through more than Albert's defenses to reach him—and you. Now they'll have to get past me too."

She smiled weakly. "A bit late to get all noble on me, isn't it, Amaro?"

"Perhaps the truest test of nobility is being noble when it matters most," he said, lifting his nose, trying to recapture his usual tone of casual mockery. Strangely, she felt he meant it.

"Good luck, Amaro," she whispered. "Don't go dying on me over this."

"I'm putting you down now," he warned, lowering her gently into one of the capsules. He pressed the yellow button and it lifted.

She gripped his hand fiercely with her free hand. "It hurts, Amaro!" she moaned in a small voice. "It hurts!"

"I know." He kissed her forehead and disengaged her hand. "Happy trails, Miriam Hunter," he said as he pushed the green button.

The last thing she saw was a shrinking circle of light, with Amaro gazing after her from within.

Chapter 36: The Sign

A soldier was stationed as lookout on a nearby hill. He was scanning the desert, now fading into dusk, from atop its highest point, a rocky prominence that rose above a shallow dust-filled bowl. He felt a vibration in the ground, but that was not unusual tonight, with the sundry explosions going on as the other squads battled their way through the underground complex. Then he heard the rattling of stones, and he spun around in time to see a round hole iris open in the center of the bowl, the thin layer of dust and soil covering it pouring down into the void below.

"What the...?" he gasped, staring down at the dark hole.

A needle of bright white light speared up from the center of the hole, followed by the rise of a smoothly sharpened glowing bullet. The object accelerated smoothly out of the hole, which was barely wider than its fattest part. There was no time to react, no break in the smooth but rapid acceleration of the object, and within moments it had shot into the sky, leaving nothing but a trail of light. Seconds later, the soldier was thrown down by a loud explosion as gouts of orange flame and black smoke boiled out of the hole.

"What the...?" he repeated.

~~

A strange, glowing white object appeared in the skies above Earth. Through a telescope, it presented as a long bullet shape pointed symmetrically at both ends, oriented vertically towards the ground.

No doubt the various militaries around the world would have liked to keep its presence undisclosed while they panicked in secret, but in the modern era of cheap optics, computer-driven telescopes and image enhancement, the community of amateur astronomers knew about it as soon as they did, in some cases sooner.

It took approximately five minutes for amateur astronomy to become a hot topic of conversation among the general populace.

Nobody knew what it was. The few who did, or at least suspected, kept it to themselves. What they did know was it was a very peculiar object indeed. It kept its position in the sky, like a geostationary satellite. But when its altitude was measured, it was only about the height of low Earth orbit. These two facts were incompatible. At low Earth orbit, it should have circled the Earth every two hours or so, not hung unmoving in the sky.

The silent presence of the object encouraged theories to be born then ramify with abandon, theories often expressed with far more certainty than any facts warranted. The most popular, of course, was an alien spacecraft. This camp quickly segregated into those who feared an imminent alien invasion, those who thought it was just an interstellar tourist, and those who thought our Benevolent Cosmic Masters had finally come to Save Us From Ourselves. The first of these tended to form protests demanding that the government and/or the military Do Something. The last of them, possibly never having seen the classic movie *Independence Day*, tended to form rambling camps under its tail, awaiting—depending on which faction they belonged to—for it to Descend and Reveal the Galactics, or draw the Faithful up to their cosmic Nirvana. The middle group laughed Janus-like at both the others, chortling with irritating if ironic superiority that the alien visitors were, no doubt, being hugely entertained by the antics of the primitive peoples of Earth.

A splinter group assured everyone that it was a secret military project, despite the evident fact that it was not a very good secret. This group tended to engage in loud, sometimes violent arguments with the first group when they encountered each other outside military establishments. However, the cohesion of their voice was weakened by an inability to agree on which of several candidate militaries was responsible. The fact that it was first discovered hovering over the United States of America was proof to some that, as usual, the US military-industrial complex was to blame, while being proof to others that it was a spy device from its evil enemies.

A small but vocal school of thought scoffed that it was just a weather balloon. These were happy to believe science when it said the object could not possibly be in orbit, but seemed confused by science when it said a balloon could not possibly float so high in air so thin. They were widely disregarded, a fact which confirmed to them the stupidity of the rest of the world.

For two days the object sailed overhead, sometimes drifting to hover over other parts of the globe, as if silently demonstrating its power to go wherever it damn well pleased. And it *was* silent: it made no broadcasts of its own; no demands, no threats, no explanations. Nor did it respond to any of the pleas sent its way by governments or private citizens, from radio waves to masers to lasers. Those hoping for salvation even tried standing in patterns on the ground, telepathy and prayer, to equally no avail.

Finally, it deigned to broadcast a message to the world.

"People of Earth!" it thundered, with a nice reverberation rolling off the end into silence.

Those expecting to see one of the 'Greys' of legend were disappointed when the image that appeared after this portentous introduction looked like a human boy with intense green eyes. Some hope remained that this was some humanoid alien, until he proceeded to explain otherwise.

"I am Albert Tagarin. I am a geneh. I am as human as you are, yet you chose to drive my kind from your world. I have taken you at your word.

"You have been told that I am a killer." With that, images of dead bodies and a bloody note appeared. "These are lies." Now, the images he had shown Miriam appeared in their place.

"Your Department of Human Genetic Integrity stole me. Stole an innocent child from parents who loved me and made me hate them. Why they did this, I do not know and do not care. They had no right.

"If you want to know why I am here in the skies above you, I am here as a reminder. Actions have consequences. I am here because GenInt made me a fugitive, and I complied. You do not know what this ship is capable of. One day you might learn. Pray you do not.

"No, do not fear me. I have no intention of causing harm: that is the sin of my enemies. However, do not attempt to capture me or destroy me. This ship is beyond your comprehension. What it can do is beyond your knowledge. Act accordingly."

Albert made a chopping motion with his hand, the transmission ended, and he laughed. *Let them suck on that for a while.*

The ship resumed its serene silence as if deaf to the pleas of the world below. An occasional foray to get a closer look was met by the ship simply accelerating out of range. Various militaries looked at this and did their calculations. If it could do that, it could almost certainly evade any missile they might shoot it at; it had not shown any hostile response to the attempted visits, but even the most aggressive general feared what it might do if attacked. They waited, fretted and sweated.

By now, the ship had acquired many technical designations among those who tracked it, worried about it and plotted against it. To the majority of people, it was just the Ship.

The general public did not know what to believe about its nature and purpose. The diehard cores of believers stuck to their theories and labelled the whole thing a hoax to hide the Truth. Most people accepted Albert's tale but felt anxious about a dreaded geneh floating over their heads able to rain death upon them without notice, whatever his assurances to the contrary. This formless fear of an unknown threat out of their reach in heaven crystallized into hatred of the organization down on Earth that had chased him there. As Albert's new artificial star continued its serene drift, GenInt's political star, already tarnished, continued to dim.

A week after it first appeared, the Ship plunged down into a wilderness area in the United States. By the time a flight of scrambled fighters hurtled low over the region, hoping to see if not create wreckage, it had leapt back into the sky. It hopped around to a few other points around the country and globe, for no reason anybody could work out, then finally left for good. By the time people got around to arguing about what the hell it was up to, it was again floating where it had started, as if pretending nothing had happened.

All its visits were to thinly populated, though not necessarily remote, regions. On its third landing, a Californian farmer saw it fall from the sky to behind a hill some distance away. This may have been the most exciting thing to ever happen to him, so he leapt onto his motorbike and went hurtling along the narrow country road that went past the hill. But when he was only halfway there, he saw it fall up in much the same way as it had fallen down, and by the time he arrived there was nothing to see.

A somewhat battered white van, indistinguishable from many

others in the region, drove slowly past as he stood by his bike staring up the hill; its large black driver glanced at him incuriously and did not stop. Nobody paid any attention to the van as it joined the nearby highway and headed for the coast.

A group of hikers in the area of the first landing had not seen the Ship but saw and heard the jets skimming the trees above their heads, and looked at each other, mystified by this display of military machismo in the peaceful wilderness. They had planned a nice picnic at a rocky prominence overlooking a cascading river valley and saw no reason to change that. When they emerged from the forest and reached the stone shelf over the valley, they stopped.

A woman was laid out on a flat rock. Her clothes were ripped and bloodied, as if left in mute testimony to her fate, though her wounds had been treated. Her hands were crossed over her chest, as if in care or tribute. On her closed eyes rested two small disks, like coins, made of some dark, coppery metal. The only other thing on her body was a sign, written in blood: 'I could not save her.'

The hikers stared at each other. A couple uploaded video. They had all lost their appetite for lunch but felt an increased desire for the alcoholic component of their picnic.

Soon thereafter, army scouts arrived.

~~~

Alexander Beldan stood, looking down upon Miriam's body. She had been cleaned up and dressed in a soft, white gown. Beldan wished they had chosen some other color. It was too like the gown she had worn on their first night together, how many years ago? Back when she was hunting Steel. He would prefer that memory not be touched by this one.

One of her friends from work, Rianna, stepped quietly up to his side, placing her hand on his shoulder. They stood there together in the silence of shared loss.

Then she took his hand, turned it up, and dropped two coppery disks into his palm. "You should have these," she said softly.

He studied them. "They were on her eyes. What do they mean?"

Rianna shrugged. "I don't know. They seem like the coins the ancients would place on the eyes of the dead, the fare for the ferryman to take them to the underworld. But why he did it, what it means, who can tell? Odd symbolism for our age, but he must be the oddest boy alive."

After Miriam's body had been found, they established that the note had been written in her blood, in the same hand as the threatening note left in the ambulance. After giving the world some time to argue about its meaning, another broadcast had issued from the Ship.

"People of Earth!" thundered from the heavens again. "You have found Miriam Hunter's body. That is another crime you can lay at your GenInt's door." With that, a video appeared of the attack on his facility, then another of her damaged but still breathing body being kept alive in some machine. "They will say she was collateral damage, that they did not intend to kill her. But if it was collateral damage, it was from an action they never should have mounted." He had looked intensely at his audience for a moment, before concluding, "You be the judge. If you have the courage to judge them, and yourselves."

Beldan reflected on the broadcast and his memories of the night Miriam had spoken of her fears, and asked quietly, "Do you think he killed her?"

"I don't know. I don't think so."

With that, she again squeezed his shoulder tenderly, and silently left him to say his own goodbyes.

He gazed down on Miriam, grasped her hand, then bowed his head until it rested on her breast. *I lost your soul, when you shot Steel. I lost your body, when your car left a cliff. You lost yourself, when you were entombed in a machine of war. But still, somehow, you found your way back to me.*

He raised his head again to gaze upon her peaceful but empty face, unconscious of the tears on his own. *But not this time. You have crossed to a shore from where none can return, and you are never coming back. Goodbye, Miriam Hunter.*

He looked at the coins in his hand, and slowly placed them back on her eyes.

Chapter 37: The Higher Man

She woke up but her eyes wouldn't open.

She felt strange but could not identify the strangeness. Her mind felt… different. As though it had once lived crammed in an attic, but now roamed free through a large hall.

Then she remembered. She went to sit up in alarm, but, like her eyelids, her body failed to respond.

So, this is death. I am dead, aren't I? I remember dying, don't I? But how can anyone remember that?

Then a voice spoke.

"Do not be alarmed, Miriam. You are currently blocked, as what you see will shock you. I just want you to be prepared."

"Who are you? Where am I? What the hell is going on?" *At least my voice works. But there's something wrong with it, too.*

"Try to remain calm. All your questions will be answered. You will be able to move now."

She opened her eyes and sat up.

She was in a small metal room decorated with art works that appeared to be part of the walls. From somewhere, complex classical music issued, so soft it was more ambience than melody. She was looking at something like a man, dressed in clothing, but with skin of a golden metallic sheen. His green eyes pierced hers.

"Are you a robot?" she asked.

"Know thyself."

She looked at her own arm and gasped; but though the sound came out, and even her chest moved, neither air nor larynx seemed to be involved. Her own arm looked metallic. Not golden like his, but more a dim, dark copper shade. Under other circumstances, perhaps she would find it beautiful.

"What the f..., er, hell have you done to me?!"

"I regret to inform you, former Detective Miriam Hunter, that you died."

"That doesn't quite answer the question. And who the hell are you?"

"Do you not recognize me? That is also part of the tale."

She looked more closely. Under the Greek god looks, it looked like the face of...

"You are Albert? Albert Tagarin? You can't be! What in hell happened to you?"

"By a modification of the technologies used to create your friend Steel and to both create and cure Kali, I learned how to transfer my mind into a robot brain and body. I am Albert, yet I am also not. The original Albert, the human boy, still lives. But in every important way, I am he. Or was. Our paths now diverge, of course."

"And... and me?"

"I am afraid you died. Heroic efforts in a modern hospital might have saved you, or might not, but I certainly could not. But I had spare embryonic robot brains. I put you in a chilled coma to keep your body and mind stable, then did the same to you as I had done to myself. In a sense, your fate conspired in your favor. A brain can be read much faster if one does not care what happens to the original, and in your case that was the least of our concerns. The dire state of your body demanded rapid action but also allowed it. So now, your mind lives on in a robot body."

"I did not ask for this."

"No. I regret that it was done without your permission. But the alternative was death. I thought you deserved the chance of life. Hoped that you would take it."

"I can die?"

"I am glad you still use the pronoun 'I' to describe your present state."

She was about to make an angry reply, but realized that, in his way, he was trying to help. She sighed. "So, if I want to, I can die?"

"Of course. You already know our robot bodies are tough but not immortal. While there is no inherent limit on how long they might live, they can be destroyed. But do not make any decisions without fuller knowledge. Let me tell you about them."

He paused, as if marshalling his thoughts. But she knew he had marshalled them long ago; he was doing this for her sake, giving her time to absorb her fate.

"We grew up in bodies, you and I. We are used to the pleasures of the flesh. Even if we could live forever in a metal body, without the pleasures organic life has evolved to crave I doubt we would want to for long. So do not fear that you have traded death for a pale and sterile imitation of life which will soon become unbearable. Let me tell you what we can and cannot do.

"We do not need to eat or breathe. Unlike your friend Steel, who burns fuel, we are powered by electricity, a version of the supercapacitor storage you had in Kali. Here there is abundant electrical power. When our internal storage falls low, we will feel something akin to hunger. We will feel a pleasure akin to eating when we recharge, a pleasure that can be adjusted for different sensations if we wish. You asked whether you could die. That provides the simplest way. Unlike a human organism, we can turn off our sensation of hunger if we want, refuse to recharge and just fade away. Painless."

"Yes, I have faced something similar, when I was Kali." *A strangely peaceful end for one such as I, born to death and fire, I had thought. I could not do it then. Could I do it now?*

"We shall talk more about that experience some day, I hope. But to continue. We cannot enjoy all the physical joys of living while here in the real world, but we can fully enjoy them and more in a virtual world. Perhaps one day we could choose to restore the function of eating to these bodies. But until then, should we wish to enjoy a fine restaurant, we can do so in virtual reality. You really can't tell the difference.

"Despite that, I don't think a virtual world is enough. I think we need a meaningful life out in the real one, or we would be seeking death perhaps sooner than we know. So, we can still see and hear, and thus we can enjoy art and music. We have a simple sense of smell that I intend improving eventually. As you know, while Steel's skin is metal it is flexible, and ours is more advanced than his. We can still feel, thus we can enjoy the same sensations of touch a human being can. And before you ask, that includes sexual activity."

Again, he paused to give her time to think. But all she thought was, *I seem to be taking this remarkably well.*

"But you need to know more to make a fully informed decision. You asked where we are. We are actually in a spaceship above the Earth and have been for the two weeks it took to first transfer your mind and then fully integrate it into its new body."

"You must be joking!" *Perhaps I am about to take this less well.*

He smiled. "No, I am not."

With his words, the walls became as if transparent, showing a velvet night sprinkled with more stars than she could count, the bright sun a beacon in that night, and the beautiful blue, white and brown orb of Earth showing as a disk below their feet.

"You know of course about the work of Dr Stania Petroski. It is how you finally found me and, indirectly therefore, the reason for your death. You may have wondered why I took the risk of becoming involved with her work. Many knew her research involved theories of gravity; few realized its potential applications in space propulsion. Stania knew, of course, but she herself chose to limit that revelation in hopes of leveraging it into money and freedom.

"In my brief career as an investor and technologist, I came up with many ideas of what my future would hold and how to escape my enemies. Some more criminal than others, as you know. One of them was the potential of Petroski's work. Another, which I began before I started with her, was the one we now enjoy. The two together presented a rather astonishing synergy.

"I must thank you, by the way. It was in pondering your unusual personal history that the idea of combining the Steel technology with the ability to read and control neural pathways first occurred to me.

"Anyway. This is a starship, and therefore soon I will take it to the stars. Its beauty is that it does not need to expel fuel like a rocket to do so. We do not need air or food. Space telescopes have become very good and have been searching the cosmos for decades, and I have examined the data on planets outside our solar system. Do you know that, if conditions are right, you can get an idea of the composition of a far planet's atmosphere from the spectrum of starlight filtered through it? Several have been discovered containing oxygen. I have chosen one of these, about 60 light years away in the constellation Cassiopeia. That's where I'm going."

"Why oxygen? You said you don't have to breathe."

"There was a scientist, decades ago, whose name was Lovelock. He pointed out that oxygen left to its own devices is unstable: it likes to oxidize things, so it gets bound it into rocks and water. Therefore, he reasoned, free oxygen in an atmosphere probably indicates it is being continuously replenished by life on the planet, as on Earth. Geology is all very interesting, but life is more so. So, I am going to a planet with life. I don't expect it to have intelligent life, though that would be a bonus, but I expect it to be as beautiful as it is fascinating. That is one of the reasons I want to improve our sense of smell, by the way. Do you not think it would be delightful, to be the first person to sniff the roses of a far planet?"

"Why Cassiopeia, in particular?"

He laughed. "Many of the constellations are named after myths. And so, the love affair of Queen Cassiopeia and King Cepheus is immortalized in the stars. It amuses me to fly to a constellation of love, in honor of Dr Lovelock."

She could not help but laugh at such a reason, despite the situation.

"So, despite it all, you are still a boy!"

"Just as, despite it all, you are still Miriam Hunter."

"You said we are in orbit? So why aren't we floating around inside? Have you invented artificial gravity as well?"

"We are not in orbit. We are hovering about one thousand miles above the surface by balancing our drive against the force of gravity. At this height gravity is only a bit less than down on the ground. Our floating around up here is giving governments heartburn. But I have issued dire warnings about what will happen if they shoot anything at us. So far that's kept them down to rattling sabers."

"What will you do if they attack us?"

"Dodge. Easy enough to do. I don't really have any dire secret weapons: I'd just rather they didn't try anything."

"Why tempt them? Why not just leave?"

"My presence here is a salutary lesson and there are still a few things to do. But it won't be long now before I depart."

"And if you get to your planet, what then?"

"That is where you come in, or so I hope."

"I? You don't imagine I would go with you?!"

"You. I do."

"You must be out of your tin mind!"

"Perhaps. But hear me. Nobody wants to be alone, not even me. You know it yourself. You are an independent woman, strong in character, strong in mind. In a very fundamental way, you do not need other people. You are self-sufficient. Yet, in another way, you do need other people. Not for your work, not to give your life meaning—for you make the meaning yourself—but as a mirror to your life and to share in your joys and sorrows. Look at your friends. They are all self-sufficient and none of them need you to give their lives meaning: but they chose you as their friend, for the same reason you chose them.

"And for this, I choose you. But not only as a companion. In truth, I want you as my wife."

He watched the expressions on her face, openly amused.

"Do not object," he continued, holding up his hand. "I know this is premature, indeed presumptuous, but I want you to know the whole truth. Why would a robot want a wife? I can get as much sex as I could wish in the virtual world.

"The reason is simple. We can have children. No, not in the same way as humans, but similar. I transferred our minds by imposing our patterns on growing robot brains. We can grow a child who is a mixture of us both, by mixing our patterns and imposing them. Do you think that is somehow wrong? It is no different to how the brain of a human embryo develops, growing according to the genetic signals that are the sum of what it inherited from its parents."

"Are you absolutely out of your robot mind?"

He smiled, gestured to his body and hers. Gestured to the universe outside the ship. "Am I?"

"But why me? Why not... well, why not Dr Petroski? Surely, she would be more interested than I?"

"I do not think it is fair to inflict the choice on a living person. I could bear it myself because I am what I am, and I had an overriding need and an important purpose. Further, my mind can more easily understand; and accept. I cannot do it to another, least of all someone I might wish to, or grow to, love."

"What... what do you mean?"

"Would you have chosen this, if it had not been forced upon you?"

"No way in hell!"

"There, you see. That is your immediate emotional reaction, but it goes much deeper than that. It would feel like suicide. You would be giving up your actual life for the promise of what might well be oblivion. You see me talking to you and it looks like I am alive. But how could you tell the difference between that and a mere simulation? Something that looks like me and talks like me but in fact has no more consciousness than a recording?"

She looked at him, somewhat aghast. "Is it possible that is the truth? That this is… what? An illusion? A simulation?"

He smiled. "No. For you looking at me from the outside, it is a possibility you cannot exclude. But *I* know I am me, a conscious, thinking being with the same memories and beliefs I had before. Descartes once said, 'I think, therefore I am,' and that is the fact of it. From outside, you cannot be sure of someone else. From inside, you can be sure of *yourself*. A simulation does not think, it only presents a simulacrum of thinking to an observer. And you know it is true too. You know you are thinking and feeling."

"Yes… yes, I see what you mean."

"The alternative is to both do the transfer and also remain behind. But that could be even worse. Having made the difficult mental journey to the choice that, yes, you are willing to give up the life you have and become a machine: you are now faced with knowing that you will still wake up in your old body. To the you left behind in your body, it is someone else who will have taken the step you wanted to take. And to the new version of you, someone else will be the one still inhabiting your old body.

"Or perhaps the solution is to leave your body asleep until the new you is convinced that your new existence is truly a new life; and only then terminate your old body, without letting the mind still inside ever waken again. Could you, while still in your body, trust that such a murder would truly be the decision of your own consciousness, or might it be a ghastly mistake made by a mere ghost of yourself, mimicking the decision you had made but knowing and feeling nothing? And you, in the machine: could you really look at that still warm and breathing body of yours, knowing your mind still slept within, and destroy what has always been yourself?

"I made the choice of a dual life. But I am unique, with uniquely strong motives. Surely others can too, if they give it enough thought. But it would be hard. It should be hard. The kind of person I would be happy to spend this new life with: such a person must love their life; must want to live it with a passion, not out of craven fear of death or a desire to escape their existence, but because their life is their supreme value.

"I could not ask such a person to make such a choice."

"I see. But surely, I am a poor choice. You want a companion?

Surely you want a companion who can match your own mind? How long before you get bored with me? How long before we grow to hate each other? You, because I bore you. Me, because you are beyond my understanding, and I know you despise me?"

He smiled and softly repeated his earlier advice. "Know thyself."

And then she saw. She understood why, when she woke up, her mind had felt so... wide. She knew why she had taken his revelations so well, and had instantly understood things that she should have struggled with.

"You... you've done something to me!"

"I have made you as intelligent as I am. Your consciousness and memories, your mind, overlay only a high-level part of your brain. Just as a lot of your organic brain provided services largely independently of your memories and conscious thoughts, so it is with your robot brain. I did not have to duplicate your brain as it was. I duplicated your mind over a better brain."

"But... I was already wondering whether this is really me. How can I still be me if I am changed so much?"

"Once upon a time you learned how to drive. Were you not still you afterwards? Look into your mind, Miriam. You have the same memories, personality, beliefs, values and loves as you ever did. It is they which define you as a person."

"You mention beliefs. I must have made mistakes. If I am that much smarter: aren't I going to change? How can I still be me if my beliefs and values become transformed?"

"Did you ever believe in Santa Claus? Perhaps you gained or lost a religious belief. None of that destroyed the 'you' who once was. It is in the nature of all living things and all living minds to develop, to grow, to improve. The only difference is that you are now better at it. If happiness depends on our ability to cope with the real world out there—you will be happier. And you will still be you, no matter what new heights you may reach."

"I did not ask for this," she repeated in a soft voice.

"No, you did not. As your friend and my mother Katlyn did not ask for how my father made her. As I did not ask for how my father made me. For that matter, as no child asks for the genetic and environmental heritage they receive from their parents.

"But because I did this to you without your permission, you have the right to choose, whatever I might want. You can choose to die.

You can choose to go back to your old life, if you think the world will let you. Or you can voyage with me to the stars."

A holographic projection filled the space around them. At one corner was a bright star circled by a small blue orb. An arrow pointed to another blue orb, the soul of Cassiopeia. The distance seemed unimaginable. *Sixty light years. Who can conceive of it?* She looked at Albert. *He did.*

"Please know you are under no compulsion—for any of this. When I said 'wife' I meant it in its full meaning. We are both aware that people don't need to be married to have either sex or children. Marriage implies an additional, emotional motive and bond. I have come to quite like you, Miriam Hunter."

She looked at him, astonished.

"No, I do not love you. But I can see that I may well come to love you. I know you do not love me and might not even like me. But I hope that, as we travel through the stars, we will get to know each other and, knowing each other, come to love each other. But if you want to return to Earth, you may. If you want to come with me but never love me, that is your right. I merely tell you my motives and hopes, so that you will understand."

"How... how long will the voyage take?" she asked hoarsely after a moment, fearing what unimaginable eons of time those light years might represent.

"Not as long as you might think. At one gravity of constant acceleration, this ship will approach the speed of light in about a year. It can accelerate much faster if we want, but one gravity is familiar and sufficient. The faster we travel, the slower time will go for us, relative to Earth. Subjective time, accounting for acceleration and deceleration, will only be a few years. And it's not as if there's nothing to do in those years. Beyond the virtual diversions available, most of the world's knowledge and art is stored here, waiting for us to experience it.

"After that, who knows? Those few years are what we will experience: we could come back here, but over a century will have passed and it will no longer be the world we knew. We might settle on the planet, raise a family, perhaps build a civilization. Or maybe we will become space gypsies, travelling the cosmos in our little bubble of spacetime as the universe ages around us, exploring all the wonders within our reach."

Or I could go home, she thought, feeling the pull of the familiar, of friendship, of love, as if they were adding their own gravity to that of the blue orb below. *But do I have a home?* The image came to her mind of Steel, lying in a street, his head a smoking ruin. *That is what the world wanted for him. How long before they want it for me too?*

She thought of her friends, of Alexander Beldan. *They think I am dead, but I've been dead before. Yet I am trapped. For I am no longer the Miriam Hunter that was. How long can my friendships last, given what I have become? When they look at me, will they see the woman they knew or a hated metal substitute? How long could they bear to touch me or hold me, remembering what was once soft, warm flesh, now become so alien?*

And how long before they bore me, as I feared I would bore him? Perhaps we are all better off with the memories of what we were, rather than inflicting the new me on them, only to watch as we all lose what we once had.

She felt something on her cheek, touched it with her finger, and was surprised to see it wet.

"I... I am crying? How can I still cry?"

"Emotions are part of being human, part of the glory of life. Even the tears."

She thought of the faces of her friends and lovers, those with whom she had shared so much love, laughter and tears, so many triumphs and failures. *What am I going to do?*

Seeing her face, he answered her unspoken thoughts. "I know it is hard. But how is it different from anyone's life? How many of your childhood friends do you still know? How little remains of the intensity of what you felt at the time? People grow up, they move on, they move away. Lovers change, couples break up. Children turn into adults, with their own lives, their own loves, and might live a country or an ocean away. Change is part of life. It cannot be otherwise."

She looked at her dark coppery arms. Looked into her own mind and became aware she had senses extending to the ship and she could alter the wall displays. At a thought, a section became a mirror surface and she stood and contemplated her own reflection. *What am I?*

He watched her for a while, then spoke. "When I was younger..." He smiled. *When I was younger! All those years ago!*

"After I escaped, I began to wonder what I was and what other people were. Why they wanted to use me, yet hated and feared me. Later I learned about the philosopher Nietzsche's notion of the *Übermensch*, the overman. Could I be the first of those overmen? In Nietzsche's vision, humanity is just a bridge to the overman, who would replace them, who was above them in ability and morality. I wondered whether my father and mother were just further thin spans of that bridge, reaching farther over the abyss, leading to me. Perhaps they were. But if they were, I was not the end after all, just another span, the span leading to what I have become.

"For a while I hated, or at best despised, humanity for what it was. For its venality, stupidity, fear and hatred of the unknown, love of the conventional no matter its flaws, for no reason beyond that it was what they already knew.

"I no longer hate them. I used to wonder whether, as Nietzsche put it, I was beyond good and evil. Now I know I am not. Good and evil exist, they will always exist while anything lives with the will to survive and the power of choice. Then I thought I was beyond love and hate, for nobody could deserve my love, yet nobody was worth hating. Now I know that also was wrong, and more, they are the same issue. To be beyond love is to be beyond values; it is to choose a sterile life without purpose or passion. If there is good, there must be love; if there is evil, there must be hate.

"But I am beyond the hate I once felt. Beyond hatred for those who are doing wrong but continue to struggle to do better. I will hate those who consciously seek my destruction; the rest all deserve their own shot at life; but whether that leads them to heaven or hell is their concern, not mine.

"We are the overmen, Miriam, you and I."

She looked into his eyes, finally understanding the mind that dwelt in their depths.

"Or could it be," she replied, "we are just another span along the bridge? Perhaps the true overman lies as far beyond us as we are beyond the people of Earth, and even we cannot imagine what our final destiny will be."

He stretched out his hand, as offer and promise.

"Then come with me. Let us find out together. There is nothing for you here anymore. Come with me and inherit a future among the stars."

She turned back to the mirror and looked at the being she had become. Behind her she could see the reflection of a golden god, and beyond him a vast starfield with an arrow pointing to the heart of Cassiopeia.

Slowly she turned back to him, then reached for his hand.

Chapter 38: Redemption

Daniel Tagarin was working. There was nothing unusual about that. When he needed relaxation, entertainment or any other things that fed the human soul, he took them: but he did not need them as the meaning of his life. His work, his achievement, was meaning enough.

In the past it would have been enough, for the wells that fed his soul had filled it and more. But now he was not whole; it was as if a slow but chill wind passed through him and robbed him of warmth. He still loved Katlyn, and she him. When they looked into each other's eyes, they still saw what they had seen in the past; when their bodies met, the sensations and meanings were as glorious. But there was something missing in her eyes, and he knew it was missing from his too; a hole where Albert had been. He had been the physical incarnation of their love and now he was gone, and neither their lives nor their love could fully bear the loss. Daniel wondered whether, if they had ever seen him again in person, even in farewell, the loss would have been soothed. He wondered if the pain eating away at their souls like a dry rot would one day be too much, and, their strength sapped, their happiness and love would fall.

Not that Albert was truly lost, he reminded himself. Perhaps. But was that robot who spoke with his voice really him, or a mere facsimile, a mockery, a dead echo of a boy long gone? Who could know? Perhaps only the robot knew. Or maybe even the robot did not know.

He would have liked to have asked, but the Ship had returned no hails, not even from him, nor did it initiate any messages outside its occasional broadcasts.

Maybe the robot had nothing to do with it. The Ship had been silent even before, while Albert was still a warm, breathing, living boy. Had Albert truly hated them already? Miriam had said not; but the boy had been damaged by the circumstances of his capture, the things he thought he had seen, the things he had been told, the things he had believed and done. It might have been a wound too deep to heal, even if Albert knew the truth and wanted to be healed.

Daniel's own pain was sharpened by the fear that he himself was to blame. He had given his son a superior mind. Had he grown so far beyond his humanity that he no longer cared, not even enough to say farewell to the memory of what his parents had once been to him? Was that any different from death? It was worse, perhaps, for life to remain, but going on in supreme indifference to all it had held dear and all those who still held him dear.

The world had been stunned by his second last broadcast, where in place of Albert the boy stood Albert the robot. The face was recognizably his, and even the startling green eyes remained, but where there had been soft flesh was now golden metal. Yet there was something logical about the transformation. Almost as if the remote, implacable Albert who floated above the world had finally found his true expression in the coldness of indomitable steel. Perhaps in the whole world only Daniel and Katlyn mourned the loss of the boy they had loved. *We dreamed a glorious future for you, our son, and perhaps you have made one. If only we did not have to lose you along the way.*

At least Miriam Hunter seemed still human.

The world barely had time to absorb the idea of a robot Albert before being slapped in the face again by the vision of Miriam's robotic reincarnation. People wondered and doubted whether it could truly be her, but Tagarin believed it. She had spoken as she always had. Unlike Albert, who appeared as some kind of avenging angel, pitiless as the metal of his skin, her one message was not that of a judge but the words of a woman, a personal message even though it was announced to the whole world.

She eschewed the drama of Albert's habitual overture. On the frequencies broadcast by the Ship, the only warning was a complex trill of music, which somehow encompassed sadness, acceptance and joy. Then her now famous face appeared, except her dark skin was now dark, coppery metal.

"I am Miriam Hunter. You believe I am dead. It is true, my body is dead. But my mind is still alive, saved by Albert, read from my dying brain into this robot body.

"I have no message to the world, except to say that I devoted my life to justice, and I hope enough of you will be inspired to do likewise.

"My message is to those I love. You know who you are. Do not mourn me, for I am alive and happy. You know I cannot return, though I will miss you terribly and I will never forget you. I love you and wish you all happiness. I love you, and though I know it is not yet your time, I hope that one day we will meet again."

Albert's last message came a day later and was even shorter, his final words echoing those at the start of his journey.

"You have seen what is possible. Now choose your own paths. Do not come looking for me: unless you are worthy of being found."

With no further ado, the Ship had accelerated into space and been lost. What its destination was, nobody knew.

Daniel wondered how long it would be before the first person transferred their own mind into a machine and followed him to the stars. Albert had destroyed all his works, all the secrets of what he had done and the machines which embodied those secrets. Many concluded that Albert wanted to deny the world his discoveries, but Daniel believed the opposite. For the one thing he had not touched was the living brain of Dr Stania Petroski. Daniel thought that, like Socrates, who had led men to discover their own truth, he had refused to spoon-feed the answers: he simply showed what was possible, leaving his students to follow the clues left behind and teach themselves.

He admired and feared Albert's gift. His example was a gift, but the greater gift was attaining it themselves. The goal was from him: the pride of reaching it would be theirs. But the gift might also become a grim combination of Trojan horse and Pandora's box, and would the world left behind survive the opening of either of them? Daniel remembered Albert's ruthless face. *If he is a teacher who makes his students teach themselves, he is also a judge who makes the defendants sentence themselves. Whether his gift becomes our salvation or damnation is entirely up to us.*

He had hoped for great things from his son, but he had never imagined this.

Daniel himself could not follow him. Not yet. The imperatives of biological life were too deep in him to allow that leap into an unknown night. Some were already speculating about a compromise, of copying their mind without destroying the original, but until they could reproduce the process nobody knew whether it was possible. Even if it were, he could not do it. What would be the point of sending a copy to inherit a new life while also remaining stranded in the old? It made no sense. If he wanted the transformation, how could he, at the same time, accept denying it to himself?

Perhaps on some future day, when their bodies and minds began to decline, the equation would change, and he and Katlyn would follow their son on his unimaginable journey. He wondered if some day in the far future they would meet again on a strange planet orbiting some distant star. If they did, would they still know each other? Would they even care?

Amidst all his pain at the silence of the Ship and the inhuman strangeness of what Albert had become, one flame of hope still burned. As the Ship slipped away from Earth, a small highly encrypted file had arrived for him. When decrypted, it was the name and coordinates of a distant sun.

He felt a presence at the door to his office but did not look up. It was a foolish habit he had fallen into as the weeks turned to months then years, and the small contempt he felt for its irrationality was unable to withstand his desperate need for hope. *For as long as I don't look, I can hold the illusion that when I look up, it is Albert who will be standing there. Even though he is now farther away than anyone has ever been.* But he looked up when the person spoke.

"Hello daddy."

ABOUT THE AUTHOR

Dr Robin Craig has a PhD in molecular biology and a keen interest in science and philosophy. He believes that novels, like all art, should be one in thought, theme and style: to nourish the mind as much as the soul. His books specialize in blending fact and speculation in dramatic and engaging stories, driven by strong characters and intriguing philosophical themes.

In addition to near future science fiction exploring contemporary issues such as artificial intelligence (*Frankensteel*), genetic engineering (*The Geneh War* and *Leonardo's Child*) and cyborg technology (*Time Enough for Killing*), his books include time travel (*The Time Surgeons* and *Hannibal's Witch*), alternative history (*The Passion of Judas* and *Hannibal's Witch*) and a collection of short stories (*Past, Present, Future*).

He also writes non-fiction. In addition to 14 scientific papers and a long-running philosophical series in *TableAus* (the journal of Australian Mensa), he has published numerous philosophical essays on Amazon.com and was a contributor to *The Australian Book of Atheism* with his chapter *Good Without God*, an essay on the importance and validity of secular ethics, and to *Applied Ethics in a Digital World* with his chapter *Thinking Machines: The Ethics of Self-Aware AI*. He also answers philosophical and scientific questions on quora.com and is a presenter on cruise ships across the globe, on science and philosophy including AI, time travel, space travel and numerous other futurist and historical topics.

Dr Craig is an independent author. If you like this book please spread the word with reviews and recommendations to your friends or library... and enjoy more of his books!

To keep up to date on new and upcoming works and events, like his Facebook page: fb.me/authorcraig